GREGORY BLAKE THOUGHT HE WAS THE BEST PRIVATE INVESTIGATOR IN CHICAGO. But maybe it wasn't so smart to take on a client marked for destruction and try to save him. Now he was forced to deal with crud like Frambeen, who was pushing a gun into his back.

"Move . . . take off his gas mask," Frambeen ordered, pointing to Billy. "Remember, I have little use for you alive."

Blake didn't budge. He was trying to figure his odds.

"You can take off his mask or I can shoot him. Your choice."

Blake didn't think much of Frambeen's abilities with a gun, but at point-blank range he didn't need much ability. With that bit of keen logic motivating him he reached over, pulled off Billy's mask, and watched him collapse in seconds.

"Okay," Frambeen said. "Now take yours off. . . ."

BODY
MORTGAGE

Richard Engling

AN ONYX BOOK

NEW AMERICAN LIBRARY

PUBLISHER'S NOTE

This book is a work of fiction. Names, characters, places, and incidents either are the product of the author's imagination or are used fictitiously, and any resemblance to actual persons, living or dead, events, or locales is entirely coincidental.

 ONYX TRADEMARK REG. U.S. PAT. OFF. AND FOREIGN COUNTRIES REGISTERED TRADEMARK—MARCA REGISTRADA HECHO EN DRESDEN, TN, U.S.A.

SIGNET, SIGNET CLASSIC, MENTOR, ONYX, PLUME, MERIDIAN and NAL BOOKS are published by NAL PENGUIN INC., 1633 Broadway, New York, New York 10019

First Printing, March, 1989

1 2 3 4 5 6 7 8 9

PRINTED IN THE UNITED STATES OF AMERICA

For Gail

Special thanks to my fellow members of the Chicago Writers Group and to Robert Engling and Eddie Williams for suggestions concerning this book.

1

Private investigator Gregory Blake entered his office to find his secretary in the center of the room, everything turned upside down around her, files thrown everywhere. The chairs lined up in a row, tipped over near the wall, their legs sticking up. Drawers lay stacked next to his desk, their contents spilled out on its top. There was something almost orderly about the chaos, as though the most polite of cyclones had blown through the room.

Mona looked up at him and smiled a slight, crooked smile. "There's no mistaking it," she told him. "Somebody's been in here."

"Well, this is a kick in the ass," Blake said. "I hope they got what they wanted."

"At least we know they've been here." Mona often kidded Blake that he was probably the only boss in the city who still made his secretary file paper in the old-fashioned metal cabinet.

"Go ahead and laugh," he told her. "If this were on the computer, they wouldn't even have had to walk in here."

"You know that isn't necessarily true."

"Maybe I know that. But I'm not so sure." Blake was really less concerned with computer theft than with his own dependence on machines. He wanted to be able to reach into a file anytime he wanted, Mona at work or not. "At least we haven't lost all our files." he said.

She looked at the paper scattered over the room and laughed. "Nope. Plenty of those left. But something must be missing."

"I don't imagine they turned the place upside down to amuse themselves," Blake agreed. He picked up a large manila envelope from his desk. It had no writing on it. He noticed it was sealed, probably the only thing in the room that could make that claim. He smelled the seal for traces of chemicals and held the envelope up to the light. He rattled it, shook it, and felt along its surface. It did not seem to be dangerous.

"What have you got?" Mona asked. "The Trojan Horse?"

He carefully opened the envelope. From inside he pulled a few sheets of newspaper dated November 16, 1998—five months old. He looked them over. There were no marks on them, no sections cut out. Among the articles he noticed the name of his "old friend" Murray, but nothing else.

Mona moved over to look with him. Blake caught the warm fragrance of her scent and noticed uncomfortably that he enjoyed the closeness of her body. He'd noticed that more and more over the two years she'd worked for him. She put her hand softly on his forearm as she examined the clippings. He looked at the gentle curve of her eyebrow, and felt pleasure at her touch.

He handed the newspaper to her and stepped away. "What do you think?" he asked.

"It's not yours?"

"Nope."

"Then I think it's a time-waster," she said. "They leave a phony clue to keep you busy while they do whatever they do."

"Could be," Blake agreed. "Whoever left this doesn't seem to be in the business of doing us favors."

"By the way, a John Dwight called this morning. He said he's president of Midland Waste Reclamation."

"I know John," Blake said.

"I thought you might. Anyway, they had some sabotage out there last night."

"At the plant?"

"Yes. In Lincolnwood."

"Was anyone hurt?"

"I don't think anyone was hurt, but he didn't want to say much on the phone. I promised him you'd be out there sometime this morning."

"Good," Blake said. "I'll enjoy seeing him again."

They heard a knock at the door. Mona answered it to let in a tall blond fellow. He began to speak, then stopped for a moment when he noticed the chaos in the room.

"Are you Gregory Blake?" he asked doubtfully. Blake looked him over for a moment. He looked like a California-beach-boy movie star. His clothes were rumpled, but of fair quality. And he was pale—paler than his blondness would have made him naturally.

"That's right," Blake said finally.

"The detective?" the man asked.

"You're in the right place," Mona smiled. "We're just trying a new filing system." Blake thought he noticed her wink at the guy.

"It looks like you have enough trouble already," he said.

"Don't worry about this disaster," Mona assured him. "Blake's the best in the business."

The man sidestepped as the detective grabbed a chair and flipped it upright. He stood still in one clear spot on the floor and watched silently as Blake righted the chrome-and-leather furniture.

"Have a seat," Blake told him, indicating the chair he'd set closest to his desk. "Start sorting this garbage, will you?" he asked Mona.

"Sure," she said, still with a slight smile in her eyes. Blake knew the closer she could get to the middle of the action, the better she liked it. And she seemed to like looking at this new client, as well. There was a clear sharpness to his features and a wary intelligence in his face. But there was something about him Blake didn't like.

He swept the mess off the top of his desk into two empty drawers, then sat down. "How can I help you?" he asked.

The man shrugged as though the situation were slightly ludicrous. He crossed his legs and looked sidelong at Mona behind her desk. She nodded encouragement.

"I've developed a valuable piece of new equipment," he told the detective. "An elemental processor. There's nothing else like it in the world. What I need is protection for a week while I set it up, operate it, and deliver a product. After that I'm in the clear." The phone began ringing and Mona answered it.

"Sounds simple enough," Blake said. "Who's trying to bother you? Why do you need protection?"

"Do you really need the details?" the man asked impatiently. "How about if you just take me and my equipment somewhere safe?"

"Just a minute," Mona said into the phone. "Blake, this man insists on speaking to you. He wouldn't give his name. He says it's an emergency."

"One moment," Blake said to the blond man. He reached automatically for his phone before realizing it was not on the desk. He glanced at Mona, who raised her eyebrows and pointed downward with her index finger. He found the phone under a pile of papers beneath his desk.

"You got a guy named Jeremy Scott in there with you?" the voice on the phone asked.

"Who's this?" Blake asked.

"We're in the same business," the voice said. "Scott defaulted on his HRL. We got to pick him up. You hold him for us, you get the standard payoff. Just don't use a buzzer. We need him clearheaded."

"What's this guy look like?" Blake said, glancing blandly at the man in his office.

"He's a tall blond guy in a bum's suit. Looks like he could've been on TV."

"Sorry," Blake said.

"Come off it. We know he's at your place."

"Maybe he got delayed. Give me your number, and I'll ask him to phone you."

"That's not funny, Blake."

"Sorry." He hung up before the other man spoke again, then sat staring at the customer in his office.

The man stared back, beginning to look apprehensive. "What's wrong?" he asked.

"I make it a practice not to do business with dead men, Mr. Scott," Blake said. "It makes it hard to collect my bill."

"I'll have the money in a week," Scott said. "I'll pay you and the loan without a problem."

"The gentleman on the phone said you'd already defaulted. They want to come and pick you up. They want to lay out your organs in the deli-counter window."

"The loan doesn't default until Monday. I'll have the money in a week."

"Jackass!" Blake said. "A week is too late. You knew what you were signing. I ought to let them chop you up."

Scott pulled himself up and squared his shoulders. "It was a gamble. I knew that. But the payoff is big. I'll double your usual fee."

Blake looked at him coldly. He hated that stupidity that led anyone to sign a Human Resource Loan contract almost as much as he hated the collectors and detectives who picked up the defaulters for easy bounty money.

In an earlier period of wild deregulation, Congress had made citizens the legal arbiters over the fate of their bodies—in certain instances, at least. By clever manipulation of the voluntary euthanasia law, combined with the rights of citizens to will their organs to the recipients of their choice, a person with healthy organs could take out a loan with only his body as collateral. If he defaulted, collectors picked him up, doctors plucked out his organs for transplants, and the cadaver was dried and ground for fertilizer. Toxic pollution kept the demand for organs high. The whole business made Blake sick.

The process was clearly illegal, but each of the participants—banks, doctors, and collectors—covered the legality of their specific contribution, and there was no one left to prosecute. Anyone could sign his life away for a pile of quick cash. And yet one practically had to have a doctor's prescription to buy a pack of cigarettes.

Usually Blake just stayed out of HRL situations, figuring anyone stupid enough to sign one deserved to pay the price. But he didn't like the way that collector on the phone had said they were in the same business. And he'd said not to use a buzzer on Scott. That was odd.

Collectors wore buzzers on their palms, like the novelty-shop toys that shocked gag victims with a handshake. This latter-day buzzer, however, was a hypospray jet injector, a device which shot a stream of fluid though an orifice of fifty microns. The collectors slapped the buzzer onto a victim's forehead, injecting a chemical through skin and bone that ulcerated the frontal portions of the brain. The personality and will were destroyed, but enough of the cerebrum remained to keep the body living for several days—plenty of time for doctors to ravage it for spare parts.

The detective looked at Scott again. He didn't trust the man.

"Isn't there something you can do for him?" Mona asked.

Blake looked at her in surprise. She seemed truly concerned. He hadn't liked the way Mona looked at the guy, and now he realized that that was part of his resentment toward Scott. Since Blake studiously avoided on-the-job romance, he thought he'd better drop the on-the-job jealousy, as well. But most of all, he hated that a collector thought he would accept bounty money.

"Come on," Blake said finally. "We'd better get out of here before they're busting down the door."

Scott stood up. "Thank you, Mr. Blake," he said coolly. "I was a dead man without you."

"Yeah," Blake agreed. He turned to Mona. "You better take the rest of the day off. The collection boys aren't going to be happy when they find we're gone."

"I can handle them," she said. "I've got to get through these files and see what's missing. It could be important."

Blake hesitated. "I suppose you're right," he said. "But don't let them in. And if you get a chance, take a look at that paper."

"I think it's a time-waster," she said lightly.

"Probably, but maybe not. Give Jake Fishman a call and tell him I'll need his help. I'm taking Scott over there. Then I'll get over to Dwight at Midland Waste."

"Good luck," she said.

"You too. And whatever you do, don't shake hands with a collector." He winked at her.

"Buzz me later, if you get the chance," she replied, arching an eyebrow. Blake winced.

"All this jocularity is doing nothing to boost my confidence," Scott told them.

"Too bad," Blake said. "Lock the door behind me," he told Mona.

2

Blake led Scott down into the basement of the building, making sure they were neither seen nor followed. The first thing to do with Scott was to get him out of sight. Blake planned to hide him at Fishman's for a time while he worked on more pressing concerns—like taking care of John Dwight, a real paying client—and finding out who'd ransacked his office. Paying the rent and protecting himself came before the problems of an egghead who'd signed his life away. But Fishman would keep Scott safe until Blake could do more.

Jake Fishman was an odd-jobs man. Blake had used him a number of times in the past, mainly to dredge up information, to pass messages or money, and occasionally to keep someone safely locked up—and not always willingly.

Blake led Scott to the door of a basement maintenance room. He used a key to open the door and unscrewed a flat metal panel from the lower wall inside. He turned off the overhead light before he removed the panel, then shone a pocket flashlight beam into the opening.

"You first," he said to Scott. "It's an air duct to the Crosstown Subway. Be careful of the edges on that hole."

Blake watched the other man fit himself down into the air duct. It felt good having Scott drop down the passage first. When he didn't want to be confronted at the doors to his building, the unfinished tunnel made a good escape. But Blake was not the only one to use it. He didn't like running into strangers, since no one had any legitimate reason to be down there. If bullets started flying when they dropped through the ventilator, Scott would be the first to take them. Blake's client might bleed, but at least his organs would be safe from collection.

He followed Scott into the duct, climbed down a few rungs of the emergency ladder, and pulled the metal panel back into place. He lowered himself into the dark, his eyes blinking wide and nonsensically against the blackness, until he felt the last rung beneath his foot. After that came ten feet of empty space and the floor of the abandoned subway tunnel below. He climbed down hand over hand, hung from the last rung, and dropped onto Jeremy Scott's back. The blond man cried out, and Blake clapped his hand over the client's mouth. He pressed his lips close to Scott's ear and whispered, "You make another sound down here, I'll slit your throat."

"Someone told me contacting you would be a mistake," Scott whispered angrily.

Blake let it pass and looked up toward the ladder and duct overhead. Invisible. Even people who'd come through here more than once couldn't find this entrance. Down the tunnel he could see more easily. At long intervals, safety lights shone from behind wire-mesh guards, illuminating small sections of the elliptically shaped tunnel, creating a series of diminishing archways of light punctuated by long passages of dark. Blake knew they would have a long walk, probably an hour and a half before they reached Fishman. They walked in silence, the impatient Scott several yards ahead of Blake.

On the left side, occasional short alleys opened onto a parallel tunnel meant for train traffic in the opposite direction. It was from one of these alleys, as Scott stepped into an illuminated section of the subway, that he heard a voice telling him to stop.

Scott yelped his surprise. From the darkness of the passageway emerged a large, broad man carrying a gun. He grinned with the pleasure of having the upper hand.

Blake froze in the darkness where he had not yet been seen. "You looking for a train?" the big man asked Scott.

Blake recognized the voice at once. It was Billy. Blake looked at him carefully. The big man's face looked thin and his eyes were sunken. He looked a little shaky on his feet. Billy was a strong-arm man whom Blake had hired in the past. A nice guy. Mona especially liked him. Nobody had seen him in a while, and now he looked strange. His short brown hair was normally combed straight back and neat. Now it looked matted and dirty. A few days' growth of whiskers on his square chin accentuated the unusual redness of his lips. The rims of his eyes and even his bulbous nose had taken on a red tinge, as well.

"What do you want?" Scott asked. Blake hoped he would have the sense not to look back, not to give Blake's presence away before he assessed the situation.

Billy smiled derisively. "I work for the mayor's office. I keep these empty tunnels secure." Billy gestured with his pistol to the blond man, his voice slightly slurred. He took a step forward and cocked the gun. The shadows from the wire grid on the light slid down over him like prison bars. "The mayor said I should collect from you. I need some money."

"Blake, where are you?" Scott said in panic. "Where's my protection?"

"Blake?" Billy said, dumbfounded.

The detective sighed. Damned fool clients, he thought. "Don't shoot anybody, Billy," he said aloud. "It's me." He stepped slowly into the light.

"Oh, crap, Blake," Billy said. "I need cash. This guy has got to give me some money."

"Sorry, Billy," the detective said.

"Come on. Don't make a big deal. Put it on this guy's expenses."

Scott backed off a few steps.

"He ain't a client," Blake told him. "This is my brother-in-law. I'm helping him hide from my sister."

"Listen," Billy stammered, "you don't have any sister. I know that. So don't bullshit me. I had this guy pegged fair and square." He gestured toward Scott with the pistol.

"Don't let this idiot shoot me, for God's sake," Scott yelled. "Can't you put down that gun?"

"If you don't give me some money," Billy told him, "I'm going to smack you in the head and take it." He lifted the gun threateningly, but Blake jumped forward, grabbing Billy's gun arm and kicking sharply into his kneecap. Billy screamed as his pistol blew a slug into the tunnel wall, deafening all three men. As Billy fell, Blake knocked the gun away and jumped in with a knee on his solar plexus and the tip of his stiletto tucked under the big man's chin. From its point of contact, Blake's knife drew one small drop of blood.

"Now, I want you to come round to my office tomorrow, Billy. We're going out for a drink, and you're going to tell me why business is so bad you got to pull this kind of crap." Blake could tell by his breath that Billy had been drinking quite a bit already.

"I say we shoot him right now." Scott stood with the recovered pistol clutched in both hands.

Blake looked at him, then looked back down. "And I'll explain to you how I took a nitwit like this for a client," he said.

Billy grinned nervously as the detective got off him. He wiped the blood from beneath his chin as Blake took the gun from Scott. Blake tossed the pistol back to Billy. Scott looked dumbfounded.

"Are you crazy?" the blond man asked. "What's to stop him from doing it again?"

"If he does, he knows I won't buy tomorrow," Blake said.

Scott turned angrily away, then noticed Billy hobbling off into his tunnel. "What?" Scott said in surprise.

"No more noise," Blake said, leading the way on again through the tunnel.

They walked a long time through the alternating light and dark, watching for figures in the side tunnels and stopping silent when Blake heard noises.

Then the tunnel dipped, and water stood in the deepest parts underfoot. Blake knew they were passing under the Chicago River and Goose Island. Another mile and they'd be out.

When it finally came, the change of smells gave great refreshment: fresh air blew in their faces, stripping away the wet-cardboard aroma of the tunnel. Then the darkness ended, opening into a large abandoned pit meant someday to be a Crosstown Subway station. They climbed up the steep road the heavy-equipment operators had built. No trucks had driven it in some time.

The Crosstown was a study in the Chicago style of public works. The plan was to provide good transportation from the Northwest to the Southwest side of the city, with easy connections between Midway and O'Hare airports. A good idea. However, subway construction had halted two years earlier, tangled in legal right-of-way and funding problems. And the only part of the underground tube that had been started was the least important part, the spur to connect the main part of the Crosstown with the center of town, hooking under Blake's building through the fashionable Near North Side.

In building the spur, the city had found it necessary

to condemn and knock down a whole section of slums south of the Cabrini-Green housing project—which is why, Blake thought, this spur had come first. Cabrini-Green was an embarrassment to the city. As the Near North's popularity began to spread to neighborhoods further west, the Cabrini housing project stood as a fatal barrier to rising property values: a whole series of high-rise housing projects in one compact area. Too many poor blacks in one spot. Too much crime.

The city had not found it necessary to knock down the modern building that housed Blake's office, however. They had managed their construction past it, though it was as close as many of the slums they had knocked down.

At the top of the incline, Blake unlocked the fence gate leading to the street.

"How did you get that key?" Scott asked.

"I didn't," Blake answered. "I cut off the construction company's lock and replaced it with my own."

Scott laughed appreciatively as Blake closed the gate behind them and made it secure again. He looked around, following the detective. "I know where we are," he said.

"Good for you," Blake replied. He led the way up the block to a small coffee shop on Milwaukee Avenue. They could hear the sound of traffic on the Kennedy Expressway nearby.

"What's this? You're stopping for lunch?" Scott asked.

Through the large plate glass windows Blake glanced over the five booths and the two small round tables inside. Customers hunched over on the stools at the counter like people doomed to a life of gruel. One of the customers was a man Blake wanted to see. Beyond him, the cook flipped eggs at the grill.

"Business," Blake said. He pulled the door open and pointed Scott back to a sixth booth, out of sight in the corner. Then he sat on an empty stool next to a gray-headed man reading a newspaper.

"Know anything about a sabotage last night? It was at a waste-reclamation plant up in Lincolnwood," Blake said, looking straight forward.

"I know enough to wonder what the hell you're doing on the street," the man said quietly.

"What does that mean?" Blake said.

"Stay seated and don't look at me," the informer told him. "Don't try to contact me. I don't want to get dragged down with you." He got up, turning away from Blake as he rose and left the shop.

What the hell? Blake wondered.

The cook set a plate of eggs on the counter. "Where's Bowens?" he asked.

"He left."

"Where? This is his breakfast. Where'd he go?"

"Didn't say," Blake said.

"Shit," the counterman replied. "You hungry?"

"No." Blake looked at the headline on the newspaper Bowens had left behind: "Plans for 2000 Fest Mired in Council Bickering." Blake had heard this on the radio. "The Changing of the Millennia Ball." Some jackass had got the idea of enclosing the entire length of Navy Pier in a clear plastic bubble. Then people could dance in the moonlight and enjoy the open skyline, warm on a frigid New Year's Eve. On New Millennium's Eve, he should say. The mayor loved it. But the projected costs, as always, had been grossly underestimated.

Next to the main story, Blake noticed the sidebar, "But it's 2001! Prof Says." Some University of Chicago professor was protesting the 2000-Fest, since the millennium wasn't ready to start until 2001. But the mayor liked 2000. It was like the excitement of a car's odometer flipping over to all zeros. Personally, Blake didn't give a shit.

He flipped the paper over. "Police Investigate Bank

Bombing," the front-page headline read. "Seven Killed at First National." A large color photograph showed bodies strewn in the rubble.

Fucking people, Blake thought. They'll do any goddamned thing. He got up, signaled Scott, and walked outside. The blond man joined him.

"Let's go." Blake led the way down the street, heading back southeast toward Chicago Avenue.

"You get what you wanted?"

"No," the detective told him. Blake wished the informant had stuck around. Since he was delayed in getting up to Dwight's plant, he'd hoped to go with a lead already in hand. Instead he got a warning that was no warning.

"We need to pick up my equipment," Scott said. "You told me we were going to somebody named Fishman. Is he going to help us with that?"

"No," Blake said. What was it about Scott? He was good-looking, obviously intelligent. Why did Blake's mind's eye insist on seeing him as the high-school president of Future Scientists of America, surrounded by pimply technology nerds running arcane computations on mini-terminals? Because he'd signed an HRL?

"I've got other commitments," he told Scott. "You'll have to sit safe at Fishman's for a while." The scientist grunted his irritation.

"What does your machine do, anyway?" Blake asked.

"It's an elemental processor."

"A what?"

"An elemental processor."

Blake stared at him.

"It's a simple concept," Scott said impatiently. "Every compound is made up of elements with specific atomic weights and charges. Each compound, at the molecular level, has a weight and charge determined by its atomic makeup. With a machine programmed to attract molecules of one specific weight and charge while repelling all others, one can extract pure substances from adulterated ones."

"That's what it does?"

"As simply as I can put it. Unless you want a more technical explanation."

"I got the picture," Blake said.

"When will I get my equipment?" Scott asked.

"When I'm done with my other business, we'll see about picking up your machine."

"I've got to have it right away, Mr. Blake. There are adjustments to make." He snorted a laugh. "You can't expect me to just sit and play cards with Mr. Fishman."

"Listen, Scott," Blake said, pushing his client out of sight into an alley. "Deep down inside"—he patted his chest for emphasis—"way deep down in my heart, I feel like a jackass for having anything to do with you." Scott tried to protest, but the detective raised his left index finger for silence and cupped his right hand gently over the man's mouth.

"Starting Monday, Mr. Scott, you will be an outlaw. You signed the paper. The bank has the right to repossess your ass. If I were a right-minded individual, I'd turn you in, collect the reward, and take my secretary out to a well-deserved dinner." Blake released Scott's mouth and wiped his hand on Scott's shirt.

Scott smiled oddly. "I don't think you like me, Mr. Blake."

"There's no percentage in you," Blake told him simply. "A man who won't pay his bill when his life depends on it gets a lousy credit rating in my book."

"But why are they after me already? This is only Thursday."

"You tell me."

He walked back out of the alley and down the sidewalk, Scott following. After the second block, they went past a man sprawled on the ground like a fallen scarecrow, his head propped against the wall in an attitude of drunken repose. Across the street a woman sat on the curb, her purse emptied on the ground beside her, bobbing her head like a quizzical sparrow.

"Has she been robbed?" Scott asked. The woman began howling in an incoherent guttural rasp. The man bellowed behind them and rolled off the sidewalk to kick his legs twice. The woman threw her purse.

Blake looked into her face and saw the horror of her eyes. "Jesus, God," he said. He dug quickly into his pocket and pulled out a slender case with two capsules in it.

"Quick, take one of these," he told Scott. Blake opened one of the capsules and sniffed a pinch of thalamin powder up each nostril. It burned like hell, but he couldn't take any chances. He wanted it working fast. Then he put the capsule back together and swallowed the rest of it dry. Scott stood, still holding the thalamin in his hand.

"Hurry up," Blake told him. "You want to be jibbering like these poor gooneys?"

Scott looked at it. "I can't," he said. "I've seen what happens to people from this stuff."

"Don't be an asshole. Look what happens without it." The woman on the curb began rubbing lipstick all over her face.

"I'm a scientist," Scott explained. "I can't afford to lose my edge of clear thought." He stopped and looked around. "I don't smell anything. It's probably blown away." At that moment the breeze picked up a sheet of dirty newspaper from the gutter and swirled it toward them like an airborne dervish. From around the edge of a grocery store ahead, Scott saw the faintest wisps of yellow fog curling in the air. "Oh, shit," he said. He tried to take the antidote capsule, but in his haste, dropped it. The capsule hit the sidewalk, bounced on the edge of the curb. and arched through the sewer grating like a tiny Olympic diver.

"I dropped it," he said.

"That was the last one," Blake told him. He could feel the thalamin turning the air viscous, slowing him down, making him dull and woozy. That would change soon enough.

"How long can you hold your breath?" he asked Scott, grinning stupidly. Then he felt the sting of QDT on his eyes. He smelled its acrid flavor: like barbecued bug spray.

"I've got to get out of here," Scott said. Blake forced himself to dive hard and tackle his client before he ran away. He held him to the ground as Scott's senses began to scramble.

QDT, originally developed by the Army, had become a popular "disambulant" with police and military forces all over the world. It affected its victims like an airborne LSD—and certainly left them "disambulatory." It knocked everyone on their collective ass.

"I may have to start playing nursemaid now," Blake said slowly, though he suspected Scott could no longer understand, "but I'll be damned if I'm going to chase you." Scott began making small noises, and the detective got up. "You won't get far now," he said.

Blake felt the first rush of QDT fighting with the antidote in his system. All his drowsiness fled as though he'd shot a heavy dose of amphetamine. He'd have to be careful. His thoughts would come fast again, but they'd be skittish and unreliable.

He wondered who'd put QDT in the air. There hadn't been riots, so it probably wasn't the National Guard. The police? Fishman would know. He had to get Scott safely to Fishman's.

Blake walked up to the grocery store. A middle-aged man with a Manager patch on his uniform lay on his back near the door moaning, "Oh, no." Blake leaned over him, and the man shrieked in terror.

"I know how you feel," Blake told him. He flipped one of the shopping carts over the barriers, wheeled it back to Scott, and hoisted the wriggling man into it.

"Get to Fishman's place," rattled on in Blake's mind. "Stick to original plan." Blake wheeled his load swiftly away.

The detective knew why Scott had hesitated to take the thalamin. When the drug first hit the underground market, a number of political dissidents had taken it too often. Excessive use of thalamin left them permanently dull-witted. The police then found it easy to capture and lobotomize them, turning their bodies over to redemption centers and collecting the exchange for themselves. By one means or another, police never lacked for exchange organs. And thalamin was still illegal without a permit.

Blake pushed on with the cart, using the alleys like cockroaches use the insides of walls, trying to stay out of sight. Being mobile and coherent in a QDT "control zone," led to questioning by the police, something Blake definitely wanted to avoid.

But there were worse problems. When the police deserted a "control zone" and the incapacitated victims were left helpless at the site, the results were sadly predictable. Up at mid-block, five gang kids swung into the alley like jackals smelling blood.

Blake let his head bob twice as the cart with Scott swerved into the brick wall of the building to his right. Blake moaned and twisted his head as he banged the cart into the bricks like a violent spastic. The police would not be deceived by his act. One look at his eyes and they'd know. But the boys he might be able to fool.

He allowed his head to loll in their direction. The gang members all wore gas masks: customary QDT looting attire. One had a pistol stuck in his belt, one dragged a chain, and the other three carried bags for raiding the stores.

The lead boy pulled the gun from his waistband and held it high over his head. The others stopped behind him. He gestured graciously toward the two men. Scott rattled himself violently in the cart while Blake hung his head slantwise, watching the boys out of the corner of his eye.

"What have we here?" the boy with the gun exclaimed. The others laughed as he pranced up to the men. "It's another couple of gooneys!" Through the gas mask, his voice sounded like it came from a tin can. He looked like some horrible human insect.

Gang kids had originally coined the term "gooneys." It sounded so appropriate for the awkward victims of QDT that "gooneys" had been taken into general usage.

As the boys approached, Blake lurched sideways against the cart and lolled his head, moaning again.

"Let's string up their balls for bow ties." The boy with the chain leered at them. The detective picked up his head and let it roll back. They had gathered in a semicircle around him like a pack of wolves.

"Just get their wallets," a third said. Blake saw this was one of the bag boys. He swirled further so his back rested against the cart's handle and his arms hung forward like an ape's.

"Before we make any decision, my friends, let's see how much they'll pay for our protection," the gun boy said. He walked up to Blake and reached his arms around behind him to feel for his wallet. Blake grabbed the boy's gun and slapped his gas mask straight up off his head. Blake's fingers fumbled in drug panic, but he held on to the pistol and spun the boy around, putting a choke hold on his neck. He pressed the gun barrel to the boy's temple and looked at the other four, who had frozen. Blake watched the chain carrier's surprise turn to a challenging smirk. The kid he held whimpered, and Blake felt the warmth of blood on his trembling wrist. The gas mask had caught the kid's nose on the way up. Blake saw from an angle that the boy sported a new red mustache and goatee.

Blake's heart pulsed at tremendous speed as adrenaline continued to pile onto the confusion of QDT and thalamin in his system. He forced himself to speak slowly:

"I think you boys came shopping to the wrong store." Blake's body trembled and his hands shook continuously. He couldn't think of anything else to say.

The chain boy's smirk deepened. "Look at this guy," he said. "He ain't going to shoot nobody. He's scared shitless."

Blake felt the danger of being so misread. As a kid, he'd survived some trouble himself, and he wanted to let the boys down easily. He wished suddenly there were more QDT in the air to take out the kid he held, but Scott had probably gulped the last blast concentrated enough for the job.

The boy blew some blood out of his nose and then spat, trying hard to keep the trembling out of his voice. "Shut up, you asshole," he said to the chain carrier. "He's got a gun to my head."

"He's harmless as a fly." The kid began reeling in his chain and smiling directly at Blake.

"He busted my fucking hose!" the first one said, sounding on the verge of tears.

"You was too sloppy." The three other boys backed off as the kid began to swing the chain over his head, quickly letting out links to increase his range. Blake kicked the first boy's feet from under him and knelt hard on his back. With two hands he pointed the pistol at the chain swinger.

"Now it's you . . ." Blake started, but the slap of the links stung his hands, and the pistol rattled onto the pavement. They dove simultaneously, with the boy's hands reaching it first. Blake pulled him up by the wrists hard, knocking him backward off balance. As he fell, the kid jerked the pistol suddenly from Blake's grasp, and it slapped down into his own gut at the moment it discharged. Blake snatched the gun away.

Beneath the goggles of the mask, the boy's face twisted up in pain. "God damn it! God damn it!" he cried. He curled up like a hemorrhaging fetus. Blake stuffed the gun in his pocket and ran down the alley, pushing Scott in the cart.

"Take care of him," he yelled back at the four other boys, who were still paralyzed with shock. The sound of Blake's voice broke them out of it, and they all ran, disappearing between buildings and behind garages.

"You shits," the wounded boy shouted, having pulled off his gas mask for air. "You chickenshit pigs!" he yelled.

Blake ran on, then shoved the cart into a garage. The overhead door had broken off its runner on one side and hung down diagonally. He leaned against the back wall, out of sight. The horrible drugs and tension shook his body, then suddenly seized his middle like a gigantic hand, squeezing everything up out of his stomach. He was hallucinating now, he realized, as he saw his vomit swirl. He stepped away from the mess and wiped his mouth on his shirt sleeve. Some of the QDT had gotten through his antidote barrier.

He felt bad about the kid and angry that his reactions had been slowed. He couldn't escape the boy's tin-can voice repeating "God damn it!" in his mind.

Blake inhaled deeply through his nose and smelled the burnt-wire odor of his own chemical sweat. He looked around and saw odd swirling shapes in the dark corners of the garage. Over his vision floated a film of tiny colored dots, turning the world into a study in pointillism. He felt his skin tingling, especially in his face, as though he were faint. He had to take it easy now, calm his blood.

Then he noticed the sound of crickets. Thousands of crickets chirped in the garage around him. The racket deafened him to all else. He put his hands over his ears, but that merely changed the tone of their buzz. *Dammit, dammit, dammit,* they chirped. Blake's stomach twisted, and he bent over, retching dryly. He looked at the vomit on the floor. It moved toward

him! He was sure of it. He stepped back with a shiver
of fear and turned away. Then Blake saw the wounded
boy. He was sitting in the shopping cart, his entire
front drenched in blood. He saw the boy's chain
wrapped around his gas-mask neck. His tongue hung
out, blue, and his eyes gazed blankly dead. Blake
lurched away in panic. When he looked back at his
shopping cart, his client was in it again, pulling at the
upper lip with his fingers. The detective sat down on
a cinder block with his eyes closed and waited for
the sound of crickets to subside and his vision to
return to normal.

He remembered being the kid's age. He remembered working on Jacky Valdez's old Dodge Dart in
the garage behind the Valdez two-flat when they were
kids. Blake had been adjusting the extension light
over the engine. He turned to grab his soda and saw
the head silhouetted in the dirty garage door window—a
head wearing the Raider gang's short-brimmed cap.
The Raiders had been pressuring Blake and Jacky to
join. Now they were watching them. Somewhere outside a car's tires squealed.

In a moment's bravado, Blake grabbed a broken
pellet gun from the work bench and pointed it at the
window. The head bobbed back in panic, then flashed
out of sight in a scream of automobile tires and human
pain. Blake pulled out the cord on the extension light,
and the two boys cowered like criminals beneath the
door window.

The Raider boy's skull had split like a dropped
melon when a speeding car knocked him to the alley.
The boy in the car was a Street-King proving his
bravery by cruising Raider turf. It took six months for
the two gangs to stop killing each other over the
accident. Young Blake joined the Raiders in guilt, but
he never confessed his part in the death.

Blake thought back to the gang boys who'd just
attacked him. Through the chemical fog in his brain,

the memory of the shooting in the alley had lost its hard sense. Had it been a hallucination? He pulled the gun out of his pocket. It still felt warm. The gun looked very real. It had happened, all right. He found a tube of glue on the floor of the garage and carefully filled the gun's barrel and chamber, wiped it for fingerprints, and put it under a flowerpot against the wall.

When Blake dragged the cart with Scott back out into the alley, the shock of seeing the wounded boy not even a block away almost pushed him back into hallucinations. He'd felt as though he'd run miles from the shooting.

"You fucking assholes!" the boy screamed, his voice fading into pain at the end. Blake hesitated, then started moving toward Fishman's again. The kid looked too feisty to accept anything but hate. That spirit ought to get him through the bullet wound, at least.

3

Mona had locked the door after Blake left with Scott, then stood with her back to it, surveying the wreckage. "No disasters of the magnetic age for us," she said aloud, and sighed, resigned to the task ahead of her. She called Jake Fishman to let him know Blake and Scott were on the way.

"I'm sure this comes as no surprise to you," Fishman told her, "but I'd rather not see your boss around here today."

"Why not?"

"You mean aside from the fact he's got every shvartzer in Chicago out for his ass? He should go to Milwaukee and hide out for six months."

"What's he done, Jake?"

"Hear it from your boss. I don't butt in. I'm amazed you don't already know."

After that she could get no more information. Jake could be a pain sometimes. Mona didn't really like him.

Jake could be trusted to get a job done, but he never let loyalty stand in the way of profit. She knew he had worked both sides of certain situations, selling information to opposing parties. But since he limited his dealings to exactly what each customer requested, he believed he treated everyone fairly.

Mona knew Fishman's loyalty would not be an issue in this case. When hired to protect someone, even he would see the conflict of interest in selling that person to the competition.

She began making stacks of paper and file folders for the long sorting process. As she crouched down to pull a pile of messed billing forms from beneath his desk, Mona noticed out of the corner of her eye a small shiny object.

Here's something interesting, she thought. She reached up and peeled an electronic-surveillance device from the panel next to the drawer above her head and carried it out into the light for examination.

"Nasty little bug," she said. It reminded her, for some reason, of the newspaper Blake had found in the mysterious manila envelope. She grabbed the envelope and took it back to her desk. While she browsed through the sheets from inside, she kept the bug clutched tight in the palm of her hand, knowing that confining the mike often produced ear-splitting feedback. She smiled, imagining an agent bouncing out of his chair as though electrified, clutching at the headphones.

The sheets of newspaper were out of sequence. She rearranged the yellowed pages, noticing the "Fin de Siècle" and "Changing of the Millennia" sale ads had already started then, in November of last year. By the time New Millennium's Eve arrived, they'd all be sick of it. And they'd probably have to suffer through it twice, since the new millennium was actually to start in 2001.

Running through the pages, she noticed a continuing feature on Joseph Murray and his City Action Coalition. She knew about them. Over a year ago, Blake had been hired to free a young man from the Coalition's influence. His parents were convinced the boy had been brainwashed.

Murray's Coalition was essentially a group which fought for civil justice. But because they took on unpopular causes and were not afraid to use direct confrontation to achieve their goals, much of the public preceived them as glorified hoodlums or urban terrorists. There had been violence connected with some of their activities, but it was seldom clear whether the violence had originated with the group or with the police. The City Action Coalition was very unpopular among the police.

Blake freed the boy from his captors, which meant, actually, that he kidnapped the kid and returned him to his middle-class parents. But it was an unfortunate case. Blade had ended up more in sympathy with the Coalition than his employers. The kid returned to Murray, the parents were mad, and there was bad blood all around.

As Mona began to skim the article, she heard footsteps approach and stop outside the office door. The knob slowly turned. She felt a surge of fear go through her chest like a voltage spike. The collectors? Or was it the angry blacks Jake had warned about? In either case, she wasn't ready.

She moved quickly and silently, closing the window shades, turning out the lights, then running to wait with her back against the wall by the door.

Can it be Blake? she hoped. She heard metal slide into the lock, followed by the exploratory clicks of a pick-key. She found herself wishing she'd taken Blake's advice and spent the rest of the day at home. The metal tabs of the pick clicked into place, and she heard the inner bolt slide with a long scraping sound, raising a fearful tingling in her body. She felt foolish, realizing she still clutched the bug in her hand. She needed a weapon! Then she felt sickened, remembering the pistol Blake kept holstered under his desk. Would it still be there? She wanted to rush to get it, but it was too late. The knob turned and the door swung open.

"Shit," a man said from the hallway. He walked directly into the room and stood still for a moment, as though waiting for his vision to adjust to the darkness. Mona kept a nervous eye on him as she crept behind his back out the door. She turned to escape down the hall and saw the palm of a large hand zoom in and smack her hard against the forehead. Small lights flashed across her vision and ran up behind her eyeballs as she fell backward to the floor.

A man with short-cropped red hair stood over her and laughed. "Hey, Brubaker," he called into the office. "Look what got past you."

Brubaker came out. "It was dark," he said. "I thought they were gone. Let's pull her inside before someone sees." The two men each grabbed an arm and dragged her into the office, closing the door behind. The red-haired man flipped on the lights.

"What'd you do to her?" Brubaker asked. He crouched down and examined the large red patch in the middle of Mona's forehead.

Mona moaned and rolled to her side, instinctively rubbing the back of her head where it had hit the floor.

"You're lucky you ain't buzzed, honey," the red-haired man said though Mona was not yet hearing him. He raised his bare palm to show Brubaker. "I wasn't wearing one."

"Yeah," Brubaker said. He bent to rub a thumb across her forehead. "She'd have a bruise popped up by now."

Mona pushed the hand away and sat up. Waves of dizziness swirled through her head and she noticed, oddly, that her left fist was clenched tight. Inside she could still feel the small hardness of the bug. She thought of Blake's gun.

"Come on," Brubaker said. He pulled her to her feet, and she leaned dizzily against him, her left hand above his waist. Brubaker's jacket pocket pushed open, and Mona dropped the bug inside, unnoticed. She pushed away from him and sat back on her desktop.

"Where'd Blake take Scott?" Brubaker asked her.

"I don't know," she said.

Brubaker slapped Mona hard across the face, tumbling her easily off the desk. She ended kneeling on the floor, facing away from the two men, her face throbbing and hot. Silently she thanked Brubaker for knocking her closer to Blake's desk.

"Ain't no need to get rough," the red-haired man said. "I'm sure the lady wants to help us out." Mona turned to see him strapping a buzzer onto his palm, his face a grinning obscenity. "Now, why don't you answer the man's question," he suggested.

"I don't know where they went," she said, rising from the floor.

"If I slap you in the head again," he said, "you ain't going to get up a second time." She backed away from him, hating him, and moved around behind Blake's desk. "You look kind of scared, honey. You've got good reason." He held up his palm, exposing the buzzer. "You ever seen a brain after one of these hits? It dissolves a little section. Looks pretty fucking ugly."

"No," Mona cried, outraged and angry. "Leave me alone." She collapsed, kneeling behind the desk, feeling nearly as hysterical as she sounded.

"Just tell us where they are," Brubaker said impatiently.

Mona reached cautiously beneath the desk and thanked God, it was there. All her fear channeled into rage and loathing. She stood suddenly, her arms fully extended with two hands wrapped around Blake's gun, the muzzle pointed straight at the red-haired man's chest.

"Get out of here," she said, her voice still quivering.

"Now, you ain't going to shoot me," the man said quietly. He ran the fingers of his buzzer-less hand through his short-cropped hair. "We don't want you or your boss. Just Scott. He owes us." The man made a small sideward gesture, and Brubaker took a step to separate himself from his partner.

"If he takes another step," Mona said loudly, not moving the gun, "I shoot you."

"I never meant to hurt you," the red-haired man said. "We just want information."

"Shut up!" Mona shouted. She shot a bullet into the floor between his feet. The man yelped and jumped back.

"You got three seconds before the next one crushes your sternum," she told him, her body trembling in anger.

"All right," he said indignantly. "Just have Blake call us. Carlyle and Brubaker. We're in the book." He unstrapped his buzzer and walked out the door, Brubaker following sideways like a crab, keeping his front to her.

Mona moved from behind the desk and went out to watch them down the hall. Other people passed in the corridor. Some glanced at her furtively, but no one asked about the shot or her gun. She relocked the door and stood by her desk, still holding the pistol and shaking all over.

"God damn it!" she screamed with all her might. She kicked a stack of folders from the floor up into the air. "Stinking shits!" she shouted. "Look at this!" She stamped her foot onto the wound in the floor. Where the bullet had dug in, wood splintered up like the earth around a tiny animal's burrow. " 'You look kind of scared, honey,' " she said, mocking Carlyle's voice. That two agents as moronic as these could have got the upper hand on her, even for a moment, made her furious. And then to threaten her with a buzzer!

Mona hurried over and pushed back the shade in time to see Carlyle and Brubaker climb into a black gas-driven car. The doors closed and the engine started as she pushed open the glass, leaned out with both arms, and fired a slug through their back window. The auto jerked hard into the car parked behind them, then popped forward into the street with wheels spinning, cracking the outside back taillight of the car ahead. She watched it speed off around the corner, squealing tires all the way.

"I should have killed you when I had the chance," she shouted after them. Behind her a train's wheels screamed as it rounded the curve on the elevated tracks one block away. Mona closed the window, slid back the shade, and paced the room, cocking and uncocking the gun.

She finally sat down in her chair and tried to calm herself by reading the article from Blake's mysterious manila envelope, a long, rambling piece from the Chicago *Reader* on Joseph Murray and the radical activism of his City Action Coalition. It came as a confusing blur of words, some parts praising Murray for his action on behalf of the people, some parts damning him for his violent methods. Murray, the protector of the weak. Murray, the terrorist. She couldn't concentrate enough to make sense.

Then the phone rang and startled a yelp out of her. She calmed herself and picked up the receiver. It was the police.

4

Blake pushed the cart with Scott down the last alley and through the gate into the yard behind Jake Fishman's building. Inside the door to the back steps, Fishman waited.

"I heard a gunshot and thought maybe you'd taken it," Fishman said offhandedly, but with a slight edge to his voice, as though disappointed. The odd-jobs man slouched in the doorway. He was tall, in his forties, bald on top, with large protruding eyes.

"I almost did," Blake said. "A gang kid took it instead. Give me a hand with this gooney."

Fishman didn't move. "Mona called me," he said. "This is the guy you're protecting?"

"Yeah. Let's get him inside," Blake said.

"You're out of your mind bringing him here. You jeopardize me. You jeopardize yourself. Now look at him. I had no intention of letting you in here."

"I can't go on carting him around the streets, Jake. And being outside is making me nervous. How about we talk upstairs?"

Fishman grunted ill-temperedly, and they pulled Scott out of the shopping cart and half-carried, half-dragged him up the stairs.

"Why didn't you give this guy some thalamin?" Fishman asked, out of breath, as they pulled Scott into the apartment on the top floor of the three-flat.

"I did. He dropped it down a sewer." They dumped

him into a kitchen chair. His arms rose up and jerked in palsied motion. He began muttering nonsense syllables. Fishman patted Scott on the back. "You're a bright boy," he told him.

"He's a winner," Blake agreed. "Maybe you can give me a clue to the kind of hospitality I've been getting. I go to see Bowens at the diner—he's a regular source for me—and he walks out. Now I came here, you don't want to let me in the door."

"You're breaking my heart," Fishman told him. "What are you doing with an HRL defaulter?"

Blake shrugged. "If he doesn't pay his bill, I can always turn him in for the deposit."

"Anything for a buck," Fishman said dryly. He turned to the refrigerator and pulled out a tray of ice. He handed the ice and a kitchen towel off the back of a chair to Blake, indicating his reddened hand. "That looks swollen."

Blake sat down at the kitchen table across from the babbling Scott and applied ice where the kid had chain-swatted the gun from his hand.

"What the hell are you doing in this neighborhood?" Fishman asked.

"I don't get you," Blake said. His two middle fingers felt stiff as he flexed them, and he wondered if a bone had been broken.

"They picked up Joseph Murray for bombing the First National."

"I saw a photo of the bombing in the paper. Unbelievable. Did Murray do it?"

"You'd know better than me," Fishman replied.

Blake let that one pass. "They sprayed that QDT in taking Murray?" he asked.

"I imagine."

Scott leaned in his chair like a tree about to topple. Fishman pushed him up against the table.

"Why Murray?" Blake said.

"Very coy, Gregory. But there's no use trying to

impress me. Word's already out that you co-opped
Murray on the bank bombing."

"What?" Blake said. "I don't cooperate with the
law. You know that."

Fishman looked at him, his bug eyes expressionless.
"Didn't you give Murray's boys trouble once before?"
he asked. "If they find you, I hope you've written
your last will and testament. Personally, I hate the
sight of blood. That's why I don't want you around."

"Come on, Jake," the detective said.

Scott flailed his arms wildly and knocked a drinking
glass from the table to smash on the floor. "Why don't
we put Lightning in the crib?" Blake suggested. Fishman
nodded. They pulled Scott out of his chair and dragged
him into a large walk-in pantry. All the shelves had
been stripped from the walls. They put him on a
narrow cot, locked the reinforced door, and sat back
at the kitchen table. Blake felt a pinch and stood up.
A section of yellowed plastic upholstery poked up at
him like a finger. Blake curled it back and sat again.

"The First National doesn't seem like a Murray
job," Blake said. "People were killed in there."

"The old radical gets hard. Cops or customers, they
all blow up the same."

"So, the People's Man, Murray, blasted the People
into hamburger, and I cooperated him right into the
slam. That's what you think?"

"You known me too long, Gregory. I don't think.
To me, a fact is what the majority believes—unless I
got hard info otherwise. I used to make judgments. I
got surprises. Now, I don't judge."

"Do you mind?" Blake took the receiver off the
phone on the wall. Fishman shrugged. Blake dialed.

"Hello?" Mona's voice said.

"Thank God you're there," Blake told her. "I need
a little sanity. I had a hell of a time getting over here,
and now Jake Fishman is treating me like a leper."

"Cut it out," Fishman muttered in the background.

"It hasn't been great around here either," Mona said. "And the police just phoned."

"The police?" Blake looked at Fishman. "What did they want?"

"A Detective Lieutenant Ahern said he needed further cooperation on what he called the Murray/First National case."

"Shit. Even the police believe I co-opped Murray."

"That newspaper in the envelope had a long article on Murray too. I haven't found anything else. Except we were bugged."

"Great," Blake said. "Now we're shoved into another case. It was probably Murray's people who ransacked our place."

"Maybe," Mona said. "But I don't think so. I have a funny feeling the mess in here had something to do with Scott."

"Any reason for that feeling?"

"Not really. Just a feeling."

"Has Murray injured citizens since we investigated him?" Blake asked her. "Bystanders? A bombing like this doesn't seem like his style. The Coalition never hurt any civilians that I recall."

"Well, you and I both know how ruthless they are when crossed," Mona told him. "But that's more personal. I don't remember anything like terrorism. And I read through the article from that envelope. It says the Coalition tries to get power for the poor. They've taken actions against the Chicago Housing Authority. A lot of protests against police misuse of force. They have done some property damage, but even that's rare."

"Have they ever used actual kidnapping? Any kind of real violence?"

"Not publicly. As far as I remember, the only time people were injuring was during clashes with police. The article seems to back that up. The Coalition is most respected for cutting down the black-on-black crime around Cabrini-Green and the Taylor Homes. All their propaganda is antiviolence. But they've taken a lot of heat because they haven't had any effect on the black-on-white crime in those same areas."

"The guy's addicted to his own adrenaline," Fishman insisted loudly. "A radical shvartzer. What do you expect?"

"Jake was mad when I called him," Mona said. "He didn't want you around."

"I know," Blake told her. "Anyway, why don't you get on the terminal this afternoon and see if you can trace who owns Scott's HRL. If you have a feeling about him being connected to our office break-in, follow it up. Your hunches have saved my ass at least once."

"You are very sweet to admit it," she teased. "Should I try hacking into the banks' HRL files?" she asked.

"Yes. The guy on the phone told me not to buzz Scott. And his HRL doesn't actually default until Monday. Something's fishy."

"Okay."

"And get a police ambulance two or three blocks south on Fishman's alley. There's a kid with a gunshot wound. Use a pay phone."

"Anything else?"

"Got a rocket pack to rescue me out of here?"

"I wish," she said, and hesitated. "Two collectors were here."

Blake felt a sudden surge of concern. "What happened?"

"They were pretty awful. I took a shot at them."

"Christ. Did you hit them?"

"I don't think so. No. I'm sure I didn't."

"Why don't you go on home now? I hate to think of you being in danger."

"Well, Blake, what a nice thing to say."

He heard the lilt in her voice, and it made him smile

foolishly. What the hell? After two years of working
with Mona, was he falling in love?

"Go on, now. Go on home."

"No. I put a good scare into them," she said, beginning to feel good about the occurrence for the first
time. "In fact, I think I scared the hell out of them.
I'm keeping the office gun on me."

"All right," he said. "I guess you can take care of
yourself."

"And you take care of yourself. Don't shake hands
with any militant political activists."

"At least they don't wear buzzers," Blake replied.
They hung up, and he turned to face Fishman. "Can
you rent me your car?"

Fishman looked at him for a long moment. "I don't
want you seen in my car," he said. "And I don't need
you seen around my place either. Ever since the city
dug up the subway and knocked down those slums, all
the Cabrini shvartzers moved over here. I thought this
neighborhood was on the way up. That's why I bought
this dump. Now look at it."

"Never speculate on real estate, Jack," Blake said.
"Not unless you're in with the big boys."

"Thanks for the late advice. But the last thing I
need around here is you. My new neighbors all think
Murray is God. So send somebody else tomorrow to
pick up Pretty Boy."

"If I go on foot, I may not be around tomorrow,"
Blake told him. "You want to be stuck with somebody
too dumb to take a pill?"

Fishman stared out the window down at the bare
yard below. His eyes, lips, and Adam's apple pro-
truded so far it seemed his head was pumped full of
air. "Why does April in Chicago always look like
October in Chicago?" he asked. He didn't look at
Blake, and Blake didn't answer. "Come on," Fishman
said. "Passover is coming. I'll emulate my great ances-
tor and lead you out of the desert." He got up and

opened the back door. "You crawl down the stairs so nobody sees."

"You didn't make this big of a deal when you kept me standing on the back sidewalk," Blake said, getting down below window level.

"So maybe I'm tormenting you," Fishman said. "Keep quiet." He led the way to the bottom and motioned for Blake to wait. Then he pulled Blake's shopping cart from the yard into the enclosed landing at the bottom of the stairs. He brought a box up from the basement and lined the inside of the cart with rags. "Climb in there and crouch," he told Blake.

"Now I know you're trying to torment me." Blake took two steps up the stairs and lowered himself into the basket like a jack going back into the box. He bent over so his face rested on his knees.

"You look like a Mohammedan bending to Mecca," Fishman said.

"You make me glad I'm trusting you. I hope I can return the favor."

"What favor? You'll get a bill." Fishman dumped the rest of the rags on top of him and heard a muffled "Jesus" followed by a sneeze.

"Sorry. They were dusty," Fishman said. "Quiet, now. We're going." He pushed the cart out the door, down the walk to the side door of the garage. As he unlocked the garage, two men walked up to his fence.

"Jake," the taller of them called. "We need to talk."

Fishman looked involuntarily at the cart. He quickly shifted his gaze to the two men. "What do you need?" he asked.

"We know you work sometime for thees fellow Gregory Blake," the second man, a curly-haired Hispanic, said. "We want some informations from him."

"You could've heard Murray's arrested," the first man said. "We want to talk to Blake about the defense."

"Where can he find you?" Fishman asked them.

The two men looked at each other. The Hispanic smiled. "He come to Biltey's Tavern in Pilsen. You know that place?"

"I could find it," Fishman said.

"What have you got in the basket?" the taller one asked.

Under the rags, Blake felt his stomach start churning. If he tried to get his hand to his pocket for the stiletto, he'd give himself away. He damned himself for allowing Fishman to make him so vulnerable.

"Just a bunch of old clothes," Fishman said. Blake heard the hesitation in his voice. "I'm taking them out of here," he said. "Giving them to the resale shop."

"Got anything in my size?" the tall one asked.

"Hee-hee, you *polaco*," the Hispanic giggled. "You always the same."

"Take a look for yourself," Fishman offered. Blake tensed, ready to spring. He tried desperately to remember in which pocket he'd put the knife.

"Great," the Polack said. The sound of the rusty fence gate squealing open ran through Blake's spine like cold steel.

"Only thing is," Fishman said, "these clothes are full of crabs."

"Crabs!" the Polack backed off.

"Crabs?" the Hispanic asked. "What? Those fishes?"

"No. They're fucking crotch bugs," the Polack said, closing the gate behind them. "Let's get the hell away from here."

"Man, you give away fucking crotch bugs?" the Hispanic asked, backing off. "*Mierda!* You are one sick fucking man, *hombre.*"

"I'll take them to the Laundromat first," Fishman promised.

"We'll see you later," the Polack called, already well down the alley.

"So long," Fishman told them. He waited until they

were well out of hearing. Then he struggled the cart over the garage-door threshold, working as awkwardly as a lobster on dry land. He closed the door behind him, opened his car trunk, and pulled the rags off Blake.

"Get in there," he told him quietly.

"Pretty quick thinking," Blake whispered as he wedged himself into the tiny trunk.

"I don't know," Fishman said. "I just told them the truth." He closed the trunk door.

Once they were on the road, the two had to talk loudly to be heard through the material of the back seat. Blake told Fishman to take him to John Dwight's Midland Waste Reclamation. After a short time, they fell into silence.

Curled tight in the rubber-scented darkness of the trunk, Blake was trapped in with reflections on his sometimes sordid, sometimes absurd livelihood. The year 2000 sprang to his mind like a conditional response. The politicians and media flashed it in the public's face as a beacon of hope, a day of new beginnings, a clean slate for all. But in fact, the city was exploiting the coming of the year 2000 as shamelessly as the retailers promoting their "Sales of the Millennium." Even atop Blake's own office building, an elegant billboard pictured the 2000 Fest couple in evening dress dancing under moonlight. "Changing the Millennia Ball," it proclaimed. "Midnight, 1999. Navy Pier."

With all the buildup of hoopla and despair, New Millennium's Eve was sure to be explosive. An incredible number of people were looking toward it with real dread. And there was a hard-core crew of fanatics making sure they never forgot that dread.

For the first time since the Middle Ages, public self-flagellation had come back into style. Flagellants roamed the streets, whipping themselves to atone for their own and the world's sins. The end of all time was imminent, they said, and they had to make ready the way for the Lord. To most people, believers and non-believers alike, this was not the way Jesus would want his way prepared, and the flagellants were routinely harrassed by citizens and police.

Worse than the flagellants were the Apocalytes. They wore white biblical robes and took all their misdirected cues from the Book of Revelation. The Apocalytes spent a lot of time on busy street corners screaming about the whore of Babylon and the scarlet beast. They shouted about Jezebel and invited passersby to join the triumphal rainbow around the throne. But their main refrain was that the seals had all been broken and Gog and Magog were upon us. Only those servants who were sealed over to God could be saved. At this point they would raise one poor recruit above the crowd and "seal" him on the forehead with a battery-operated branding iron in the shape of a cross. Blake had been present at one of these "sealings," and the smell of burning human flesh had been nauseating. People had shouted their outrage, and those Apocalytes involved were arrested shortly after.

In Chicago, a punk gang calling themselves the Anti-Christers had taken up the attack. At several of the demonstrations, Anti-Christers had broken in and branded the Apocalytes with "666" on their foreheads, the apocalyptic mark of the Beast, before they could be "sealed to the Lord." Blake had heard rumors that the Anti-Christer movement was beginning to follow the Apocalytes to New York and London, as well. He wondered if the same company were producing the battery-operated branding irons for both the Apocalytes and the Anti-Christers.

Blake tried to shift to a more comfortable position in the trunk, but only bumped his head against something sharp. He tried moving his hand to rub the sore spot, but found he was too boxed in to reach it. Lying still with his head stinging, he smelled faint gas fumes swirling around his nose and hoped the trip wouldn't take much longer.

The gas fumes reminded him of paint. He thought of kids he'd seen painting fire hydrants to look like mushroom clouds. It was like a horrible, nihilistic twist on the patriotic fire hydrants all the kids had painted before the national Bicentennial, when he was young. Blake had painted one himself, though his father had made fun of it—not made fun particularly of Blake's efforts, but fun of the whole thing.

Blake's parents had both been political activists during the 1960's. His dad suspected all patriotism was a blind cover-up of national crimes.

"Always remember you were born in the sixties," his father occasionally told him. "Don't forget what that means." Blake would nod when he heard that, and it surely meant something to his father, but Blake really couldn't remember if he'd ever figured out what it meant himself. Something political, he suspected. His father had left them before Blake had ever thought to question him about it.

His mother, on the other hand, had mellowed her idealism from the political to New Age spiritualism.

"Someday, Gregory," she had told him, "science and religion will merge." He remembered her standing over him with her hand on his shoulder, her curly hair shining in the light behind her head. He sat at the tiny kitchen table with his homework in front of him. Seventh grade.

"When we know all there is to know, it'll all be in the same book. The source of creation and the creatures of the spirit world will be facts like the structure of the atom." Her eyes glistened, and an excited smile wrinkled up the lines above her cheeks. He smiled back, feeling warm and happy with her. The smells from dinner still hung in the room.

"Maybe you'll make some of those discoveries. Maybe you'll show us ignorant peasants what's what."

He had giggled as she hugged his head to her side. She released him and went back humming to the dishes.

Gregory had looked out the kitchen window at all the back porches lit in bubbles of electric light. Maybe I will, he had thought. Maybe I just will.

The memory of his hopes made the trunk even more stifling. He felt the car pull to a stop and Fishman get out. Then the trunk door opened, and Blake climbed out to find himself in a park. "Where the hell are we?" he asked.

"McCormick Boulevard, just north of Devon." Fishman slammed the trunk closed.

"Midland is still four blocks away. What're you letting me off here for?"

"Life is a lonely process," Fishman told him. "Death even more so. I don't intend to horn in on yours."

"Thanks," Blake said.

"Not at all." Fishman got back into the car. "And remember," he called out the window, "send somebody else for the gooney tomorrow."

Blake stretched his back and turned a few neck rolls to get out the kinks. He remembered the cars of his childhood. Oldsmobiles. Pontiacs. Those were cars you could live in. He remembered his old Uncle Bob: "I got me a big Buick," he'd say, stretching the word "big" as long as his car. In Uncle Bob's trunk, Blake probably could have stretched out comfortably and taken a nap.

Blake started walking north across the new April grass of the park toward Midland. He wondered how serious the City Action Coalition threat was. He wondered if Fishman had been right to be so cautious. Would someone be waiting at Midland?

5

"Take a look. Yesterday this tank was full of pure liquid mercury." Dwight's voice squawked from a voice wafer on the chest of his black coverall. A clear Plexiglas helmet completely encased his head. He led Blake up a set of stairs to the platform over a round tank the size of a backyard swimming pool.

Blake had entered Midland without incident. He and Dwight had donned protective clothing and proceeded to the "scene of the crime." Now the problem was making sense of it. Blake edged forward on the platform, slipping between a computer control terminal and a stand of interconnecting chrome pipes and swirling glass tubes. Below, the material in the tank was a crusted mass of solid vermilion.

The detective tilted forward, turning to get a good look past the reflection of his face on the inside of the helmet. The hiss of the air purifier in his suit and the continuous plastic around his head clouded his senses. Beyond the tank a row of huge waste-cracking reclamation towers dwarfed the two men. Blake turned back to see Dwight frowning from behind his mask.

"Now what the hell am I supposed to do?" Dwight asked. His lips seemed to move a half-second ahead of the voice from the wafer on his chest. "The mercury is already ordered. I have to ship next week."

"Let's get out of these God damned suits," Blake said. "I feel like I'm in orbit."

Dwight went down the stairs from the platform. Blake took another look at the sabotaged mercury. High overhead, colored gases spewed from pipe ends and valves, their blasts adding to a roar which shook the air like a giant waterfall. Blake's head felt as though it were packed in cotton.

He descended to the bottom of the platform and sat down backward behind Dwight on a three-wheeled electric cart. They drove fast to the other end of the complex, zipping through the aisles between huge open holding tanks, and climbed the steps through the air lock to Dwight's office, dropping their coveralls and breathing apparatus in the uniform room.

It was good to breathe and move freely again. Blake stood in front of the large window to the side of Dwight's desk and looked out over the complicated array of separation and distillation equipment. Engineers and workers in blue and black coveralls and Plexiglas helmets punched commands at control terminals. They monitored huge robotic arms and set up commands for the mixing and distilling of chemicals. Others whirred through the long complex on electric shop carts like programmed automatons.

Dwight approached Blake from behind and stood with him by the window. "It's a hell of a thing to lose," he said.

The statement surprised Blake, and he looked at the other man. New wrinkles lined Dwight's long face, and his wide shoulders drooped. Dwight had always seemed more at home in his business than anyone else he knew. Certainly more so than Blake himself. Blake tried to stay clean as a detective, but sometimes the work got dirty. Dwight's operation was impeccable.

"You look like hell," Blake said. "It can't just be the mercury."

"I'm sure I don't look as bad as you," Dwight replied. Blake brushed at the patch of dried blood on his jacket sleeve. When he'd washed his face in the men's room, his skin had looked very pale. The after-effects of thalamin.

"But you're right," Dwight said, "It's not just the mercury." The businessman moved behind his desk and pulled out a bottle, pouring himself a drink and offering one to Blake. Blake took it and looked at the clock on the wall: 1:17 P.M. Dwight drained his glass.

"Do you remember how I lost my petroleum company?"

Blake sat in the overstuffed leather chair to the right of the desk. He sipped his drink. "That was before I knew you."

"Hostile takeover," Dwight told him. "Apollo Oil wanted drilling rights I had, so they started buying up our stock. I tried to find a white knight—some conglomerate to take ownership who wouldn't interfere. Nobody had the capital. Apollo grabbed up a majority of our stock and forced a merger." Dwight shrugged. "I tried to run things as I'd always done, but they replaced me. Then oil prices dropped. Apollo sold off my fields and equipment for a loss." He walked to the window and looked out. "When I started Midland Waste here, I swore never to sell stock."

"So what's the problem?" Blake quietly poured half of his drink into the rubber-tree pot next to his chair. Dwight turned to face him.

"There's a new kind of hostile takeover for hardline independents. If you don't have stock, they do what it takes to ruin your company and drive you bankrupt. Then they take you to court and buy out your assets by force. They get you cheap." Dwight looked bitterly into his glass and pulled out the bottle. He made the offer, but Blake held back his glass. Dwight poured into his own tumbler and put the bottle away.

Blake brushed his fingertips over his thick black eyebrows, wondering how much of Dwight's suspicions about the mercury might be pure paranoia. "Who'd be after you?" he asked.

"Rengore," Dwight said.

"Aren't they the people who make QDT?"

"The crowd-control gas. Yes, that among other things. Rengore Chemical is their biggest division. The sabotaged mercury was earmarked for them."

"Why should they bother you?"

"They've made offers for a buy-out. An outfit like ours would be a big benefit for them. There's a government incentive for waste reclamation. Congress wants to encourage new facilities. The problem is, corporations who create the wastes, like Rengore, can also get the tax write-off for buying existing companies."

"What about accepting Rengore's offer?" Blake watched the creases deepen below Dwight's eyes and down his cheeks.

"Once the contract is signed, it's all over. They'd bring in their own boy." Dwight rubbed his fingertips over his temples as though the conversation were giving him a headache.

"You'd have the money," Blake suggested.

Dwight slammed his hand on the desk. "I don't want the money! I got money when Apollo fucked me in the rear! I'm tired of building businessess for other people to ruin." He sat for a moment, then spoke again, softly. "I need to know if that mercuric sulfide is Rengore's trick. We've got to stop their next move if we can, so don't keep me waiting." He drained his glass and turned to stare out the window.

Blake looked at the executive surveying his domain. The last days of the century, and running a business there's still one honest man, Blake thought. John Dwight, Dinosaur. He set down his drink and left.

The detective passed through Midland's offices to the reception area and had to wait for people entering the building to clear the final air-lock chamber before he could exit. When they cleared, he got into the chamber with a businesswoman wearing a pleated skirt.

The door sealed shut behind them. As the suction fans in the ceiling began dragging in outside air through the grid beneath their feet, the woman's skirt flew up around her. She impatiently pushed it back down over her thighs, angered by this affront to her dignity.

Blake couldn't even enjoy a wry smile at her expense. The rushing air and change of pressure left him slightly disoriented as the air-lock doors opened onto the outside world.

The businesswoman scurried off as Blake took a moment to catch his bearings. He damned the government for this superfluous torture. The plant area where all the actual chemical processes took place was atmosphere-isolated from the office area as well as the outside world. To also require that the office, which was no more dangerous to the environment than any other kind of office, have a seperate sealed air system reflected the legislative overzealousness of the earlier nineties. Driven by scandalous excesses of mob-run disposal and reclamation outfits, Congress responded with regulations that plagued businessmen and allowed government inspectors to line their pockets with shake-down money.

After lunch at a restaurant down the street from Midland, Blake decided Rengore, Inc. would be his next stop. He needed to see if Dwight's paranoia had any foundation. He called a cab and gave the driver the address.

As they traveled down Lincoln Avenue toward Peterson, they drove under a viaduct spray-painted with "199-8, 199-9, 199-NADA!" The end of the century. This attitude was honest, if nihilistic. But still, it irritated Blake to the point that when they reached Lake Shore Drive, not even the sight of the city's beautiful lakeshore or steel-glass-and-stone skyline helped lighten his mood.

As they crossed the river into the Loop, Blake remembered Fishman's caution in approaching Midland,

and he directed the driver to drop him on Lower Wacker Drive. Blake had a better chance of avoiding anyone waiting in ambush by entering through the basement delivery door than at the well-traveled Michigan Avenue entrance.

The driver turned off down the ramp into the eerie green-lit lower level of Wacker Drive. Blake had the cabby stop where Lower Wacker met Lower South Water, just a few blocks from Rengore's delivery entrance on Lower Michigan.

Far off to his left as Blake walked, concrete pillars gave way to open space and the river. Three feet above on his right ran a walkway, though no human could walk it. Every four feet, another stout wood beam leaned drunkenly into a plank. Wedged in, the planks held back the crumbling brick of the walls. What skyscraper sits on top of that? he wondered.

Blake didn't like being underground. The concrete overhead was etched with cracks dripping tiny stalactites of white lime. The air felt damp and unhealthy.

At one time, of course, all this "underground" had actually been street level. In the early part of the century, this land had been the south Water Street Market, where ships and barges unloaded their wares from the river—mainly foodstuffs. Ramshackle warehouses, shops, and wagons dotted the area. By the 1920's South Water had aged into an eyesore. Truck delivery lowered the importance of the river, so the city moved the market out of the Loop and covered this land over. Main street level for Wacker, South Water, Michigan, and a few others all moved one flight up, keeping the unsightly commercial traffic underground. Out of sight.

That was the way Chicago worked, Blake knew. If you didn't like the way something looked, pave it over. Cover it up. But down here, even the original cobblestones still lay exposed in patches of the street.

He turned away from the river, taking a last look at

the natural light filtering through the girders of the
Wabash Avenue bridge—light rendered stroboscopic
by the movement of traffic above. The upper level
would have been exhilarating: cars and buses travel-
ing, pretty women carrying packages or briefcases,
and lovers at the railings looking down over the water.
On the lower level Blake walked alone. Even delivery
trucks seemed to move furtively.

He turned off Wabash toward Michigan, walking
slowly and watching for anyone who might be watching for him. Concrete, brick, and asphalt, lit by overhead vapor lights, surrounded him. On the subterranean
truck docks, workmen looked like criminals loading
stolen goods. The cars parked might all have been
waiting only to be chopped or disguised. Out of the
pavement, parking meters stuck up like odd jokes on
legality, many of their unbreakable Plexi faces frosted
over with spray paint.

The entrance he sought lay a half-block east of
Michigan in an alley that dipped deeper underground.
At the bottom he opened a steel door next to a tall
sliding truck entry and walked past the truck dock and
receiving area to the elevator. As he waited for the
car, he felt half-surprised no one challenged him. The
elevator took him to the ninety-first floor, and he
entered the executive offices of Rengore Chemical.
Time to stir up a little trouble, he thought.

Blake got a peculiar look on telling the receptionist
he wanted to see the president. She looked at the
remnants of the bloodstain on his sleeve. His clothes
were still somewhat rumpled from the trunk ride; his
eyes were bloodshot and his skin sallow in the after-
math of QDT and its antidote. This man wanted to see
the company president?

When she announced Blake as representing John
Dwight and Midland Waste Reclamation, it was her
greater shock to be told to send him right in.

"Mr. Blake," Byron Frambeen said, looking at the

detective quizzically and slightly amused. Frambeen
wore a blue three-piece suit tailored snug to his slender body. Eternalast weave, the soft metallic fabric of
his clothing, was wasted on anyone who could afford
it. The dictates of fashion would have them discarding
garments decades before the new synthetic fabric lost
its fresh look. On his right hand, Frambeen wore a
wide gold ring with an inset diamond. His hair was
trimmed and waved carefully. Even his fingernails
glowed with the subtle buff of a recent manicure.

"Mr. Frambeen," Blake said. "You'll forgive my
appearance. I was involved in a mishap on the way
here."

"Nothing serious, I hope." The two men sat down
with the president's enormous oak desk between them.
The blue waters of the North Side lakeshore extended
behind Frambeen far below on the other side of the
window. Blake noticed the executive's scent drift to
his nostrils—very pleasant—but found himself longing for the honesty of gas fumes.

"Just inconvenient," Blake replied. "I'm here about
your offer to buy Midland Waste Reclamation."

"Really?" Frambeen replied eagerly.

"Yes," Blake said. "Dwight doesn't want to sell."

"Oh." The man looked disappointed, then puzzled.
"You came to tell me that?"

"John Dwight is upset. He asked me to do some
looking around. It seems there's been sabotage at
Midland."

Frambeen gave one of the most effective shows of
minor dismay Blake had ever seen.

"Oh, my," he said.

"Yes," the detective went on. "Dwight wondered if
somebody was trying to put him in the mood to sell.
Perhaps someone in this building here."

Byron Frambeen looked surprised, then began to
laugh delightedly until tears came to his eyes. "Oh,
my dear," he said, gaining control of himself. "Yes,

my poor dear John. What he must think." He pulled a monogrammed linen handkerchief from his pocket and wiped his eyes. "Yes, yes," he said. "You know, I only make these offers to buy his business to tease him. I suppose I shouldn't do it, but it makes him so damned mad. It's just fun. You heard what happened with his first company and Apollo Oil?"

Blake nodded.

"Yes. Unfortunate," Frambeen said. "A hostile take-over can leave some bitter losers in its wake. Of course, I don't believe Dwight would ever sell Midland. Even if he did, I'm not interested."

"You'd have no motive for a takeover?"

"Oh, now," Frambeen said, waving his hand to dismiss that idea, "there's always a reason to acquire. Midland provides a necessary service. If we owned them, that service might be cheaper and more secure. But I wouldn't want to take over Dwight."

"Why not?"

"Dwight's an idealist. He takes less profit and does a better job than anyone I can call to mind. In the long run, he's good for the city. For me, it's an investment to let Dwight run Midland."

"Why an investment?" Blake asked cautiously.

"I have a board of directors who expect me to wring every dime from an operation. I couldn't make the decisions Dwight makes. As it is, I do a profitable business with Dwight, and he helps keep the city a viable base for my operations." Frambeen thought about it a moment. "If you were to characterize me as a shark," he said, looking at Blake with the barest gleam of humor in his eye, "then Dwight is my remora. The remora swims along with the shark and scavenges scraps from the kills. He even has a suction fin to cling to the shark's body and 'hitch rides.' " Frambeen gestured expressively, imitating the action of a suction fin with his palm. "Undoubtedly the shark could nourish himself on the remora, but he doesn't.

They have a mutually beneficial relationship and coexist peacefully." He finished the explanation with a flourish and a winning smile.

Blake knew bullshit when he smelled it, but this was one of the most elegantly prepared crocks he'd been served. "Then who might have a motive to sabotage Midland?"

Frambeen raised his hands helplessly. "I couldn't guess who Dwight's enemies might be," he replied. "What did they do?"

"Turned some mercury into dried red mud."

"Mercury," the executive said thoughtfully. He got up from his desk and walked to a cabinet in the wall. He pressed a button and a panel slid up like an automatic garage door, revealing an efficient wet bar inside. Frambeen served himself a glass of water, walked to the window, and stood looking out over the highrises, bright as knife blades stabbing the sky.

"That mercury could have been meant for us," Frambeen said. "You may know, we supply QDT to the government and military."

"I've heard that."

"QDT has a relatively short shelf life. It must be brought back to us periodically or it loses potency."

"How nice for you."

Frambeen looked at him uncertainly, then decided to smile. "Yes," he said. "The rejuvenating process requires surprising amounts of mercury, which become tainted. Midland purifies it for us." Frambeen stood for a long time, staring out at the lakeshore, tapping his index finger on his upper lip.

"And?" Blake prompted.

Frambeen looked at him absently, then came back to his desk. "We've had pressure from groups to stop QDT production. I don't know why," he said irritably. "It's the victims who benefit the most. Surely a few hours of delirium are preferable to being ripped by police bullets. We should use more QDT. In situations foreign as well as domestic. Our country is locked into some very backward treaties."

"So you think protesters are the culprits?"

"We are security-conscious here. It would be easier to get at us through our suppliers. But it's difficult to say."

Blake thanked him and got up to leave.

"I hope you solve Dwight's problem," Frambeen said. "This sort of thing hurts us all."

What really hurts me, Blake thought as he rode the elevator down to the main-floor lobby, are my God damned legs. It felt as though the drugs and poisons of the day had turned to gravy in the veins around his knees.

Everything had got awfully complicated in a hurry. Blake needed to discover who'd sabotaged Dwight's operation. He needed to make peace somehow with Murray's followers, and that would mean finding the real bomber to clear Murray's name. With the newspaper article he'd found, it looked like the break-in at his office was connected with Murray, as well. And Scott. Why did he take on that idiot Scott?

Then Blake remembered the look on Mona's face. She'd wanted him to do it. Suddenly he wished she were with him. Mona could help. Mona always helped. And she was beautiful. Sometimes he thought he should say the hell with his private rules. He was a lonely detective, once you scraped away the activity. When was the last time he'd kissed a woman who meant something to him? Too goddamned long.

He though again of Mona's hunch about their office break-in. At times it seemed like Mona had some kind of inside dope on the universe. It had saved his ass once. When he'd been "rescuing" the kid from Murray's Coalition. Blake had taken the kid back to his own apartment before delivering him to his parents. Some of Murray's boys tracked them there. They had

Blake dead to rights when Mona showed up, out of the blue.

She'd never been able to explain what had brought her there. It reminded Blake of the link his mother had had with him when he was a child. She always knew when he was in trouble.

Blake felt his ears pop as the elevator neared the bottom floor. He was exhausted, his hand hurt, and he wasn't sure he'd accomplished anything upstairs with Frambeen. The man seemed like the type who'd lie on principle.

Blake came out of the elevator and walked toward the revolving doors. Out on the sidewalk a young black wearing a beret stood like an island among the current of pedestrians. Blake stepped behind a large plastic floor plant and watched him through the plate-glass window. He turned to look into the lobby.

Blake had recognized him instantly. Danny White. He was one of Murray's lieutenants. He'd also been the "kidnapped" kid's trainer.

The First National was just a block away. Blake guessed White was probably covering the area in case Blake returned to the scene with the police. He couldn't deal with White or any other of Murray's men until he had something to offer. The detective waited until White turned again, then headed for the stairs to the basement.

6

Great ruffled-edged stacks of paper, standing mono-liths to drudgery, weighed down the tops of the two desks. Mona put the last of the file folders back into its drawer. Most of the files in the cabinet gaped empty and open, waiting to be fed. Mona looked at the towers of paper to be sorted into the folders and sighed. She looked at her watch.

Those are for tomorrow, she thought. She picked up the newspaper from the window sill. "City Activists Mix Violence and Grace," the title read. That re-minded her of something she could check. She pulled one of the file drawers open. Nope. It wasn't there. She pulled open another. They were both missing. She could find neither the Joseph Murray nor the City Action Coalition file.

The phone buzzed, and Mona grabbed it. "Check the mail," Blake's voice said. "I'll call you in fifteen."

A secret message, she thought. It was seldom that Blake called in with one of his prearranged codes, but she loved it when he did. Now she could act like a spy.

Mona looked at the back of the calendar for the location code of the day, then took the elevator down to the basement garage. She patted Blake's car affec-tionately on the hood as she unplugged it from its charging jack. A storage battery drove its electric en-gine. Blake had both a windmill and a solar panel on the roof of the office building to charge it up. A gas-driven generator waited beneath the car's back deck when all else failed. Still, something on it always seemed to need repair. Mona liked the car, but Blake could never seem to raise much more than a dull resentment for it.

Mona took off out of the parking garage, watching the rearview for a tail. In many parts of town there were so many cars on the road, and so many kinds of cars, that even normal traffic had a suspicious look. Tiny three-wheeled vehicles with engines like sewing machines chuffed along doing their damnedest. Larger gas-powered cars crowded the center, trying to pass. Alcohol-driven one-passenger trikes weaved through everything.

Seven minutes away from the office, feeling secure that no one was following, Mona circled back to the phone booth *du jour*. Blake called her there, thus avoiding any tap that might have been on their office phone. He told her to meet him at the underground entrance to the Randolph/South Water Street Train Station, right away.

When she pulled up and double-parked at the underground commuter entrance, only a scattering of people was heading for the trains and home. Overhead at street level, a thronging rush hour progressed.

The detective came out of the station and smiled like a good husband home to the subterranean suburbs. Mona reached over and unlocked the passenger door. When she straightened up, she shouted, "Blake!" as she saw in the rearview a man pointing a gun. Blake dropped between the parked cars as the gun fired, echoing wildly off the brick walls and concrete overhead. Pedestrians screamed and ran.

Mona shoved the car into reverse, stamping the accelerator. The man turned his gun in her direction, but Mona pulled a button under the dash and the hatchback sprang up with surprising force, knocking the pistol into the air. She hit the brakes as the bumper

thudded against the gunman's shins. He yelped and
dropped out of sight like a wooden bandit in a shooting gallery.

Blake threw himself into the seat next to her, rocking the car like a boat in water. "Go!" he shouted.

Mona shot up around the block over to Wacker and
headed west along the river's edge, the hatchback
door bouncing stiffly as she drove.

"I don't think I'm going to get that fixed," Blake
said. "That's the first accessory on this car I've liked."

"I thought it might hit him in the face," Mona
laughed, giddy with the excitement.

"That was incredible, knocking away the gun."

"As long as *you* keep *your* nose out of its way,"
Mona said, grabbing his arm and shaking him playfully. She looked over at him and smiled, still catching
her breath from the exhilaration of action.

Blake loved her incredible vitality and excitement.
He saw her flushed cheeks, the rising of her breasts as
she breathed, her happiness, and felt desire expand
inside his chest. He wanted nothing more than to take
her in his arms and make love to her that moment.

"Was that guy from Murray?" she asked.

"Yeah. That was Danny White. I don't know how
he followed me. I thought I saw him first." He squeezed
her arm back. "You were fantastic."

She smiled, and he climbed to the back of the car
and pulled the hatch down closed. "We collected something," he said. He pulled out his handkerchief and
wrapped it around the gun at the back of the deck and
crawled up into his seat. He unwrapped the cloth and
held the pistol cradled like a hot dog in deli paper.
" 'Never touch another man's gun,' " he quoted. " 'You
never know whom they've shot.' That's either Shakes-
peare or Confucius. Pull over here." Blake got out
near a sightseeing boat dock and threw the gun into
the river. His hand began to throb again. As he looked
down at the ripples in the water, he suddenly realized

how exhausted he was. Now that the tension was off, all his muscles started to ache at once.

Back in the car, he adjusted his seat to recline. "Take me somewhere I can sleep," he told her. "We better to avoid our own places till this is over." He settled back, bone-weary, and began to doze.

By the time she drove the few blocks to the ramp which took them up out of the Wacker Drive underground, Blake was sound asleep. Even when she turned onto Lake Street and the elevated train rattled deafeningly over their heads, he didn't stir.

Mona looked over at her sleeping boss and felt some tenderness welling up inside. She admired Blake. She liked his honesty—and his ruthlessness—because that was honest too. She had only seen him use it in ways that seemed just. Mona had worked for another detective before Blake. He had seemed to think that truth possessed by anyone other than him was nothing but a liability. Blake had been a refreshing change.

Mona enjoyed being around detectives. She enjoyed the action. Sometimes she thought she would have liked being a detective herself. But she never liked preparing for things. She didn't care for license applications. She loved doing the detail work in her job, but she didn't like doing it for herself, so she'd settled for being a detective's secretary for the past four years, two of those years with Blake.

She looked back over at the sleeping man's face. He was attractive. And she liked more about him than just the way he operated. But was he really her type? Being tall herself, Mona always preferred taller men. Blake was merely the same height as she.

When Blake finally awoke, they were in the outermost neighborhood of the city, parked in front of a motel oddly called the Heart O' Chicago. The car door stood open, and Mona pulled at his arm. "Come on, Snoozy." He struggled out of his seat. The last

pink faded in the sky down Peterson Avenue. Mona
helped guide him up the concrete stairs to the room
she had taken on the second floor.

Blake collapsed onto one of the beds in the small
robin's-egg-blue room. Mona went back to the car and
returned with two brown bags.

"Up, Gregory, dear," she said. "I got food. It's hot.
Let's eat."

He sat up while she pulled two plasti-cans of beer
from a sack. "Where did you get all this?" he asked.

"There's a rib joint a half-block away. I went down
there after I checked us in."

"You left me in the parking lot, alone and unpro-
tected?"

"I put my hanky over your face," she said. "No one
would have known it was you." From the other bag
she pulled a cardboard bucket, translucent with soaked
grease. On its side a smiling porker clutched a knife
and fork.

"Ribs," Blake said. "After all I've been through,
now you want me to eat ribs."

Mona pulled out a few sections and gave them to
him on the bucket lid as a plate. "Macrobiotic Blake,"
she said. "What did you want? Brown rice and beer
nuts?"

"I don't mind occasional meat, but this is catsup-
soaked fat and bone." He took a reluctant bite.

"Don't worry," she said. "I got coleslaw too."

"You know where toxic wastes gather? In pork fat."

"I thought it was in lake trout and salmon."

"You might as well drink hemlock," Blake said. He
took another bite, pulled back his lips in distaste.

"I love ribs," Mona told him. "In ten years Doctor
Sylvia is going to give me a complete change of organs. Then I can start all over."

Blake grunted. He took another bite. In a half-hour
he was asleep again, full mainly on coleslaw, fries, and
biscuits. Mona pulled off his shoes and covered him

up. She smiled at his sleep-smoothed face, clear and open as a child's.

"You're a cute guy, Blake," she whispered, and stepped out the door to take some evening air.

She walked out the gate of the parking lot, down Peterson to Clark Street. Clark was one of the few angled streets in Chicago, most of them having been built on a north-south, east-west grid system—all square blocks with right-angled intersections. But looking down Clark, she could see straight toward the center of the city. The central skyline rose above the general pink glow of the city's streetlights.

In recent years there had been talk of changing the streetlights. The pink lights were said to have an unfortunate psychological effect on the residents. Some studies suggested that a change in color could reduce violence in the city.

Mona often felt there was something dirty about the lights. Usually, one never thought about them. But from the air, she knew they were beautiful. There was nothing like flying into Chicago at night and seeing the lovely blush apricot color of the city's lights rising out of the darkness.

A vacation. Wouldn't flying off on a vacation with Blake be lovely? She surprised herself with the thought and could almost feel herself flush. Well, why not? A vacation. After all, she was already sharing a motel room with the man.

Let's make the next motel room be in the Bahamas, she thought, turning to head back to the room.

7

In the morning, Blake looked across to the opposite bed and saw Mona was already up and gone. He felt considerably, but not completely, revived. His watch read 8:17. Over twelve hours' sleep.

He went in the bathroom and climbed into the shower. Under his soles, he felt the impression of flat rubber fish stuck onto the surface of the bathtub. He looked down as he began to lather a miniature bar of motel soap. These were no bright whimsical fish with big eyes and smiles like his mother had stuck to their bathtub when he was a child. These were serious gray-colored fish with beady little eyes and straight fins whose only thought were to prevent bathroom-injury lawsuits.

He rubbed the soap into his face and hair, smelling its test-tube-lavender scent. He knew this soap would make his scalp feel weird all morning, but he wanted to wash away any residual QDT from his hair. He showered thoroughly, shaved with the disposable shaver on the sink, and reluctantly put on yesterday's clothes. He tried blotting the bloodstain on his jacket sleeve again, but it didn't do any good. For a moment he wondered how the gang kid was doing. The shock of the gunshot wound just might have started to help straighten him out. Or it might have sent him on the way to more violence and bitterness—assuming it hadn't killed him.

Blake cleaned his teeth by rubbing the towel nap over them, then went out to use the phone at his bedside to call John Dwight. After he briefed Dwight on the progress of the case, there was silence on the phone.

"I'm not sure I would've let Frambeen know we suspect him," Dwight said finally. "but you're the detective. Check out Chicago Chemical Supply. I called them to replace our mercury for the Rengore order. The same thing happened over there."

"Sabotaged mercury?" Blake asked.

"Same thing. They hadn't realized it'd happened until I called and they checked their warehouse stock."

"I wouldn't think that's Rengore's work," Blake said. "Not if they really need the mercury. According to Frambeen, they use a lot of it for rejuvenating QDT. Was that the only thing touched at Chicago Chemical?"

"Far as I know. Also, some men were looking for you here yesterday. They loitered around the building until I called the police."

"Did they say what they wanted?"

"No. And they didn't look like business types. You'd better be careful."

"Thanks."

As Blake hung up, Mona walked in carrying a tray of food. Blake noticed how cheerful and fresh she looked. "So you're up," she said. "I brought breakfast from downstairs. The man who runs this place is such a sweetheart. I told him you'd had a hard trip yesterday, and he fixed this tray for me. Coffee, juice, and Danish."

"Thanks. Really. This has got to make for a better day than yesterday," he said, reaching for a coffee from the tray. "I can use this." He held the cup to his lips and the aroma rose up to bathe his face. He took a sip, set the cup on the bed table, and began lacing up his shoes. "How did you do with the mess at the office?"

She took her coffee and a doughnut and sat on the other bed, giving him a wry look. "I've got a long way to go," she said. "I think a can of wastepaper got mixed with our files." She dipped her doughnut in the coffee, took a bite, and started talking with her mouth still full. "The Murray file is gone. And City Action. I couldn't get a thing on the terminal about Scott."

"Swallow that, will you? You make me nervous."

She rolled her eyes, chewed, and gulped the mouthful down. "Carlyle and Brubaker want you to call them," she said. "They're the collectors who dropped in."

Blake raised his eyebrows while reaching for a Danish. "The ones you shot at?"

"Them's the boys," Mona said. "They have a very efficient pick-key. Took fifteen seconds to get in our office.

"What did they do?" Blake asked, looking concerned.

"I wasn't expecting them. I just forgot. So they surprised me. I think I have a bump on the back of my head from getting knocked down. Anyway, I chased them out and put a bullet through the back window of their car."

"Were you trying to kill them?"

"I gave them that impression."

Blake sat still for a moment, looking like he'd just discovered a toothache. He put his Danish back in the bag. "Let's get over to the office," he said. "We've got to get some work done before everything blows up in our face."

Mona drove Blake's car out of the parking lot, hearing the motel's beeper sound once as they crossed through the electric eye at the gate. She pulled into the morning traffic, turning onto Ridge to take them out to Lake Shore Drive. Blake pointed out one of the fire hydrants painted to look like a mushroom cloud.

"I keep seeing more of these things all the time. They remind me of sick versions of the painted Bicentennial hydrants when I was a kid. Do you remember those?"

"What was the Bicentennial?"

"Nineteen-seventy-six. The country's two hundredth birthday. I guess you were too young."

"I don't remember any fire hyrants," Mona said.

"You were too young. People painted them to look like flags, soldiers, I don't know what else. I painted one myself."

"There's another," Mona said, pointing it out.

"I wish I could just look at these and think of regular mushrooms. It's always nuclear explosions. I'll be glad when we get to 2001, and all this new-millennium crap is over."

"*If* we get to 2001."

"Sounds like it's getting to you too."

"Not too bad, really." Mona fought to conceal a smile. Every time she saw one of the mushroom hydrants this morning, instead of a mushroom it looked to her like a stout penis sticking out of the ground. She turned away from Blake and looked out her window, almost laughing. She didn't want to have to explain her amusement.

Mona headed south on Lake Shore Drive, turning the curve around the big pink landmark Edgewater Beach Apartments building toward the center of the city. To her left the morning sun shimmered on the surface of the waves on Lake Michigan. The beaches were often closed because of the pollution count, and you couldn't eat any of the fish—some people said the tiny smelts were all right, though Mona never chanced them—but still the lake always *looked* beautiful. Chicago politicians were notorious for screwing things up, but the city had done this one right. The whole length of Lake Shore Drive, all the way south to Jackson Park on the other end of town, had a gorgeous, unobstructed view across the parks and beaches. Mona loved that about Chicago. The beauty of the lake, the sight of sailboats on the water, the sharp brightness of the skyline—all these excited her as she drove, and made her feel sharper as Blake and she talked theories on the past days' occurrences.

Mona peeled off the Drive onto Michigan Avenue and drove a few blocks past fancy stores with shoppers dressed like they'd stepped out of fashion magazines. She turned right on Chicago Avenue.

"Our neighborhood always looks so much nicer when you approach from the east," she said.

"You should have seen it when our building was built," Blake told her. "You've met Quiller, right?"

"Our landlord, Mr. Taos Hotel? Sure." Mona pulled up behind a bus blocking both lanes as it let passengers off at the stop. She thought of the Taos Pinnacle downtown, which Quiller, as the major tenant, had renamed. The Pinnacle had been the Britannica Centre back when the encyclopaedia people occupied more square footage than anyone else. But the man-on-the-street really knew the building by the eerie blue beacon at its pinnacle. The beacon, shining above the grassy expanses of Grant Park from atop its Michigan Avenue location, was shaped like a beehive, and was meant to represent industriousness.

Mona honked her horn as the bus in front of her continued to sit.

"Quiller won a fortune in the national lottery," Blake said. "That's how he started his empire. I forget how many million he got. Before that, he was a bicycle messenger in the Loop."

"Quiller?" Mona laughed. "He's huge." She tried to imagine the tall, obese man on a bicycle, his long, stringy Fu Manchu mustache and goatee blowing in the wind.

"He was a skinny hippie before he got his fortune. He and my mother used to march in demonstrations together in the sixties. He was in love with her. That's why he never raises our rent at the office."

Mona laughed again. "I wondered why our rent was low."

"Most people in our building pay twice as much," Blake said. "But Quiller had this thing for my mom. She was a very pretty woman."

"And he was a bicycle messenger. I just can't imagine him crashing through the Loop on a bike." Mona laid on her horn again. The traffic began to collect behind them.

"He stuck with it a long time. In the winter he would keep his bicycle locked to the fire escape at the dispatch office and take the el into the Loop. You know that three-flat building right next to ours?"

"With the sleazy grocery on the ground floor?" Mona looked around behind her at the string of cars waiting and sending up a chorus of horns and beeps.

"That building used to stand all by itself, one slender three-flat. Quiller said it looked like a weird finger sticking up to the sky. Open lots lay vacant all around it, filled with broken glass. It was really a shit neighborhood from Cabrini-Green to the elevated tracks and south to Chicago Avenue. But Quiller used to see that building as he rode in on the train. He loved how it stuck up there, all alone. It had a wild mural painted on the wall with the hand of God reaching down, and all these saints. Then below that were Indians and blacks and whites all confronting one another, and disembodied hands with pistols pointing at each other. It was strange."

"Sounds like it." Mona clipped the car into gear as the bus in front of her finally started to crawl forward.

"Quiller loved the building. It was the first thing he bought when he won his fortune. He rehabbed the top floor and moved in. A multimillionaire in one of the city's lousiest neighborhoods."

"Is that why he built our office building, to start bringing the neighborhood up?"

"He liked the neighborhood being lousy. That's what he was used to. He'd bought all the land around his building so it would stay like it was. But he hired this development manager to help him take care of his money. The manager convinced Quiller to build our office as an investment, but Quiller never realized where the building would be. He had purchased other property as well, but he couldn't bring himself to pay attention to it. He'd bought all these tanks of tropical fish, and he was much more interested in watching his octopuses breed."

"Lovely," Mona said. The bus had stopped again before she could get around it. She sat staring at another of the painted penis fire hydrants and imagined firing it like a missile into the bus's rear end.

"When his new office building started going up, right next door, he hated that. He screamed at the construction workers and threw garbage out his windows at them. By the time our building was complete, Quiller thought it ruined the neighborhood, so he moved out. That's when he moved into the Britannica Centre and started leasing up sections of it piecemeal. As Britannica got smaller, he took over the top floors and renamed the building."

"He's a character," Mona said, accelerating around the bus. "We're almost there. I think you'd better get down on the floor out of sight. I'll go in through the alley."

Blake strained the seat all the way back, then crammed himself down on the floor like a lobster under a rock. "'You know," he said irritably, "they don't make these damned cars big enough for this."

"Be grateful this is a hatchback," Mona said. "Otherwise you'd be in the trunk."

"Why is it I have to take orders from underlings?"

"Grovel, you dog." She slapped him playfully on the shoulder.

Mona turned up Orleans toward Chestnut. She was startled to see a train gliding by on the elevated tracks without hearing the usual grind and squeal as it took the curve. Then she remembered the city had purchased new experimental cars with flex-plastic wheels. El trains without noise seemed like a contradiction in terms. Welcome to the new millennium, she told herself. She pulled around the block at Locust and went into the alley, then down a descending driveway. She stopped at the bottom and pushed a button on the dashboard. The garage door opened like a mechanical mouth. She pulled in, watching the rearview to see no one followed. When the door shut its trap, she pulled into their slot.

"Open up," Blake grumbled. "I'm stuck."

She laughed as she rounded the car and pulled him out. "Come on, Grumpy." She led him to the elevator.

After he unlocked the office door and Mona entered, a voice came from behind him in the hall: "I waited for your call, Blake."

The detective turned to see a tall man with a long, sharp nose. His forehead sloped back to meet a widow's peak of pale red hair. He had the tiny bloodshot eyes of a rodent. As the man came closer, Blake caught a whiff of him. He had the sharp body odor of a man with bad nerves.

"Who are you?" Blake asked.

"I called yesterday. I stopped in. My name's Carlyle." He raised his hands to show them empty. "I just want to talk."

"All right," Blake said. He held the door for Carlyle to precede him. As Blake followed, he heard a double click, then saw Mona standing with a pistol aimed dead at Carlyle's chest.

"I see you two have met," Blake said.

"None of us had a real enjoyable time," Carlyle told him.

"I hope this won't inhibit your ability to converse, Mr. Carlyle," Mona said, sitting on the edge of her desk but keeping the gun pointed at his heart.

"I already done you guys a favor today," Carlyle said irritably. "Two niggers was around here looking for you, and I got rid of them."

Blake looked up sharply. "What did you do?"

"Nothing. I said you'd moved uptown. They left." He looked back at Mona and the gun, getting more agitated. "I just want to talk business," he said.

"I don't think that'll be necessary," Blake told her. She looked at him in disapproval, but set the gun behind her on the desk.

"Thanks," Carlyle said. He relaxed slightly. "First off, I ain't a collector. I don't live off bounty. I'm a detective with a client who's got a good deal for Scott."

"Why do you carry a buzzer?" Mona asked coldly.

Carlyle's voice raised in exasperation. "*Everybody* carries a buzzer. They're handy to have around."

"So what's this deal?" Blake pushed in.

Carlyle quieted. "We know you're helping Scott. Or at least you know where to find him. Right?"

Blake thought of the blond man. He wondered if Jake Fishman had let Scott out of the pantry. Jake could be negligent of the niceties sometimes. "Maybe I do. What's the deal?"

"My client purchased Scott's defaulted HRL from the bank. He wants to trade that back to Scott for the rights to a machine. Scott'll get some cash too."

"What bank?" Mona asked.

"First National," Carlyle told her warily.

"That's why I couldn't hack into anything on Scott!" she said. "Their computer's down from the bombing."

"Who's your client?" Blake asked.

"I can't say."

"How much money?"

"That's between my client and Scott," Carlyle said, getting angry again.

Blake snorted. "Scott can't come out of hiding without a straight deal. He'd be an idiot."

Carlyle looked like he was about to complain again, but instead he spun, punching Mona in the side of the head, knocking her away from the gun on the desk; then he lunged at Blake with the buzzer in his hand. Blake dodged, but the buzzer caught him on the ear. The left side of his head shot through with fire. He knocked the buzzer out of Carlyle's hand and shoved him away, grabbing for the pistol. As he turned back with it, Carlyle jumped on top and tried to pull the gun from Blake's hand, but Blake pulled the trigger as it came up. Carlyle's teeth shattered. The crown of his head blew out. He fell backward and blood spread from his hair.

Blake dropped forward to his knees between the dead man's legs and gagged helplessly. "Fucking shit," he coughed. His ear rang loud as a fire bell. He crawled over to Mona. She lay on her back, her lips moving and her eyes open. He slapped her face softly, then hard. "Snap out of it," he begged.

Her eyes rolled twice in their sockets, then focused on Blake's face. She raised her arm vaguely, for protection.

He pulled her to a sitting position. "Suck my ear. Quick. Like a snakebite," he said. "I been hit by a buzzer." The word "buzzer" alerted her like none of his slapping could. She leaned forward, found the red dot in the cartilage of his ear, and sucked.

"I'm not getting anything," she said. She turned the ear to look at the back. "I think it went straight through."

Blake turned on his side, pulled his stiletto from his

pocket, and flipped open the blade. "Take this. Make cuts all around. Hurry."

She made the first cut close to the ear canal, and Blake cried out, pulling away.

"I can't . . ." Mona started, but Blake was already lying down with his other ear pressed to the floor.

"I won't move now. Hurry!" he shouted.

She crouched over him and made X-shaped cuts all around the red dot. Tears ran out of Blake eyes, and his breath came in involuntary gasps. The flow of blood surprised Mona as it streamed from the cuts. She sucked and spat on the floor, then turned the ear to repeat it on the back. Mona found it easier to ignore Blake as his will broke down and he cried out more freely. She sucked and spat a few more times on each side, then grabbed a wad of tissue from her purse, wrapped his ear, and had him hold it.

Mona let Blake lie still while she looked at Carlyle. Blood had seeped out of his mouth and nose into a puddle. He had an ugly hole in the top of his head.

Mona's own head felt sore where he'd punched it, and sore again where she'd hit the floor. But hers didn't have any holes in it. Her vision throbbed, and she felt nauseated, and the sight of Carlyle's body made her furious.

"What the shit were you trying to do?" she shouted at him. "You pinhead knucklebrain."

"The man's dead," Blake reminded her, still lying on the floor.

"What could he gain?" Mona raged. "With us dead he'd have no contact to Scott."

"He was a jackass, all right," Blake agreed dully.

"Oh, shit," Mona said. She reached down and picked up the bug. She'd slipped it into Brubaker's pocket and now it had returned. Whose was it? Brubaker and Carlyle's? Or did it belong to some third party, and Carlyle had brought it back because he thought it was Mona's? If the bug had worked the whole time, somebody had a tape that meant no good to her and Blake. She smashed the device with the butt of the pistol and dropped it in the water at the bottom of a vase of dead flowers.

As she turned back to face the room, she let out a startled yelp. A large man with a gun blocked the doorway.

"Sorry to scare you," he said. "I heard a shot as I came into the building."

"What are you doing, Billy?" Mona asked, irritated from the shock.

"Blake told me to drop in." Billy looked down at the bloody corpse in front of him.

"Shithead Billy tried to mug me in the tunnel," Blake said listlessly. He noticed Billy had shaved, and his thick brown hair was clean and combed back again.

"I wasn't trying to mug you. I didn't know you were there." Billy shrugged. "I been out of work," he told Mona. "I tried to get some money from this guy, and Blake shows up. I don't know."

"Since when are you a thief?" Mona asked.

Billy looked back down at the corpse, but made no comment.

"Never mind. I can put you on the payroll for a couple of days," she told him.

"Sounds good to me," he said. Billy stepped fully into the room and locked the door behind. He looked at the corpse. "Who is this guy?"

"Collector," Mona said. "Let's get Gregory up. He's lying around too long."

The two helped Blake into his chair. He had a hard time keeping his head upright.

Mona gave Billy a worried look. "He got buzz fluid shot through his ear," she told him.

"Jesus," Billy said.

"Can you think okay?" she asked.

"Too tired to think," Blake said.

Mona turned away from him with her lip trembling.

She clenched her fists. "I hate this," she said. Then she shouted, "You asshole!" and kicked the corpse hard in the ribs.

"Cut that shit out," Blake yelled.

"Then quit acting like a zombie!" she shouted back. "You worry me." She rubbed the back of her hand across her eye. "You take the stiff," she told Billy quietly. "We'll go to the doctor."

She helped Blake up and led him to the elevator. Billy picked up the corpse easily, trying to avoid getting blood on himself. Mona signaled him when the hallway was empty, and he pulled the door closed behind him with his foot and followed.

Down at the car, Mona opened the hatchback and it banged into Carlyle's head, splashing blood on the window. Billy dumped the body in and wiped the glass. Mona pulled the car blanket over Carlyle, but the shape was unmistakable.

"Stupid little cars," Blake mumbled. "Can't even hide a stiff." He climbed into the back seat and lay down with his legs pulled up. Mona handed the keys to Billy.

"You drive," she said. "My head's approaching meltdown." As they pulled out of the garage, Mona sat with the office gun on her lap.

8

Dr. Sylvia Logan cocked her head to one side and looked at Blake's wounded ear. A pile of blood-soaked tissues lay on the desk next to the examination table. She looked at the front of the ear, then at the back, and shook her head. "I'd say the weapon of attack was a Rototiller."

"I made those cuts to suck out the poison," Mona told her.

Sylvia looked at Blake's ear again, then examined the scanprint of his head. "I don't think there's much I can do that you haven't done already," she said finally. "We'll dress the wound, and then Gregory should sleep."

"Isn't there an antidote?" Mona asked.

The doctor shook her head. "I don't know what's in those buzzers. It's all under special license. If you had buzzed that Carlyle fellow back, instead of shooting his brains out, I wouldn't even be allowed to redeem his organs."

"Hang on to that body, Sylvia," Blake said from the table. His eyes were closed.

"We'll see what good is left in it. You've already given me enough bodies to cover two complete transplants."

Blake struggled to sit up. He rubbed his face. "Give me a shot of something. I got to work."

"I don't want to do that," she said. "From your

scanprint, I don't find anything foreign in the blood, but I'd hate to take a chance. You're exhausted. Sleep."

"People are after us," he told her dully. "If we don't get some answers, we're in trouble."

Sylvia looked at Mona who nodded. "Four hours," the doctor said. "I could boost you now, but you wouldn't think straight. You'd get into more trouble. Four hours of sleep, and I'll wake you up and give you a shot if you need it."

"Oh, crap," Blake said.

"She's right," Mona told him. "Billy and I can take care of Scott. And we'll all stay away from the office. Everything else will wait."

Blake fell back down on the table. "You win," he said. He closed his eyes and felt the slight burn of fatigue under his lids. He smelled the dry sweetness of clinical alcohol and starched linens. His muscles relaxed quickly, and he was asleep before the others left the room.

Sylvia led Mona down to her small operating room. Carlyle lay naked on the table. A tube pumped liquid through a catheter into the artery on the inside of one thigh; another tube led liquid away from the other. A tight rubber clamp choked his throat, and white plastic material had been stuffed into the hole in his head. The scent of his body odor had been replaced by the stink of rancid meat. Carlyle's face looked as pale as if it had been carved out of soap. A trace of purple shone around his eyes.

Billy's color, as he sat on a chair in the corner, did not look much better. Even his normally red lips looked pale. The nurse took readings from a computer terminal, then proceeded to hook more wires and tubes into the corpse with all the grace of someone stuffing a chicken.

"I suggest we remove the head as soon as possible, Doctor," the nurse said. "I'm afraid toxins are entering the lungs through the trachea."

"All right, George," Sylvia said. "Prep him."

"I don't think we'll stay for this," Mona said. "Can you give me any more about Blake?"

Sylvia shook her head helplessly. "You've heard everything I know. I don't like how tired he seems. Could there be other cause for that?"

"Blake was sprayed with QDT yesterday," Mona told her. "He took thalamin."

"That could be good or bad," the doctor said. "depending on how that residue reacts with whatever's in those buzzers. We'll just have to wait. But how are you? You don't look so good yourself."

Mona told Sylvia of the beatings she'd taken from the collectors. When she learned Mona had been knocked unconscious twice in two days, the doctor ran a scan of her head, just to be safe. She discovered Brubaker and Carlyle had left their lumps, but found nothing serious.

As they left, Mona asked her to keep *all* Carlyle's remains in storage. Somewhere out there, Mona knew, someone might have a bugged tape recording of Carlyle's death. She wanted to avoid the police, but if the police got involved somehow, she didn't want to be guilty of destroying evidence. Even with the corpse in pieces, a legal autopsy could still be performed.

Billy still looked slightly green as Mona drove south on Larrabee toward Fishman's, so she slowed down to give him time to recover. "I want to know why you mugged Jeremy Scott yesterday," she said finally. "That's not your style."

"Family trouble." Billy rolled down the window and took a deep breath in through his bulbous nose. Mona turned onto Ogden.

"What kind of trouble?"

"Shit," Billy said. "My brother's in jail for selling dope again. I was trying to raise bail. He can't take it in there." Billy shook his head. "When Blake showed up, I would have asked for the money, but he hates

Jerry. Thinks he's a useless asshole. I didn't know that guy was Blake's client." Billy looked out the window.

"Jerry still inside?"

"Yeah. He's going to stay there, too. He's got to take his own raps now."

"Maybe he'll finally grow up."

"Why the fuck was I stealing for him?" Billy said. "Stupid."

They drove on in silence over the elevated section of Ogden, which carried them above Goose Island. The skyscrapers of the Loop gleamed to the southeast, while below them the island lay quiet in the river. Most of its industrial life had been gone for decades. The south end was somewhat active, but most of the island was just a way station for salt and construction materials.

On the other side of the river they pulled into a dusty, run-down neighborhood and stopped in front of Fishman's.

When they knocked, Fishman let them in, scowling. He gave Billy a cold glance, then looked at Mona.

"I'm almost sorry Gregory isn't here." He said the name Gregory as though it were something slightly ridiculous. "If he was here, I could give him a piece of my mind."

"You're better off hanging on to it," Mona told him. "Blake's got enough trouble."

"He's dumped plenty of it on me," Fishman said. "Have you moved your office uptown?"

"No," Mona told him.

"Me neither," Billy said.

Fishman looked at him, then turned back to Mona. "This place has got too hot," he said. "My clients are scared away. I can't do business."

"What kind of business?" Mona asked.

"That's none of your business. What I do for Blake, that's nobody's business. What I do for other people, that's none of your business. Everything is clean around here. Everything neat. But now everything is fucked up. I may as well move to the lobby of the police department."

"Business has been rotten for me too," Billy said. He kept a deadpan expression.

Fishman looked at him like he'd spit on the carpet. "Who is this guy?" he asked.

"Billy Rourke. He's working for us," Mona said.

"Fishman shook his head as thought the big man were the equivalent of a trained monkey. He turned back to Mona. "This Scott guy Blake dropped here has been bothering me ever since he came off the QDT. Electronic-vectors, this . . . when-do-I-get-my-machine? that. Finally I shoved him back in the pantry. The guy was like chemical rash."

"I know what you mean," Billy said. "A lot of people seem that way to me."

Fishman looked at him, and Billy looked blandly back. "Nice place you got here," the big man said without shifting his gaze.

Fishman led them silently into the kitchen and unlocked the pantry door. He stepped across the room and folded his arms as though wanting nothing more to do with the affair.

Scott came slowly out of his cell, irritated but in control, a genteel anger balanced in the corners of his eyes and lips. Despite his travails and soiled clothes, he himself looked almost fresh and unsullied. Mona felt surprised at how pleased she was to see him.

Scott stepped to the kitchen sink and washed his hands, giving Fishman a sideward glance of disdain. The bald man leaned on the table behind him.

Scott shook the water from his fingers, reached for the towel hung over the chair next to Fishman, and wrapped it quickly around Fishman's neck. Scott twisted him around backward and sent him sprawling across the little kitchen, the base of his skull bouncing loudly against the inner pantry wall. Fishman collapsed over the edge of the cot where Scott had spent the night and most of the day. He lay there stunned, rubbing the top of his bald head.

"Don't move until we're gone," Scott told him. He washed his hands carefully again, pulled the towel from Fishman's neck, and dried his hands. He tossed the towel back in Fishman's face. "You pustulant worm," he said. The blond man walked to the front of Fishman's apartment and out the door.

Billy sidled around and looked past Fishman into the pantry/cell. He whistled low. "Will you look at that?" he said. "Tiny." He followed Scott out the front.

"I'm sorry about all this, Jake," Mona said. "We'll call you when things get under better control."

"That would be great," Fishman replied too loud.

Mona followed the men out to the street. Scott climbed into the front passenger seat of the car and stared out at a yard full of unlikely statues in front of a discount statuary dealer. Frogs spurted water into fountains at the feet of devout Virgin Marys, and fire-breathing dragons dive-bombed Spanish conquistadors.

Mona didn't know if any of Murray's men would recognize her, but she didn't wait around to take a chance. Once in the car, they circled blocks and went through alleys, watching the rearview for a tail. In Fishman's bleak neighborhood, however, few vehicles moved. Most looked abandoned, parked at odd angles to the street, rusting, tires flat, some with sidings of cracked, ruptured plastic. Although the driving was easy, the look of the few pedestrians made Mona nervous.

"What shall we do for you, Mr. Scott?" she asked, once she felt sure they were not followed.

"What is this man doing in the car with us?" he asked, his voice carrying the tone of restrained rage.

Mona looked over at him. His knuckles showed

white, and he stared straight ahead. In the back seat,
his bulk huddled up, Billy shrugged his shoulders.

"He's here for your protection," Mona said.

Scott laughed sourly. "I came to Mr. Blake for
protection. He threw me down a sewer and jumped on
me. This man tried to rob me. I've been sprayed with
QDT, locked in a closet, and now the thief is my
protector? You people have a strange sense of humor." His voice broke in exasperation. "Very strange."

"I know how you feel." Billy patted him on the
shoulder from behind. Scott flinched. "I'd be upset if I
got locked up by a crabby Jew like Fishman."

"Billy," Mona warned.

"They aren't pleasant people," Billy said. "My people are Irish. They know about hospitality."

"Hospitality at gunpoint."

"You won't find me locking you in a closet," Billy
told him.

Scott let a silence drift by. "I need to pick up my
equipment. Is there a safe place, out of town perhaps,
where I could work for a week in safety?"

"I think so," Mona said.

Scott gave her the address of a warehouse where his
paraphernalia were stored. "There's no way anyone
would know about this location," he assured her.

"All right," Mona said. As she repeated the address, she smiled to herself, remembering how Scott
had handled Fishman. Jake *could* get on a person's
nerves.

She pulled the car over and went into a phone
booth. She tapped out seven numbers, waited, looked
at a card from her wallet, and tapped out a longer
series of digits again. Then she spoke into the phone
for a while. She got back into the car. "Where is this
address?" she asked Scott. "I don't recognize the street."

"Goose Island," Scott smiled. "We're just a few
blocks away."

Mona got an inexplicable chill. "Goose Island? Why did you set up there?"

"Isn't it perfect?" Scott asked enthusiastically. "It's right in the center of everything, and no one knows it's there."

Scott gave directions to a truck-rental agency, where they hired a van. Then they drove to his location on the north end of the island. A former factory served as Scott's warehouse. Just a few miles southeast, the glittering Loop rose up behind them.

Mona pulled the rented van around behind the dilapidated building to a truck dock. The concrete of the dock's rim had eroded into the bay. An easily visible crack weaved like a geometric river down the brick wall, and some of the windows gaped like broken teeth. Not thirty feet away, the Chicago River flowed by, quiet and dirty.

"What is this? A squatter's paradise?" Billy asked.

"I've done good work here," Scott said. "I'm going to buy this building someday."

"The price should be right."

"I'm sure it is," Scott told him. "And that's what's going to make this area come back. Energy costs will make steel-and-glass skyscrapers go dinosaur. You can't open the windows in those things. Climate control is a constant drain. Elevators run all the time. Water has to be pumped to the roof." He got out of the van, and they followed. "This is all decay now, but look at the location. A lot of these buildings are salvageable. The future is here."

Scott strode off to climb the stairs to the crumbling walkway along the truck dock.

Billy looked doubtfully around him. "Looks more like the past to me," he said.

Scott found a bent wire on the ground and poked it through the crack in the wall where it strayed closest to the door. He angled about until it caught on something, then he pulled hard. Three feet over, the door popped open.

"Only an inventor could've rigged that," Billy said.

Mona followed the two men into the building. Inside, she felt a shudder of expectant fear. Chilly sweat broke out on her palms. She didn't think it was the building itself frightening her, though the old place exuded gloom and abandonment. The only windows to break the dark brick peered down from high above, just below the arching roof. A sickly light seeped in through the glass, darkened by years of weather and soot. Chains hung from antiquated hoists on the ceiling beams, and the floor sloped gently up and down, sewer grates dotting the deepest centers of the valleys. And here and there stood large iron machines with giant metal wheels wrapped by belts to huge motors, standing like long-forgotten idols coated in grime. Even to Mona's untrained eye they looked incomplete, as though scavengers had ravaged their abandoned bodies.

"Organ redemption," she said under her breath.

"It was quite a place once," Scott said, standing with them, gazing quietly into the murk.

Mona looked at him and suddenly his handsomeness seemed like a cheap glaze. Her vision changed so that she could see only him and nothing of their surroundings. His outer surface was like a thin shell, a meaningless coating. It was as though she could see through that shell, and inside was nothing. Vacancy. But then that changed to a false gray fog. There was something of a lie inside him. And she sensed danger all around.

Then came sounds, and her vision was back to normal so quickly as to leave her doubting it had ever changed. She heard a noise like a heavy object being set down, then footsteps on wood, echoing off the brick walls and concrete floor.

"Are people in here?" Mona whispered.

"An old building like this makes a lot of noises," Scott told her. "That entire arched roof is wood. So it creaks. You don't see places like this built in the last forty years. The new industrial buildings are junk. Prefab. One big storm and they're down."

Mona was about to suggest they make a search, when Scott walked off toward a stairway. She wanted to call him back, but felt embarrassed because of the panic which had grabbed her insides. What was wrong with her?

She watched Scott climb up into a long enclosed loft projecting out from the wall, supported on steel I-beams. She and Billy followed. A person could hide forever in a place like this, she figured. The sooner they got out of the factory, the better she'd like it. The place didn't even smell right. It made the insides of her nostrils feel greasy.

Scott removed a padlock from a door of flimsy wood slats and chicken wire. He turned on a few fluorescent lights that hung from the ceiling. In the center of the floor stood a mechanism that looked like the torso of a dressmaker's dummy. Hundreds of tiny wires wound around its waist, sealed in by a thick layer of plastic. The wires came out in a neat vertical row and ran down to a metal box. Line inputs for computer connections covered an entire side of the box. Scott patted the mechanism's rump.

"This is the center of the prototype," he said. "Everything else is packed in those boxes." He indicated a stack of cartons piled against the chicken-wire wall.

"Here is where the processing happens." Scott smiled, putting both hands on the mechanism's waist. "The top section is essentially a funnel. The canal through the center is only a millimeter in diameter. Over a mile of wire wraps around it, interlaced with devices which induce currents and focus energies. I use microprocessors to give the exact twists of magnetism and energy into the strong and weak forces, focused by internal lasers, to break and reset the bonds among the molecules. In fact, I designed the architecture for the silicon and gallium-arsenide devices myself—as well as writing all the software. It was terribly expensive having the microchip prototypes made. But here it is: Liquid or powder comes in through the funnel canal and drops into the bottom chamber separated and purified." He smiled again. "To simplify it all ridiculously."

Billy nodded. "Sounds pretty damned good. I guess." He walked around the mechanism once, looking it over, then turned to Scott. "So how come you ain't a millionaire?"

"I haven't had a chance to run a profitable load. There are still bugs in the software, but mainly"—he smiled ironically—"it's difficult to work with collectors on your tail."

"The machine itself must be worth something," Billy said.

"I won't sell the machine," Scott insisted. "That would be it. A lump sum. I want control."

"Oh," Billy said.

"People cheat you," Scott told him. "A valuable property needs protection." He ran his hand down his creation's torso. "People disappear," he said, so low it could barely be heard.

"Let's get moving," Mona said, feeling another shudder of unease. "I want to get the hell out of here."

"Of course," Scott replied, alerting himself as though he were waking from a dream.

Billy looked at him and shook his head, thinking Scott fell within the ranks of the mystically deranged. "We'll take the boxes first," Billy said. "We can use them to cradle this whatya-call-it."

"Fine," Scott agreed. They each took one and headed down the stairs.

Descending behind the two men, Mona struggled with her purse. She had put the strap up on her shoulder as she picked up the box, but coming down the stairs, the strap slipped down to her forearm and the weight of the gun inside swung hard into the back of her leg. She held the box against the wall and pulled the strap over her head to the opposite shoulder so it couldn't fall off, then took a moment to rub the back of her leg where the purse had kicked her. She carried the box down to the van with the strap cutting into the side of her breast.

This has got to go, she thought, setting the box on the ground with the others by the truck. The two men went back for more. Mona left her purse on the front seat of the van. She hated to leave the gun behind, but she knew she couldn't pull any fast draws while carrying boxes, anyway.

Each time Mona returned to the building, she felt uneasy. And when the three of them finally wrestled the processor's torso down the stairs into the truck bay, she felt a great relief. They caught their breaths for a moment. Then, with a horrifying screech of rusted wheels, one of the garage doors opened. Brubaker walked out on the dock.

"That was damned nice of you to bring all that stuff down here for us." He grinned. A weird giggle came from inside the building. Mona felt a wave of nausea go through her, leaving her weak. Now she saw why Carlyle had been willing to kill them. Knowing Scott's hiding place, it was better to have Blake and her out of the way.

"How did you know this place?" Scott shouted indignantly.

Brubaker snorted. "Your client's a real winger," he called to Mona. "He rented space here with his own credit card." More absurd laughter broke from inside the factory. Mona tried to see where it came from.

"Blake's got Carlyle," she bluffed. Brubaker wasn't holding a weapon, but God knew what was back in the shadows.

"So?" Brubaker asked. "As long as I've got Scott and the machine, he can keep Carlyle." The laughter in the darkness howled. Brubaker grinned and turned to look in toward him.

Mona broke for it and pulled open the front door of the van, lunging blindly for her purse and the gun. From inside the cab, the palm of a large hand shot in on the center of her vision, a shiny black instrument strapped to its middle. She saw it just before it smacked into the skin and bone above her eyes and the whole world flashed brilliantly white. She felt herself falling, and she never felt the falling stop.

9

Blake jerked up and shouted, "No!"

He wiped sweat from his face, pulled the blanket up to his neck, and lay back shivering on the cot. The left side of his head pulsed with a numbing ache which inched back and settled with a jagged certainty around the cartilage of his ear.

Above him to the left was a woman. She put both hands on his arm. The pain radiating from his ear rippled his vision of her face like a standing wave of rising heat. He turned his head and strained to see her clearly.

Familiar dark hair streaked with gray was pulled back from her face. Full eyebrows arched at the outsides, giving her a look of slight incredulity. Small wrinkles had settled in around the eyes and mouth, and her nose sat small and sharp on her face. She didn't speak.

"How am I?" he asked her.

She gave a little smile. "You tell me."

"I was dreaming," he said. He tried to sit up again, but winced as a needle of pain pierced through the back of his eye socket. He lay back down and Sylvia wiped the sweat from his forehead with a gauze pad.

"Carlyle," he said, his eyes squinted closed while the sting eased back. "He kept screaming: 'Stop them. I'm not dead.' I floated up above, watching, but I couldn't speak. You and George kept cutting him, throwing off pieces like men feeding dogs. His head leaned up out of his body, watching. Finally I could shout: 'Get out of there. They got your heart.' Carlyle saw it. Horrified. A little light flew away and he was gone, but I knew he'd been deformed. His spirit. They got part of him, I thought. And that was the worst. I felt bad for him even after all he tried to do to us."

Blake put his forearm over his eyes and took a deep breath. Sylvia didn't speak. "Then I was in this room," he continued. He took his arm down and looked at her. "I saw my body lying here, and I thought: Oh, God, now I'm dead. I've got to get away. But I was dragged back against my will. And suddenly I was awake. Alive."

Sylvia sat down at his bedside. She still did not speak.

Blake remembered his mother: "You must never be afraid in your dreams," she had told him. He was ten years old, lying in the grass by the big white house of his grandmother. His mother sat under the apple tree, next to him, and smoothed her fingers through his curly hair.

"Dream monsters cannot harm you," his mother said.

It always seemed so peaceful at his grandmother's, so unlike the city neighborhood where he lived with his parents.

"When you face them, they lose their power," she had told him. "You can control them and glory in being brave."

"What about real monsters?" he had asked.

Blake couldn't remember. Had she had an answer for that? He took the gauze and wiped his neck. What he hadn't told Sylvia about his dream—what he had, in fact, been afraid to say—was that Mona's face had replaced Carlyle's for a moment.

"There's always something when a person dies," Sylvia said at last. "Some sense of their spirit passing.

Almost always. Or maybe a sense of other spirits in the room. Often it's inexplicable. But you feel it. If you let yourself be sensitive, you feel it deeply." She glanced at him helplessly, then looked down. "We redeemed Carlyle's organs while you were asleep," she said.

Blake nodded.

"You knew we were going to. It was natural to dream about it."

"Who knows what's natural?" he said, brushing the gauze over his thick eyebrows. "When I was a boy, we lived in this apartment where I was always scared. My father beat my mother. He'd never done that before. She said ghosts made him do it. She'd seen one, she said. My dad left us after that. He always sent a little money, but he never came back, even though we moved out of there." Blake looked away. "I don't know. I haven't thought of that in years. Maybe I'm just tired."

Sylvia looked at him. Then she picked up a little flashlight from the desk. "How are you physically?" she asked.

"My ear hurts." He reached up to feel it, but found it encased in gauze. "Should I remember this packaging job?" he asked.

"Not necessarily." She looked into his eyes with the light. She snapped her fingers to his left. "You hear that through the gauze?"

"Yes."

"Get up and try walking."

Blake got up slowly this time, edging himself up so that the pain didn't stab him in sharp retribution for his movement. Once fully on his feet, he waited a moment before he began to walk. He felt much better on his feet.

The doctor watched him move around the room. She tossed him her flashlight. He caught it. "Good," she said. "Still tired?"

"Groggy. Not too bad."

"I think you got lucky this time, Gregory." She sat down at a side desk and made some notes on a chart. "I'd rather not boost you. Mona told me you were QDT'd yesterday."

"I took thalamin."

"You've had enough hard drugs for a while. Mary Ann will give you some coffee in front."

"Thanks, Sylvia."

"Take care of yourself. And call me to let me know how you are doing."

"I will."

Blake walked up to the receptionist's desk and accepted the coffee gratefully. He felt disappointed Mona had called in no message. And a little worried. Still, four hours probably would not be enough time to settle Scott somewhere.

Scott was the least of his concerns. Blake had killed Carlyle before knowing whom Carlyle served. He still didn't know who'd ransacked his office, or who'd sabotaged Dwight's mercury. On top of all that, Joseph Murray's followers were after his ass. It made a hundred alarm bells go off in his head to think of walking into a police station, but Blake decided he ought to visit Joseph Murray.

The detective walked out of Sylvia Logan's offices onto Lincoln Avenue. Across the street the front half of a 1957 Chevy stuck out of the upper wall of the building. It had been originally erected to publicize a dance club which had long since gone out of business. Sylvia had told him some of the local residents were petitioning the current owner not to dismantle the car. What had begun as stupid kitsch was elevating toward landmark status.

Blake crossed the street and walked into a sandwich joint next to Bilman and Son Mortuary. A young man played Video Spritz at the machine near the door, his hands stuffed in his pockets, electrodes strapped to his

forehead. The fellow kept bobbing his head and wrin-
kling his face as color and sound flashed from the
machine.

As he looked over the menu on the wall, Blake
thought what a convenient neighborhood this was.
You could poison yourself at a Ptomaine Tommy's
like this joint, or go drink yourself to oblivion at any
one of a number of bars, then check in with one of the
doctors at Sylvia's office, or go around the corner to
Grant Hospital for the final gasp, and finally end up at
the mortuary next door—all without leaving the block.

An intense young black greeted him at the counter.
"Can I help you, sir?"

"I'll have a cheese nuke and a bottled water," Blake
said. The counterman looked at him for a moment,
like he was thinking of something else, then broke
away to set up the order. Blake watched him lay out
the bread, then walk into the back. A moment later,
the shutters opened on the partition window to the
kitchen and the counterman was looking at Blake and
glancing down at something in his hand. Blake took a
few steps back toward the door, and the counterman
shouted, "Stop him, Willie."

The guy at the Video Spritz looked up in surprise.

"You Willie?" Blake asked, grabbing the wires which
led to his electrodes.

"That's right. Hey!" Willie screamed as Blake
knocked him to the floor and wrapped the wires around
his neck. The detective took off out the door as the
counterman came running from the kitchen.

"That's the co-op man," Blake heard as he took off
up the street. He banged through the door of a theater
and nearly knocked down a woman carrying a tray of
tickets to the box office.

"Sorry," he called back to her as he ran up a flight
of stairs. "I'm incredibly late for rehearsal."

"There's no rehearsal up there," she shouted after
him.

He dashed past a placard proclaiming "An End to All Days" and into a small theater space, wondering if the play of the title were another millennial absurdity. Below, he heard the door bang open.

"Where is he?" the counterman's voice shouted.

"Who?" the box-office woman asked.

"A man just ran in here. A short white man. Dark curly hair. Where is he?"

Blake quietly closed the theater doors behind him, trying to lock them, hoping he could find another exit. He flipped a lever that slid a bolt between the double doors, but knew it wouldn't hold for long.

"He ran upstairs," the woman's muffled voice said, "but this theater is not open. You can't go up there."

The double footsteps clanged up the metal stairway toward him. Blake looked around the space. Two large sections of theater seats rose up at angles facing a wedge-shaped stage. He was tempted to dive under the curtains which masked the sides of the risers on which the chairs sat, but it was too obvious, and he would be too vulnerable.

Blake heard muffled voices and noticed two men in a booth up behind the seats. They stood with their backs to him behind a plate of glass, looking at a wall of switches and a notice board.

The detective moved toward the brick wall at the back of the stage, then realized the bricks were painted on canvas. The two bodies of his pursuers hit the double stage doors and rebounded off, as Blake ducked behind the false brick wall. He found himself in a large open area with bolts of fabric, tools, plastics, and wood arranged in place for scenery construction. Blake grabbed a hammer and crouched down behind the "brick" wall as the two men crashed through the double doors and tumbled into the stage area.

Bright light came up hot on the other side of the wall. He could see it shimmer through a tiny tear in the fabric. He looked through the hole and saw the two young men, disconcerted under the lights. Three spots of jelly Electrode-Sheen gleamed on the forehead of the Video Spritz player. Blake heard the Electrode-Sheen commercial pop up in his mind: "Boost your bio-contact for sharp delineation in all mental-machine interactive play. Electrode-Sheen!"

"What the hell are you doing?" a deep, amplified voice boomed. Blake looked around, tempted to answer.

"A guy came in here. We got to find him," the counterman said, clearly nervous. Blake noticed a coarse muslin curtain over a dirty window move in the breeze. Outside he could see the dark bars of a fire escape. He crept toward it and climbed out the open window, leaving his hammer on the sill. Behind him, the amplified voice demanded, "Who the hell are you?"

Blake ran down the alley and into a back entrance to Grant Hospital. He climbed a flight of stairs and hurried to a second-floor foyer at the front of the building. From there he phoned for a cab, then watched for its arrival out the plate-glass window in front, staying carefully out of sight at the side of an open door.

Across the street, the parking garage looked exactly like a bunker, with a flat-top roof and sloped concrete walls. I ought to be in there with some automatic weapons, he thought.

He remembered a dumpster he'd run past in the alley, imprinted with the "Garden City Waste" logo. Garden City. The official motto on the Seal of the City of Chicago was "Urbis en Horto." "City in a Garden." City in a mine field was more like it. City in a free-fire zone.

His taxi arrived and Blake directed the driver to the detective station at Belmont and Western, where he knew they'd be holding Murray. No matter how much he hated walking into a police station, he had to talk to the leader of the City Action Coalition.

10

When a person was held for any length of time at Belmont and Western, that meant the detectives wanted something. By keeping a suspect in their own house, they could watch who visited and, according to rumor, listen in on what was said. Some went as far as to suggest that pipes led from the toilet in each cell to a laboratory so every suspect's shit could be selectively analyzed for evidence. Since shit was freely given to the public sewer system, the rumormongers maintained, no illegal search-and-seizure plea could hold up in court. Blake had never heard of prison shit analysis being used in prosecution, but he had heard of suspects leaving Belmont and Western with bowels ready to explode.

When Blake announced at the desk that he had come to see Joseph Murray, he was not surprised to be greeted with an amused glance from the desk sergeant. The sergeant asked him to wait and crossed the room to use a phone out of Blake's range of hearing.

As the sergeant held an animated conversation, Blake watched a suspect being booked. The ritual of the mug shot was the same as ever: front shot, followed by side shot, but the taking of fingerprints had been streamlined to a fraction of its former required time. The suspect put both hands flat on a plate of glass at the top of a computerized Print-taker unit. A canvas belt stretched over the hands to hold them tight to the glass. The attending officer hit a button, a fan inside switched on, and an intense blue-white light flashed from beneath the plate glass. The unit instantly stored the suspect's complete handprint in a police data base. Prints from any part of the hand could then be speedily compared with prints taken at the scenes of crimes.

The younger police detectives especially loved all the electronic stuff, Blake knew. But it made a lot of them technology-lazy. If the solution to a case didn't come up on a computer screen, they weren't going to find it. And sometimes there was no substitute for hitting the streets.

If any detectives were out hitting the streets today, Blake couldn't tell by looking. In the reception area, officers and clerical workers manned the few desks and the booking area. At one side, a thick bullet-proof glass wall separated reception from the rows of detectives' desks. On almost every desk sat a computer terminal. If the personnel inside hadn't been wearing guns, it would have been hard to tell this from the city room of a newspaper. And it looked like there were enough detectives present to fill every one of the desks.

A steel door swung open in the wall isolating reception, and Detective Lieutenant Ahern emerged, smiling like an impresario. He walked straight up to Blake and shook his hand.

"I'm grateful you came in person," Ahern said, leading Blake back to an empty lineup room. "We'd really hoped to hear from you yesterday. We need more cooperation on the Murray case." He closed the door to the room. Blake could barely see the lieutenant's face. All light in the room came from the empty suspect runway on the other side of the one-way mirror. The walls and ceiling were of brown sound-dampening tiles textured like Belgian waffles.

"Somebody broke into my office the night before last," Blake said, looking at the lieutenant pointedly. "It's screwed up everything." He sat down in a blue plastic chair. His voice sounded like he was speaking into cotton.

"That's too bad," Ahern said in transparently shallow sympathy. "We all get busy. Then there's the occasional crisis." He looked at the fresh gauze on Blake's ear, then sat down on the edge of a table and smiled.

"I know how it is in private practice," he said soothingly, looking down at Blake in his chair. "You got to hustle around, try and make a buck, grab an HRL boy now and again to tide you over."

Blake handed Ahern his business card. In the small letters in the corner was printed *No HRL's*. "I don't do that kind of work," he said.

Ahern tossed the card onto the desktop like a tiny Frisbee, then brushed his hair back behind his ears with the fingertips of both hands. He gave Blake an oily smile. "I respect you for it," he said. "There's better ways to make a living." He grabbed a plain wooden chair and spun it around to sit on it reversed, resting his forearms on the back, facing Blake.

"We're grateful for your call on Murray. We put him in the slam, and we got a lead on explosives he had cached. But we don't have what we need to pin him yet." Ahern shrugged theatrically, as though that were a matter of time.

"I didn't call," Blake said.

Ahern stood up and frowned. He scratched his temple near the eyebrow and pointed at Blake. "You getting pressure on the street?"

"I didn't call," Blake said again.

"You turn chicken on us, Shortstop, and you'll be wishing you just had Murray's boys on your back. That'll look like the good old days." The lieutenant leaned over, one hand gripping on Blake's shoulder.

Blake crossed his right leg over his left. His foot hung between Ahern's calves. One quick kick upward and the lieutenant would be on the floor clutching his balls in pain. They exchanged a look, and Ahern let go Blake's shoulder. He stepped back out of range.

"You want to listen to the tape?" Blake asked.

"What tape?"

"The tape you made of 'my' voice. The co-op call. I know you boys tape everything. Should we listen to my voice?"

"What for?" Ahern asked.

"So you can hear it's not my voice," Blake said loudly. "You can run a synthesized comparison, then we can stop dancing around like a pair of jackasses."

"If you didn't call, what the fuck are you doing here?"

"Somebody here told the world I co-opped. I came to see Murray. I'd like to save my neck," Blake said.

Ahern looked at him like he'd lost his mind. "You came here to help out Murray? No fucking way!" The lieutenant leaned back against the door of the room, his arms crossed.

"Tell me, Lieutenant. Do you want to solve the First National or do you just want to get Murray?"

"I'll tell you the truth, Blake," he said, standing up away from the door. "I'd like to pin something on that black bastard. I don't give a fuck who knows it. But if I don't solve the First National, my butt's in a sling. I got to pin the bank on somebody, and I got to pin it hard."

"You don't care if it's the guilty party?" Blake said.

"Don't you listen, Shortstop? I said I got to pin it hard. When you pin it hard, the party is guilty." He turned away from Blake and slapped the door with his palm. Blake rolled his eyes. Ahern turned back.

"I want to help you do that," Blake said reasonably. "As long as you don't insist Murray's the boy."

"Sure," Ahern said. "So long as you don't insist he ain't."

11

The lieutenant escorted Blake down a long hallway with shiny institutional sheet-metal walls. After the muffled atmosphere of the lineup room, every sound here seemed harsh, from the buzzing of the fluorescent lights overhead to the rap of their shoes as they walked. At the end of the hall, a heavy steel door with a wire-reinforced window led to the lockup. An armed officer seated at a desk guarded the door. Ahern led Blake into a visitor's chamber outside the lockup.

"I'll have some officers bring him in here," he told the detective. "Remember: I want results." The lieutenant walked out, locking Blake inside.

The visitor's chamber was another sound-dampened room with foam-waffle-paneled walls. It was so quiet, Blake could hear the sound of his own breathing. The room's only furnishings were a plain wooden table and four molded plastic chairs.

Blake walked to the window and looked out. In front of the building, Western Avenue rose up on pillars in a long bridge for through traffic to bypass over the Belmont intersection. The overpass was like one huge concrete section of a roller coaster, a reminder of the long-gone Riverview Amusement Park which once stood on the site. Blake noticed the wire reinforcement in the glass in front of him. The window was sealed permanently shut.

Two officers brought Murray into the visitor's cham-

ber. They unlocked the handcuff from his one wrist
and relocked that side to a metal ring screwed into the
table. Murray looked down to see the table was bolted
to the floor. Then one of the guards showed Blake the
bell to ring when they were through, and the two left,
locking Blake and Murray in alone. As Murray glanced
around the room, the detective wondered how alone
they really were.

Murray sat on the opposite side of the table from
Blake, erect as a soldier, defying his round-molded
chair. The long head on his long neck seemed to pull
his spine upright. Graying nappy hair pushed straight
back from his dark forehead. His nose hooked crook-
edly like a hawk's beak after a bad accident, giving his
face the look of a strangely mixed ancestry. But his
eyes, with the mad intensity of a street-corner Bible
thumper, commanded all.

"You're the man who cooperated with the law," he
said, his voice a deep, stern rumble in the padded
closeness of the air.

"I'm not," Blake told him. "Whoever set you up,
set me up. Your men have made things tight for me. I
can hardly breathe."

"What do you want?" Murray pulled out a wrinkled
pouch and began pinching pharmaceutical tobacco into
a cigarette paper.

"I want you to call them off," Blake said.

"Why should I do that?"

"I'm a detective. I'll find out who bombed the First
National and turn the evidence over to the police."

Murray licked the paper and rolled it with the hand
cuffed to the table while stuffing the pouch away and
pulling out matches with the other. He leaned down to
take the cigarette with his lips and lit it.

Murray grinned. "But what if *I'm* the one who did
it?" he asked.

"Then we're both still in trouble," Blake said.

Murray laughed deep and heartily. "Well, that's all

right, Mr. Blake," he said. "I can assure you I did not blow up the First National. And who would know better than I?"

"The guy who did."

Murray laughed again and nodded. He looked at ease, but Blake sensed the leader still suspected him.

"Did the police use QDT in your capture?" Blake asked.

"I spent three hours out of my mind," Murray told him. "I came down to reality on the floor of a jail cell."

"We got caught in the afterdrift," Blake said, scratching the corner of one of his thick eyebrows. "A client of mine took a similar ride."

"I hate that QDT," Murray said. "People die in the afterdrift. Two years ago they came after me on some trumped-up charges. A little boy caught a whiff of that gas and fell out of his bedroom window. He broke his back on an iron fence. Paralyzed. And the police say QDT is for our safety." Murray spat on the floor. "They have tranquilizer bullets. They don't even use them.

"I stand for the protection of people, Mr. Blake. The bombing at First National angers me. Innocent people were killed. Folks' money is held up that can't afford to wait."

"Who do you think would frame you?" Blake asked.

Murray sighed deeply. He rolled his head on his long neck, looked up at the ceiling a moment, then back at the detective. "I have enemies. I try to shift the power around. Those that got the power now don't like that." He stared Blake in the eyes for a long moment, trying to read where Blake might stand in the scheme of things. Then he looked down at the table and shrugged.

"I don't know who would have done this thing to me," he said. "I was arrested so quickly after the bombing, I just guess the bomber himself turned me

in. A smoke screen." He looked at Blake with pene-
trating eyes again. "Why would this cooperator pretend to be you?"

"I don't know," the detective said.

Murray kept staring right at him, and a crafty grin
began to break across his face. "You wouldn't happen
to be the one," he said slowly, pointing a long dark
finger at the detective, "who blew up all those dollars,
and bonds, and people, would you?"

Blake smiled back. "I'm afraid not."

"I don't like mad bombers," Murray said, losing his
smile. He looked out the window.

"Have you done any work against QDT?" Blake
asked.

"I would like to do something about QDT," he
said. As he spoke, his voice became excessively rea-
sonable. "Perhaps we can begin a letter-writing cam-
paign to Congress. Document accidents due to afterdrift
and estimate losses from lootings."

Blake recognized the voice. Here was the Murray
who stood in front of television cameras, who gave
interviews on the radio. This character shift made
Blake aware again that the room was probably bugged.
Murray would not incriminate himself here.

"What about getting your men to give me a break?"
Blake asked.

Murray spoke toward the caged window, and Blake
realized how ill-suited the man was for prison. His
long body stretched as though straining against the
pressure of confinement. When he looked out the
window, his gaze grew abstracted and longing.

"My men are not soldiers," he said, "and I am not a
general. I do not demand perfect obedience in exchange for future freedom." He straightened his spine
even further, but did not shift his gaze from the window.

"Dr. Martin Luthur King taught his followers to
fight through nonviolent resistance," he continued.
"Yet violence followed and plagued him. After his

death, riots broke out. You couldn't say he caused the violence." He looked directly at Blake, making his decision. "If a giant like Dr. King couldn't keep the peace, I certainly cannot promise you safety," he said. "Especially not from jail. But I'll do what I can."

Blake got up and pushed the button on the wall near the door. The two officers returned. "Bring me pen and paper," Murray told them.

12

"I can't do anything with nothing to work from," Blake said angrily. Ahern stood facing him in the communications room, a wall of recorders, transmitters, and receivers gleaming behind them. They'd just listened to the co-op call that had implicated Murray, and Ahern admitted it didn't sound like Blake, though whoever it was had obviously disguised his voice.

"You got your letter from Murray. We'll let his boys call him. What more do you want?" the lieutenant asked.

"That just gets them off my back for the moment. It doesn't help solve anything."

Ahern shrugged in response.

"It's not like you're giving something for nothing," Blake said. "If I crack this, you get the credit."

"I ain't supposed to let stuff out of here," Ahern said. He'd seemed nervous the whole time he'd worked with the tape, cuing and stopping it precisely so Blake heard nothing but the co-op call itself. He was especially meticulous in guarding the cuing book from view. Blake figured there must be something on the tape Ahern didn't want him to hear. Maybe the lieutenant had just logged in his conversation with Murray. Or maybe the bug Mona had found was police property, and something in the cuing book gave that away.

"All right," Blake said. "We listened to the tape. The cooperator obviously disguised his voice. If I can

112

run a synthesized comparison with some stuff I got, maybe I can identify him." Blake wanted to check Carlyle and Brubaker's voices for starters.

"Bring your tapes in here," the lieutenant said. "I'll have the syn-comps done for you."

"I don't have time to fuck around, Ahern. If you're going to play games, you're cutting both our throats."

"You never helped us before," Ahern said derisively. "We asked you. You refused. Why should I help you now?"

"Because it's for your own good," Blake shouted. He calmed himself down, fought the impulse to stalk angrily out of the station. "You'd be wasting free help."

"All right," the lieutenant said finally. "Wait out in the front, and I'll make you a copy."

"Fine," Blake said.

"But you better do something for me. It wasn't my fault somebody leaked your name. Nobody can stop people talking."

13

When Billy heard the slap, he spun around and saw Mona fall unconscious away from the door of the van. As he rushed toward her, a man crawled out of the front seat with a gun held awkwardly in his left hand.

"Just step back and relax there, big fella," the gunman said.

Billy stood ill-at-ease. He turned his head and saw an enormously fat man—the man who'd laughed—emerge from the shadows of the factory, carrying a rifle. Billy exchanged a look with Scott, who stood by the boxes at the back of the van. They'd never had a chance.

The man with the pistol pulled back Mona's lids with his thumb and looked at her eyes. Then he peeled the buzzer from his palm, snapped the cap over its face, and put it in his pocket. He switched the pistol to his right hand.

"Are we taking her along?" he called up to Brubaker.

"Is she buzzed?" Brubaker asked in surprise.

"Yeah."

"God damn it," Brubaker shouted. "I didn't want you doing that."

"Well, how the fuck was I supposed to know?" the man called back. "You never tell me anything." He made a face of long suffering at Billy, who turned uncomfortably away. "Should we take her with?" he asked again.

Brubaker thought a moment. "No. Bring her up here," he said irritably.

Scott took a step toward the side of the van away from Brubaker. On the dock, the fat man shifted his rifle toward him. "Don't go away," he called down to Scott.

The gunman gestured with his pistol at Billy. "Pick her up," he said.

As Billy wedged his arms under Mona's limp body, he noticed the telltale small greenish bruise had begun to spread from the point the buzzer had hit. He carried her across the truck bay and up the stairs to the dock.

"Brubaker," Scott called. "We have to talk." Scott followed Billy up onto the dock. The gunman had Billy set Mona down on the concrete.

"I know who hired you," Scott said. "I know how he pays. I can do better."

Brubaker snorted. "You can't even pay off your HRL!"

The fat man giggled derisively.

"It'll take one hour to reassemble this thing," Scott said confidently, gesturing to the array of boxed equipment. "Once you see what it does, your little wages will seem inconsequential."

Brubaker thought a moment, then looked over at the fat man, who'd fallen silent. Brubaker glanced down at Mona, unconscious against the wall.

"Don't worry about her. There's money to be made," Scott said. "She means nothing to me. You can buzz the big guy too, for all I care."

Billy's fist swung out hard and caught Scott square in the side of the face. Scott's head bounced sickeningly against his shoulder, and he fell to the concrete. A little blood trickled from his nose, and he lay perfectly still.

The man with the pistol grabbed Billy and held the gun to the side of the big man's square jaw.

"You better not've damaged him," Brubaker threatened. He signaled the fat man. "Carry Scott down to the truck. He ain't in any condition to deal anymore. But watch him. We can't afford nothing else gone wrong."

The fat man dragged him off.

Brubaker looked exasperated. "I wasn't going to buzz you," he told Billy. "I didn't want this woman buzzed." He shot a glare at the gunman.

"I didn't know that," the man said defensively, his pistol still against the side of Billy's face.

"She said Blake had Carlyle," Brubaker shouted. "We could've used her for trade."

"But you said you didn't care what happened to Carlyle as long as you had Scott and the machine," the man complained. "You told me she was dangerous. I got her out of the way."

"You are the stupidest shit," Brubaker told him. "You never considered Carlyle is my partner? He pays half your wage. You never considered I might be lying to the broad? What the fuck is wrong with you?" He shook his head in disgust. "Does Blake know about this place?" he asked Billy.

"I don't think so," Billy answered.

Brubaker looked at him irritably, then down at Mona. "Let's put her inside," he said.

"You don't want her for redemption?" the gunman asked.

"We got too much to do. It's not worth the risk. If we have time, we'll come back later."

They told Billy to carry her in. He sat her up in a chair by the stairs like a rag doll, the back of her head leaning on the wall, her eyes peacefully closed. Billy folded her hands over her lap. The only thing that made Mona look like anything but a person enjoying a brief nap was the slowly spreading bruise in the middle of her forehead.

Billy felt a tightness in his throat and a pressure in

his chest. He wanted to throw himself on the two men. He wanted to stomp their ribs in. But he wanted to live too. The sight of their weapons made him ashamed.

Mona had been such a damned good-humored woman. She'd made him laugh sometimes. And gotten him work.

Brubaker looked at her propped in the chair. "What a waste," he said. "We'll take the big guy along. Maybe he's good for something."

14

Blake called a taxi from the police station to take him to Biltey's Tavern in Pilsen, where he knew he would find some of Murray's men. When he saw the ancient driver behind the wheel of the cab that picked him up, he wondered if the old man would last out the trip.

As the cabby angled down Elston along the river and then down Ashland through the old West Side industrial districts, he pointed out some of the abandoned factories.

"All those places," he said. "All shut down for years. I sprinkled every one of them."

Blake looked at the patches of flaking skin on the back of the balding driver's head and suddenly imagined he could smell stale urine in the cab. "You did what?" he asked, curious if the old man were reminiscing on lost bladder control.

"I sprinkled them," the cabby said proudly. "Used to be a pipe fitter for a sprinkler outfit. Twenty years ago. Automatic fire sprinklers." The driver waited a moment for Blake to respond, then shouted, "They spray water when there's a fire!"

"Right," the startled detective responded. "I got you."

"I worked for one outfit twelve years." He waved his hand toward the buildings on the street. "These places were already old dumps back then. We had to bring them up to code. But the company went bust in the seventies."

Blake watched out the window as the cab rolled by groups of men drinking from bottles wrapped in brown bags. The scattered shops and groceries wore metal-mesh grates over their windows for protection.

"This was a shitty area to work," the cabby said. "It got better for a while. Now it's shitty again. One time, one of the older fitters walked down to one of these stores to get something for lunch. Had a heart attack. Fell down on the street. People walked right by him. Figured he was just another wino in the gutter. Took hours before he got any help. Practically killed him."

"That's too bad," Blake said.

"He was never the same," the driver said. "Had to quit construction. Couldn't stand the ladders no more." He shook his head.

"When did you quit as a fitter?" Blake asked.

"Oh, once our outfit went bust, I got a few jobs, here and there. Finally gave it up altogether. Got myself a cab. Now I got a nice heater in the winter. Air condition in the summer. No more snow and mud boots for me. Shit." He laughed. "I thought I was stepping down to get in a cab. You don't make the money, but I never had it so good." He laughed again. " 'Course, I've had to shoot a couple riders." He pulled a pistol from under the dash and waved it over his head. "Got stabbed once myself, too. But I ain't going to fall off no ladders or freeze my ass to death." The old cabby seemed endlessly amused by that idea and kept chuckling and shaking his head, repeating, "Freeze *my* ass to death," as he drove. Then he pointed the pistol at his temple and turned to look back at Blake.

"Might as well blow your brains out as freeze your ass to death," he roared. This put him into hysterics, which ended in a coughing fit that sent the cab swerving over the center lane. A micro-tri-wheeler skidded out of their way, sending up a series of high-pitched squeaks from its horn that reminded Blake of an enraged Pekingese.

"I'm not looking to die laughing here," Blake said as the ancient driver pulled the cab back into his own lane.

"Under control," the cabby said. "Don't worry about a thing." He drove on seriously and in silence.

As they crossed the border into Pilsen, the neighborhood changed from poor, dirty, and depressed to medium poor and clean. The west end of Pilsen was populated mostly by Hispanics and artist types who came for cheap housing. Some of the Hispanics had painted their buildings in cheerful pastels. Murals decorated walls practically untouched by graffiti. At the east end of Pilsen, fashionable people had already begun following the artists into the neighborhood, driving up rents and forcing out the artists and Hispanics.

The cab stopped in front of Biltey's Tavern, and Blake got out and paid. All the way down the street, deep stairways led from the sidewalk down to the buildings' front doors. These were buildings which predated the sewer system. When the system was put in, the city found it was cheaper to raise the street than to dig underground sewers. The sewers were laid on top of the ground, and the city got rid of plenty of bothersome landfill in building the streets up over sewer level. People were able to study the underchassis of their parked cars, right from their living-room windows.

It was already late in the afternoon and the day was overcast, but when Blake walked into Biltey's he had to wait for his eyes to adjust to the gloom. In replacement for his sight came the overwhelming scent of stale beer. He'd heard plenty of voices when he opened the door, but by the time he could see again, the room had gone silent. He walked down five steps and crossed the floor to the bar with the uncomfortable feeling

that everyone in the room was on a break from looking for him. He sat down at a stool. The bartender
came over. He didn't look happy to see Blake.

"What do you want?" he asked.

Blake looked at him and wondered if the bartender
was a Murray-follower too, or if he was just uniformly
unfriendly to all new customers. "I'll have whatever's
on draft," Blake told him.

The detective swiveled his stool to face the room as
the bartender filled a mug. Two men got up from a
table and walked toward him. Their footsteps sounded
loud in the silence. They stood in front of Blake as the
other two men from their table got up and asked a few
of the patrons to leave. One fellow who complained
was pushed roughly toward the door. Blake felt a drop
of sweat trickle down his side.

"Oh, shit," the bartender said, noticing it all. He set
down the mug of beer for Blake. "You better pay up
in advance."

Blake gave him a look, but did not reach for his
wallet. One of the men locked the door and pulled
down the shade. The man on Blake's left was a short,
stocky Hispanic whom Blake recognized from the sub-
urban kid "brainwashing" case. The other was a tall,
large-boned fellow with short dirty-blond hair. Blake
looked at the Hispanic.

"There's an envelope in my left inside jacket pocket,"
Blake said. "Take it out."

The Hispanic looked at the other. The tall man
shrugged. The Hispanic pulled Blake's jacket open by
the lapel. Cautiously he reached in and removed the
envelope.

"Now open it up and read it," Blake told him.

The Hispanic tore open the envelope and pulled out
a single sheet of paper. He read the paper slowly.

"What is thees? Murray say I call thees number?"
the Hispanic asked.

"Call it," Blake told him. "It's all set up. They'll put the call through."

The Hispanic looked at him, trying to figure an angle, then pulled out some change and walked over to the phone on the wall.

"If you don't want cops in here, don't use that phone," Blake said. "You're calling a police station. They'll be tapping and tracing."

The Hispanic turned and looked at him. "You say they don't know thees place now?"

"Not from me they don't," Blake said.

The Hispanic gave him another long look, then walked up the stairs and out the door. A man locked it behind him.

"What's it all about?" the tall man asked. The detective recognized his voice at once. This was the "Polack" from Blake's shopping-cart ride under Jake Fishman's rags.

"I saw Murray today," Blake told him, just loud enough for everyone to overhear. "We had a long talk. I'm not the one who co-opped."

"That letter was from Murray?"

"His own handwriting," Blake answered. He turned toward the bar and sipped at his beer. The mirror behind the bar was etched with decorative beehives around the edges. Blake thought of the blue beehive beacon atop Quiller's Taos Pinnacle downtown. As Blake's mother's social-protest buddy of old, Quiller loved Murray and his City Action Coalition. They helped to keep the city lively. Quiller would be so disappointed if Murray's boys murdered the son of his early love. Though not as disappointed as Blake himself.

The detective smiled at the Polack on the stool next to him and raised his beer mug in a mock toast. The Polack shrugged. Beyond the Polack's head, Blake saw fuzzy dice hanging on the wall. A holy card of the Virgin Mary was stuck to the cash register. Out-ofseason Christmas decorations hung from the lamps overhead.

Blake watched the clock crawl through a long fifteen minutes while a few customers were turned away at the door. Then a rapping came at the glass, and the man on the stairs let the Hispanic back in. Blake watched as his eyes adjusted to the light and he crossed the room. He did not look happy.

"Murray think that he Jesus Christ, he so God damned forgiving," he said to the Polack.

"Did this guy do it, or what?" the Polack asked.

The Hispanic took a pull at his beer. "Murray don't think so. But, man, he does not know."

"Murray said that?" Blake asked.

"Murray don't got no proof," the Hispanic said angrily. "You say what you want. *Nobody* got no proof what you say. You speak shit. Now we trust you? You fuck us up before. You fuck us up again."

"I got no interest in cooperating with the law," Blake told him, feeling the sweat break out again on the palms of his hands. He felt his tongue getting thick in his throat.

"I'm a detective," he told them. "You know that. A private detective. This whole thing is screwing up my work. But I'm willing to put that aside. I'll work on the First National until we find the real bomber."

"Sure, you willing. Yeah," the Hispanic shouted. "You fuck right willing. You want save you fucking ass!"

"God damned right," Blake shouted back, rising off the stool. "And who the fuck is going to work harder than that?"

The Hispanic took a step back from him.

"Now what do you want?" Blake continued shouting. "You want a chance at getting Murray out of jail or do you want revenge on someone who may or may not have helped put him there?"

The two men stood facing each other. Blake felt the

hairs on the back of his neck slowly settle down as he stared into the bloodshot eyes of the other man. He broke the gaze himself, not wanting to show the Hispanic the humiliation of staring him down.

Blake looked at the men in the room. Some looked away when he caught their gaze. Then he sat back down, faced the bar, and took a sip of his beer.

"If Murray thinks he's straight, that's good enough for me," the Polack said.

The Hispanic looked at the Polack sharply. "We don't speak in front this guy."

"It's up to you," Blake said quietly, still facing away from the men. He put his hand against his pocket to feel the reassurance of the stiletto inside.

The Hispanic walked over to a table in the corner, and the other men gathered around him. Blake signaled the bartender.

"Get me a double shot of bourbon," he said.

Blake had sipped halfway through his bourbon when the ad hoc City Action Coalition contingent approached him again at the bar.

"You got one week," the Hispanic told him. "You can't get no evidence in thees time, *hombre*, I ain't responsible what happen to you."

Of the five men who faced him, the Hispanic looked most angry. If any of them were to be "responsible" for injuring him, Blake thought, it would probably be this man.

"All right then," Blake said. "I'll take the case. I don't imagine we'll have him out of jail in a week, but we might have the evidence to clear him. You know the cops are going to drag their feet about letting him out."

None of them argued the point, though the Hispanic looked tempted.

"First I need some information," the detective said.

"No, no, no," the Hispanic said. "We ain't answer no question."

"Come on, Ray," the Polack said to him. "If this guy's going to get Murray out, we got to get on-line with him."

"We got stuff we can't say. You know thees," Ray insisted.

Blake watched as the Hispanic turned from face to face, trying to pull the men in line.

"We know what not to say," a young black said finally. He turned to Blake. "I'll talk to you. I want the man out."

"Do you know anything about who actually did the First National bombing?"

The young black shook his head.

"Anybody?"

A few others shook their heads.

"If anybody got something to say about thees," Ray told them, "speak now." But no one had anything to say.

"An alibi might help. The cops might still say Murray directed the bombing, even if he wasn't there. But it would be a start," Blake said. "Murray says he was alone. He's got no proof. Does anyone have anything that proves where he was?"

"I was with the man," the young black said.

"Where?" Blake asked him.

"Wherever he says."

"No," the detective told him. "That won't work. We got to deal with the truth."

"We can make this story straight," the black said.

"We can't beat the district attorney at proving bullshit. He's got more experience. The only way we win is by proving facts."

Blake waited until it was clear no alibis were forthcoming.

"Anybody think of any good reasons to *want* to blow up the First National?"

"It's full of money," another Hispanic suggested. The others laughed. "I could use some money," he added. "Blow some cash out the window, I'll pick it up."

"How about Midland Waste? Somebody sabotaged a tank of mercury there a couple days ago," Blake said, seeing if he could get anything on the other case. When he had questioned Murray about it, Murray's answer had been too diplomatic to be real. "There could be a connection to the bank," Blake lied.

"What connection?" Ray demanded.

"I heard Midland was an inside job," the black said.

"You hear shit," Ray told him.

"What did you hear?" Blake asked.

"Just that it was an inside job," the black said, looking back at Ray.

"Where'd you hear it?" Blake continued.

"Some guys talking. I don't remember."

Blake sensed he knew more, but anyone could see Ray would kick his ass if he said another word. The detective stuck his business card in the black kid's pocket.

"Give me a call if you remember anything else. There was another mercury sabotage at Chicago Chemical Supply. Anyone know anything about that?"

"Never heard of the place," the Polack said.

Blake threw a couple more cards on the bar, along with the money for his drinks. "If any of you remember anything about anything, give me a call." He took a last sip of his bourbon and headed for the door to phone a cab. Asking questions here was a waste of time.

15

A half-hour later, Blake walked into his office, flipped on the lights, and tossed the cassette tape he'd got from Ahern onto his desk. The office looked like preparations for moving day, what with all the stacks of paper everywhere. Mona hadn't had much time to be a secretary lately. If this kind of action kept up, Blake thought, he'd have to make her a partner and get a new secretary.

He went over to the window and slid back the shade to look out. The day had faded into evening, and the streetlights came on. A man got into a car and started the engine. Blake backed off from the glass. He didn't want to take a potshot from one of Murray's boys who hadn't yet got the word.

He sat down at his desk and rubbed his hands on his forehead against the fatigue. He had Dwight's mercury sabotage to solve. He couldn't pretend he'd gotten far on that, though from their caginess at Biltey's, it looked like Murray's boys maybe did have some involvement. Dwight had hired in some extra security, so he was safe for the moment.

As much as Blake hated it, he'd accepted the Scott job too. He'd have to see him through. And now there was the First National. He still had no real clues as to who'd ransacked his office, either.

He dialed his answering service, hoping someone had left a message with the solution to all his problems, but the only thing the service had to report was an anonymous obscene phone call. He tried calling Sylvia's office to see if Mona'd left a message there. No luck. He didn't imagine she would have had any trouble settling Scott under protection, but it bothered him that there'd been no message from her. He was reminded again of seeing her face in his nightmare of Carlyle's dismemberment, and he tried to push down the anxiety that memory brought him.

Taking Ahern's tape of the co-op call from the desk, he went over to the computer console. He really needed Mona for this. She could run synthesized comparisons in no time. It would take him hours. Mona could even hack through protection codes and into corporate files with the pleasure and finesse some people had for crossword puzzles.

He flipped the computer to audio mode, and a signal came up on the monitor. "Important Message," it read. "Code 29."

He knew Code 29, thank God. Mona had created that code for him to phone in and secure information he didn't want left with the answering service. He pulled the card out of his wallet and punched in Code 29: "5B76CA4." He put on the headphones and hit Enter, but instead of hearing any message, the words "Unscramble Code" flashed on the screen.

"Unscramble Code"? He didn't know anything about any "Unscramble Code." Mona always retrieved these things. He looked at the screen for a moment, then typed in "Override Unscramble Code" on one line, "Play" on the next, and hit the Enter key again. An unintelligible squawk came through on the headphones. He punched Reset. "Unscramble Code" reappeared on the screen.

Blake got up and looked through Mona's desk. If she had a code book, he didn't know about it. Her desk was still practically empty after the break-in. He'd been so damned picky about leaving anything valuable in the computer, now he couldn't get at the message.

"Unscramble Code."

He went back to the console and looked at the monitor. Then it occurred to him to think of "Unscramble Code" as a command rather than a request. He looked at Code 29: "5B76CA4." That wasn't too hard to unscramble: "ABC4567." He entered the code, gave the "Play" command, and a beautiful sound came through the phones:

"Hi, Blake," Mona's voice said. "I imagine I'll be back at the office before you, so you'll probably never hear this. Anyway, I thought I'd drop some bread crumbs on my path, just for fun. We're going to pick up Scott's equipment at 1220 North Hooker. Then I'm taking him out to Kane County. I'll try to set him up in Waverly's barn. If that doesn't work, I'll leave a message there, or I'll call you at Dr. Sylvia's."

There was a break of silence; then Mona spoke again, hesitantly. "I hope you're going to be okay, Blake." Another pause. "I just hope you're okay," she said quietly. The tape clicked out. Blake smiled at the tenderness in her voice and shut down the console.

He wasn't smiling, however, after he phoned Waverly's, then Sylvia's again, and finally Mona's residence: no messages at the first two and no one home at the last. He ran down to the basement to see that his car was still absent from its stall; then he phoned for a cab.

"Twelve-twenty North Hooker," Blake told the cabby as he climbed into the back seat.

"That sounds like the wrong end of Goose Island," the driver said.

"Yeah?" As long as this cabby didn't put a gun to his head, Blake figured he could listen.

"That's right across the bridge from Cabrini-Green. The niggers from Cabrini walk across that bridge at night to go mug queers. They jack on down to the

south end of the island and grab the fags coming out
of that yuppie gay bar by the big loft building." The
driver turned up Orleans toward Division. A silent
flex-plastic-wheeled train slid by on the elevated tracks
into the night.

"A regular procession, huh?" Blake said doubtfully.

"What, you don't think they do it?" the cabby said.
He turned his flabby head on his fat little neck to look
back at Blake. "Don't fucking kid yourself."

"I suppose that's why Goose Island never revived
like it was supposed to."

"Shit no," the cabby said. "That ain't it. Hell, fags
love to get mugged. Why do you think they're fags?
The one who stopped Goose Island is Laudner."

"Who's Laudner?" Blake asked.

"Laudner. Are you kidding? The mayor has to call
Laudner every morning to ask if it's all right to get out
of bed. He's got his finger in everything." The driver
waved his fat right hand expressively as he spoke.
"Laudner owns Construction Materials south of the
island, across the river. He owns Industrial Salt on the
west side of the island. If Laudner decided to raise the
price of a yard of concrete by five bucks, half the
construction in Chicago would grind to a halt." He
turned left onto Division, toward the Cabrini-Green
housing project and the island beyond.

"Laudner bought in here about ninety-one. Figured
he could make a bundle. Then when the yuppies moved
into the renovated lofts," the cabby continued, "they
started complaining about Laudner's cement dust floating through the windows and collecting on their art
prints. Laudner's salt was rusting their BMW's." He
laughed derisively. "Poor babies. So the courts told
Laudner to hose down his cement dust. He had to
slow down his salt conveyors. He didn't like that shit.
He was here first. So every time a building on or near
the island comes up for rezoning, Laudner's lawyers

block it. Progress stops. That's why the north end of the island still looks the same as it did ten years ago.''

They drove across the old metal bridge, and Blake looked down at the murky waters of the Chicago River. In the darkness, he could see barely a glint of reflected light.

The cab took a right at the first street and pulled up to a desolate building.

"This is some God damned address," the cabby said.

The old factory looked just as much like a trap to Blake as it did to the cabdriver. The streetlights were sparse, apathetic sentries as evening fled into night. The area looked as deserted, but felt as malignantly populous, as a graveyard in the dark.

"Wait for me," Blake said as he climbed out of the cab.

"I'm an independent businessman," the cabby said. "I don't wait for nobody when I don't want to."

The detective tried showing his license. The fat little driver looked at it skeptically. "That don't bend my rod," he said.

"I'll double the fare," Blake said. "A woman could be hurt in there."

The cabby thought about it. "Triple," he said. "And the meter runs the whole time."

"Jesus Christ," Blake said. "All right." He pulled a flashlight out of his pocket. "You leave me here, you better hope I never find you." He walked around the car and headed toward the front door.

The driver slid down his window. "I ain't hanging here if somebody starts shooting," he called.

Blake ignored him and looked over the front. The metal tape on the windows for the security system had aged and peeled. He doubted if it were connected to a live alarm. Nobody used metal tape anymore. Laser eye installed easier.

The main entrance was a cement-filled steel door in

a steel frame with a wire-reinforced glass window. The office space inside looked as vacant as a long-burgled tomb. Blake walked back toward the cab.

"Let's go around behind," he said.

"You go around behind," the driver told him. "I'll wait ten minutes."

Blake shoved the cabby's sliding window all the way down. He leaned in close enough to see the wrinkles in the driver's fat face and smell the onion on his breath. "You leave me here," Blake told him, "I'll take your car apart piece by piece."

"I'm insured against that."

"But then I'll make you eat it."

"I haven't seen dollar primera uno from you."

Blake handed him a twenty. "Don't move," he said. The detective took off toward the corner of the building.

"Fifteen minutes," the driver called after him.

He ran down to the end of the factory and stopped. Between the old structure and the building next to it, refuse and twisted sheets of rusting metal writhed on the dark ground. Blake picked his way through carefully and rounded the back corner to the truck dock.

He tried the garage door on the dock platform and the personnel door at the end. All the locks were too old for the pick-keys he carried. He scanned the truck bay and the alley. Deserted. The buildings looked abandoned even for daytime use. This was no time for delicacy. He kicked in one of the wood panels in the first garage door. The old wood splintered more easily than he'd expected. He pulled away the shattered pieces and crawled through the hole, his flashlight glowing on little patches of space before him.

The hills-and-valleys floor spread a series of black pits before him. The abandoned machinery squatted like hulking brutes under grimy chains from the ceiling. When his flashlight played down the stairway from the loft and caught Mona's pale, pale face looking up, her head tilted back against the wall, Blake gasped first in shock, then in recognition.

He put his hand on her throat and felt the pulse, light and irregular. He shone the light in her face to look at her eyes and noticed the small green-brown bruise on her forehead. He looked closer and saw the tiny red dot in its center.

Jesus God, Mona, he thought. His knees trembled. He felt suddenly weak, and stretched out his arms to lean on the wall above her seated body.

"Mona," he said aloud. He turned away from her and took a few deep breaths. Then he opened the personnel door, picked up her limp body in his arms, and carried her out into the night.

When the cabby saw them coming, he jumped out to get the door. "What happened to her?" he asked.

"I think they drugged her," Blake lied.

The driver helped him prop her up on the seat. Her head rolled back, and the overhead light caught the bruise on her forehead. The cabby looked at it, then looked at Blake.

"She was your friend?" he said. Blake nodded, walked around the car, and got in beside her. The cabby shook his head and slid behind the wheel. Blake gave the driver Dr. Sylvia Logan's address, and the cab took off.

Blake looked at Mona's face. It reminded him of the pale, fevered face of his mother, decades earlier, sunk back in her pillows. The image of his mother's face was so strong, it took him back to that day, though he hadn't thought of it in years. It was the day he realized she wasn't just sick, but dying. The details came to him like it was yesterday. He recalled the strange smell of his mother's breath, like pork going sour. He remembered the lost, hollow feeling in his chest when he looked at her.

Young Blake had held her hand. "There's no family fortune," his mother had told him, smiling weakly.

She lost her breath again and pushed up on her elbows, struggling for air. Gradually she settled back into the pillows, taking shallow breaths.

"I couldn't breathe," she had said, raising her eyebrows like this was a kind of mysterious joke.

Blake had found out three days earlier she had much more than a cold. Her lungs were filling with fluid, the doctor told him. He wanted young Blake to convince her to come to the hospital, but she refused. "Horrible, ghoulish place," she called it.

"Your father will help you," he remembered her saying, barely loud enough to hear. "You can go to him." But she wouldn't allow Blake to call him while she was still alive. After she was dead, he never could find his father, and he went to live with Quiller until he could take care of himself.

"Make me tea," she whispered.

The boy walked to the other end of the room and put the kettle on the stove. His mother's bed rolled out of the couch in the living room. The kitchen began where the living room ended.

When the kettle boiled, he poured the water over the leaves in the teapot and put the remainder in an open pan to steam moisture into the air.

When he took the teapot to his mother's bedside, her eyes would no longer focus. She clutched for his hand and held it tight. Air hissed in her throat, but no words would come. After a tight struggle, even the hissing stopped.

Young Blake felt her wrist and her neck. No pulse, no breath, no sight in the eyes. He laid her hands, already turning cold, onto her chest and stood up by the bedside, alone.

He looked around him and saw a lightness in the air, a subtle shift of the colors in the room. She hadn't gone. She filled the space around him, abandoning the dried shell on the bed. She wanted to tell him something.

"What is it?" he said aloud, his voice sounding foolish to him.

She wanted him to understand something about his future. He could feel it. She wanted him to know. He had to attend to something.

"What?" he asked.

The presence closed in on him, vibrating his nerves. He thought he knew—what she had always wanted him to be: a seeker of truth. He must fulfill his past life.

As a small child he'd had a vision. She'd been with him, and he'd described it to her as he saw it. She wanted him to fulfill the life that had been cut off.

"I'll do it," he had told her spirit. "I'll do it."

The warmth blossomed around him, then left him alone with the cold corpse of his mother.

Blake looked back at Mona's face beside him. Eyes open. Vacant. Mindless. He had failed both women.

Mona suddenly slid over against him as the driver turned north sharply onto Lincoln Avenue from Ogden. Somewhere along the way the driver had apparently decided this was an emergency.

"Let's not get the police involved," Blake told him. The driver grunted and brought the cab back nearer the speed limit.

A half-block short of Sylvia's, Blake had the cabby turn left onto Webster and go north into the alley to enter the doctor's office from behind, out of sight. The driver was still overly anxious and scuffed the fender of his cab against a steel plate bolted onto a telephone pole to protect the pole from exactly that kind of abuse. He cursed as he finished the curve around the pole, his headlights picking up "Redbones" spray-painted in huge red letters on a garage door.

"This is it," Blake said as they rolled up to the parking lot behind Sylvia's office. On the roof of the building a few drunken couples sat on lawn chairs in the eerie green light of an outdoor chem-lamp. A man sitting on the guardrail leaned back his head to finish his beer and almost toppled backward four flights to the parking lot below. The others laughed as he yelped his surprise and recaptured his balance.

"Pull underneath, right up to the door," Blake said. The first row of parking spaces was under a recess in the building, where cars couldn't be seen from above. Blake didn't want to risk being spotted. If the authorities knew about Mona, they'd confiscate her body before Sylvia could try to save her.

The cab pulled up to the door. The driver helped Blake carry Mona in, his flabby face going red with the strain. When he left, he would accept only the regular fare.

"I don't take no profit from misfortune," the driver said. "I don't need that kind of luck."

16

Blake used his pick-key to break into Sylvia's. It took her only ten minutes to reach the office after he'd called her. She began attaching tubes and running tests the moment she arrived, her initial look of fear being quickly replaced by the calm of those who thrive on emergencies. Blake stood by, awkward in his ignorance, helping when he could.

"Once a part of the brain is removed," Sylvia told him when the initial work finally slowed down, "we can't guarantee the integrity of the mind." She circled the examination table, looking over Mona's face. Mona's body, now naked under the single sheet, lay perfectly still. With her eyes closed, she looked like a woman asleep.

Sylvia rechecked the tubes running to her arm. "I wish we could do a complete transfer," she said. "But that's too traumatic. I'm replacing her blood as quickly as I think she can stand. That will reduce the effects of whatever might still be in her system."

Blake sat on the edge of the side desk, fighting down his sense of urgency. He knew Sylvia needed time to think this through. They couldn't ask advice from a buzz-fluid expert. That would only get them co-opped for practicing a specialty without a license. If they were caught, they could both go to prison.

"I feel like I'm getting too deeply in your debt," Blake said.

"After what you did for my father, I thought I'd never get out of yours," she told him.

Blake remembered the time, ten years earlier. Dr. Samuel Logan was being sued for malpractice in the poisoning death of an extremely ill young patient. With the girl's death, her divorced mother was left all alone, and seemed to want nothing more than to destroy Sylvia's father. The case was going against him, and because of the alleged criminal liability, his insurance would not cover the damages. With some intense digging, Blake had been able to prove that the girl's father had performed what he felt was a mercy killing. The girl had had an advanced and painful cancer of the cervix. The father had never discussed the deed with his estranged wife and seemed willing to let Sam Logan take the rap.

"I don't think about debts between us anymore," Sylvia went on. "These are tough times. It's not right for friends to keep a tally." She put her hand on his shoulder and stood next to him, looking down at Mona's body.

"Tell me about transplants," Blake said.

"For Mona to recover, we may have to replace the destroyed section of her brain. It's a difficult procedure." She stood looking into empty space, then focused abruptly on Blake again. "Just a few years ago, surgeons discovered the 'personality transplant.' They replaced the pineal gland of the subject brain into a host brain, transferring the personality of the subject to the host. The idea came from an old theory. Descartes claimed the pineal gland was the point at which man's body and soul interact." She moved over to look at Mona's tubes again.

"What we might have to do is different, but this can give you some idea of the problems. You see, the pineal gland did seem to have this, I don't know, 'seed' of personality. It was sometimes thought to be a vestigial eye, the famous 'third eye' of the occultists, although no one could determine what use an eye would be in the middle of the brain." She brushed away the hair at the sides of Mona's face with her fingertips.

"In virtually all pineal transplants the personality was confused by operating within a new brain. Catatonia, schizophrenia, and convulsions were so often the result that the technique was given up." Sylvia looked him in the face again. "Replacing damaged portions is almost as difficult. When you put in a new section, it has vestigial memories from the donor. Echoes of the donor personality remain even though we do an electrical process to 'clear its circuits.' The resulting confusion can be as catastrophic as the pineal technique."

"What are her chances?" Blake asked.

"I don't know. We have to see how much damage there is," she answered. "It's not my specialty, you know. That won't help."

Blake nodded.

"And you will be assisting me."

"Me?" he exclaimed.

"George is a good nurse, but I can't ask him to do this—for his sake or mine."

"You don't trust him?"

She shrugged. "We've never done anything illegal. He might try to stop me."

Blake sat and thought for a long moment. He didn't want Mona's life depending on his hands, but there didn't seem to be an alternative.

"What's our next step?" he asked.

"Brain scan." The doctor got up and started moving the machinery into place. She had put off the scan, telling herself the blood transfer was more urgent. But she knew she just did not *want* to see what lay inside Mona's brain case. If the buzzer had caused too much damage, she would have to declare Mona brain dead. She couldn't face that prospect easily.

Sylvia pulled a white plastic rod with a shallow bowl

on its end out of the examination table. It stuck out like a little beggar's arm. They slid Mona forward on the table until her head rested in the plastic bowl suspended over empty space. Sylvia pushed the scanner into place so that Mona's head split the area between its two shiny glass eyes.

"Let's step out into the hall," she told Blake. They walked out of the room, and she flipped two switches on a control panel in the hall.

Blake watched through the window as the glass eyes twirled slowly around Mona's head. He heard the stillness of all the empty offices around them and felt the darkness of the night muffle the building. The muted clicks of the working scanner sounded melancholy through the thick glass in the door.

Mona, he thought, the sound of her name humming emptily in his chest.

He glanced at the doctor. She looked tired, watching through the glass, and old.

"Let's go," she said when the cycle clicked off.

Inside she adjusted the controls on the developing machinery, then pulled the scanning sensors up away from Mona's head. Blake helped her slide Mona's body back fully on the table.

"I wish we could get information," she said. "With anything else, I could have dozens of articles and diagrams brought up from the data bases on my terminal. But they haven't even released the chemical name for this. 'Buzz fluid.' That's all we have."

Blake didn't say anything. The only person in the room with the talent to break into forbidden medical computer files lay on the table, helpless.

A ping sounded behind them, and three prints of Mona's brain began rolling out. Sylvia picked up the first of them, and Blake sat down at the desk.

"This is odd," she said.

She pulled the second out of the rollers and looked at it more carefully, pushing Blake aside momentarily to take a large magnifying glass out of the desk. "I don't understand this," she said.

She tossed the two prints on the desk in front of Blake and turned to get the third. Blake looked over the prints. They meant nothing to him.

"I've got to have an enlarged foresection," she said.

She tapped out the coordinates on a tiny keyboard at the front of the developer, and it began working again, giving off a faint odor of ammonia, a series of clicks, and a hiss like the sound of bacon frying in the next room. The doctor removed the fourth print and looked at it carefully with the magnifying glass. Finally she set down the glass and the print and turned to Blake.

"What is your understanding of the action of buzz fluid?" she said.

"What did you find?" he asked her.

"Please, answer the question."

"The buzzer shoots fluid through the bone into the brain. The fluid acts like an acid and eats part away. It leaves enough brain working to keep the body alive until redemption."

"Yes," she said. "That's what I thought. Whatever gave us that idea?"

"Shit," Blake said. "It's common knowledge. I remember seeing articles in the paper when buzzers first came out. There was a lot of bad feeling against collectors and the whole HRL system. Doctors came out and calmed it down: collectors were a necessary evil, they said. No one forced anyone to take out an HRL. It all came out back then."

"Have you seen buzzed people?"

"I've seen some," Blake said.

"Look carefully. Examine her." The doctor pulled away the sheet to reveal Mona completely.

Mona's naked body lay long and sleek on the table. Blake felt a guilty stirring of desire. "I never saw a buzzed person undressed," he said uneasily.

Sylvia covered her again. "Then just look at the face and hands. Whatever you've seen before."

Blake looked at the bruise on her forehead. The tiny red dot in its center looked like a speck of blood in the dirt. He pulled back her lids and looked at the eyes. He looked at the color of her skin and at her hands and shook his head.

"It seems the same as any buzzing I've seen," he said. "What did you find?"

"There is no ulceration in the frontal lobe. Or anywhere else," the doctor said. "There is a tiny column of dead brain cells where the fluid entered. I don't think that's permanently significant, and I'm certain it's not what's causing her present condition. Either buzz fluid is not what we've been led to believe, or these fellows had something different in their buzzers."

"How do we treat her?" Blake asked.

"You won't have to worry about being a surgical nurse," she smiled. "At least not tonight. I'm going to take a bone culture—a scraping from where the fluid shot through. Whatever it is, there will be traces remaining in the bone."

"And you can analyze it?"

"Unfortunately, I don't have the proper equipment. It's going to be a small trace, hard to separate. I'll have to take it over to Grant Hospital."

"Isn't that risky?"

Sylvia shrugged. "I don't think it'll be too bad. They have no redemption center at Grant. If this is buzz fluid, it matches no one's preconceptions."

Blake watched as the doctor took a large spoon-tipped needle and dug out a tiny sample of skull material from beneath the red dot on Mona's forehead. The young woman stirred slightly as the doctor gouged into the bone.

"That's a good sign," she said. She looked at Blake's face and smiled. "Don't look so worried, Gregory. If she felt pain, you should be glad."

"What do you want me to do?" he asked her.

"Go home. Get some rest. But make sure you contact me in the morning. I may still need your help."

When he got home, Blake sat on the stairs outside before he went up to his apartment. A thick cloud layer crowded down over the city, reflecting back sour pink from the streetlights. The April dampness chilled Blake's skin and filled his nose with must. Even April felt like November in this town, he thought. And November felt like loneliness.

Loneliness made him think of Jake Fishman. Fishman exuded the emptiness of a solitary life, and made Blake see it closing in on himself too.

And now Blake had jeopardized the one person in the world who made him feel less alone. The vacant stare on Mona's slack face in the warehouse on Goose Island flashed back into his vision, and he shut his eyelids tight against it. Then he saw her face in the cab again, mouth drooping open, head tilted back while they drove to Sylvia Logan's. The shiny red spot of the buzzer wound caught the glint of a streetlight as they passed. And he saw her face yet again from his dream of Carlyle's dismemberment. Mona buzzed. Ready for redemption.

Blake rose from the step and brushed off the seat of his pants. He walked through the gangway to the tiny backyard behind the six-flat. He plucked a spring blossom from an overhanging branch of the neighbor's tree and looked at it. How many years had he been renting an apartment in this building? He didn't even know what kind of tree this was. He crushed the blossom between his fingers to release its fragrance, and the scent took him back to his cab-ride reverie about his mother's death and the past-life vision she had thought so important for him. As it came to him, he felt how odd it was that he'd been thinking about his mother. She'd been dead so many years. And

Quiller. The strange man who'd been his second father. For some reason he could not fathom, it seemed
important to remember. Important especially in the
midst of the danger to Mona and to himself.

He remembered being very small, sitting on a branch
in his grandmother's apple tree in her quiet yard. His
ears began ringing, and he looked up through the
branches toward the glare of the sun, shaking his head
to clear it. The scent in the air changed from the
aroma of the tree and cut grass to the smell of salt
water and fear. Where branches had stirred in the
breeze, now swung ropes. His legs were caught in the
ropes. The ship beneath him was going down into salt
water far from land. Men jumped overboard below,
and men screamed and swore. The water rose up over
the deck, and he could not free his legs. The waves
climbed the mast to meet him, then surrounded him,
and his chest cried out in panic. Underwater. Alone.

He felt none of the pain of death, watching the
vision from outside the body which he had had. He
could see his old self dragged under the water, tangled
in ropes beyond help. He saw his panicked face in
great detail, and understood the frustration of that
death.

"What do you see, Gregory?" his mother had asked
him, standing next to him on the ground. Her voice
carried the scent of ripening apples.

"I died, Mommy," he told her.

"What happened?"

"I was a sailor. And I was scared and mad. I didn't
know something."

"What didn't you know?"

"I can't remember. I wanted to know something
very big. That's why I became a sailor." A tear broke
from his eye, and his mother gathered him up from
the branch and cradled him to her breast.

"Gregory," she whispered, and kissed him behind
the ear.

"I was mad 'cause I couldn't find out. It was too late. I was alone."

"It's all right, honey," she said. She sat down in the grass and rocked him in her arms for a long time. "Someday you'll find out," she said. "You'll be a seeker of truth. A holy man, maybe, or a scientist."

She had been the seeker, Blake thought as he looked up at the overcast sky. But she had died and left him alone. Now it was as though her memory was trying to tell him something he had missed. Something he hadn't thought about in years. He turned to climb the steps of the back porch to his apartment.

He'd been too busy chasing facts to find anything she would have called the truth.

17

Blake heard bells ringing in his dreams long before he realized it was the phone next to his bed. Then he had to pull himself hard out of sleep before he could reach up and take the receiver off the hook.

"Sylvia Logan," the earpiece told him.

"Wait," he said. He struggled to sit up and swung his legs over the edge of the bed, then rubbed the puffy flesh of his face for a moment. He saw the doctor's face on his telephone monitor and swung his hand over to flip his camera off.

"You're looking good this morning," she told him.

"You saw me, huh?"

"Like a hibernating bear coming out of his cave. Didn't sleep well?"

"I had something on my mind." He looked at the phone monitor again. Sylvia had left her camera on. Even on the little screen he could see deep bags under her eyes. He guessed she'd been up most of the night running tests.

"All right. I'm awake," he said. "What did you find?"

"We have something odd here. The analysis shows Mona was shot with a fairly common anesthetic. Her vital signs are getting stronger."

"She'll be all right?" Blake asked, feeling suddenly alert.

"I'm going to do another bit of blood transfer. That

146

will speed things. She already looks much better. Want to see her? She's right here next to me."

"Sure," Blake said. His picture wobbled as Sylvia picked up her phone.

"Do you have a color monitor?" she asked.

"Of course. Only the latest in pointless equipment." Blake watched as the picture focused in on Mona's face. Although his picture phone had been expensive and not often very useful, he was grateful for it now.

Many professionals had invested in the audio/video service. Private eyes got them for long-distance assessment of evidence. Doctors got them for telephone diagnosis. As time went on, however, it became clear most people weren't buying the service. They didn't *want* to be seen while they talked on the phone. The existing units were few and far between.

Sylvia managed to stabilize the picture of Mona, and Blake took a close look. The bruise on her forehead looked worse than ever, but color had come back to her cheeks and lips. She looked much more alive. He pushed a button on the side of the phone and a color print of Mona's face slowly emerged from the bottom. He felt suddenly desperate for her to get better. He wanted to hold her in his arms.

"Her pulse and blood pressure are much improved," Sylvia said. "It's brought the life back to her face."

"She looks really good," Blake said, finding his voice a little thick.

"Before we get too overconfident, we've got to remember, even the safest anesthetic isn't the best thing to have shot into one's skull. But at least I'm certain now she'll live."

"Brain damage?" Blake asked.

"I can't know that yet. She might come out unscathed. The brain scan showed minimal immediate damage. I'm certainly grateful for Mona's sake. Can you guess why these collectors would have anesthetic in their buzzers?"

"I don't know," Blake said. "I thought buzzers were sealed at the source."

"I'm going to look into this," she told him. "I never liked doctors being involved in HRL redemptions in the first place. I want to find out what's going on."

"Be careful," Blake told her. "I don't want to have to rescue you."

"One doesn't necessarily have to be a private eye to know how to take care of oneself," she said.

"Sure," Blake said. He hung up the phone and pulled himself into the bathroom for a shower. He had enough work for a half-dozen cases, and it was time to get moving.

He let the hot water run over his head and began kneading shampoo into his scalp. Somehow he felt if he could just solve these cases, it would help Mona get better. He had a morning appointment to check further on the mercury sabotage, then he wanted to find the collector who'd buzzed Mona. He wanted that bastard to pay.

18

A fine drizzle blew into his face as Blake paid off the cab which had brought him to Chicago Chemical Supply. He couldn't help feeling there was something significant in CCS being just across Goose Island from where he'd found Mona. Driving past the site had given him chills and made him long for revenge.

Like the abandoned warehouse, CCS was on the north end of the island, where renovations had never had a chance to take root. Chicago Chemical Supply was housed in an old brick building along the river. Only the hardiest, coarsest weeds clung to the discolored earth on the bank side. Just across the water, a rusting barge was docked at a gravel yard.

After Blake announced himself to the receptionist, Lester Dorr, the warehouse manager, came out to greet him.

"I'm real glad to see you coming round here," Dorr said as they shook hands. He led Blake into the warehouse. "We had the police. They were curious about the whole thing, but they didn't seem inclined to do anything. If they got an investigation going, they're keeping it covered up real careful."

Dorr looked sideways at Blake as he walked, the front flip of his gray pompadour bouncing with each step. His voice twanged with a strong hint of the Tennessee hills.

"Doesn't surprise me," Blake said.

"Mercury is one of those liquids we keep in one tank, so they got the whole batch at a crack. We always filled our orders as they came in." Dorr turned down an aisle, stepped up onto a short ladder, and pulled the top off a tank the size of a large barrel. He climbed off to let Blake up.

Blake stepped up the ladder and looked down into the tank. "I've seen this before," he said. He leaned in and chipped a piece out with his stiletto. "You mind if I take this?"

"Help yourself," Dorr told him. "It's some kind of mercury compound now."

"Mercuric sulfide," Blake said. "That's what it was at Midland. Do you think this could be an inside job?"

Dorr scratched at the edge of his hairline and leaned against the rack behind him. "I can't think of anybody who'd want to do that. Everybody gets along pretty good around here." He thought about it a moment longer.

"No, I can't figure it," he continued. "We hadn't had anything but a small mercury order about ten weeks ago. Then we got two big orders and discovered this."

"Two?" Blake asked.

"First from your client, then from Rengore Chemical."

"Rengore," Blake said. "Are they a usual customer?"

"We get some fair business from them. They've ordered big quantities of mercury before."

"Did you find anything out of place here?"

"We didn't find anything at all. Couldn't even tell what door they came through. If the police found anything, they didn't tell me."

Blake circled the aisle. "Sounds like a clean job," he said. "I may want to come back."

"We'll be right glad to see you. Especially if you figure anything out," he smiled.

"I'll let you know what happens."

"Appreciate it," Dorr said. "I hate to think of this thing repeating itself."

After calling for a cab, Blake circled the building twice, looking for any clue as to how the saboteur had gained entry. He found no evidence, but on the river side of the building he stepped into some mud which began to dissolve the bottom surface of his shoe. As he scraped his shoe on the hardy river weeds, he thought about the mutant vegetables which would surely result if some fool tried to farm the island.

What a glorious millennium, he thought. The earth will never make it through another one like this.

19

Blake's mood did not improve when the cab which came to CCS was a little tri-wheeler. He felt tempted to send the toy away, but climbed in nonetheless.

"How did you get a taxi license for this piece of junk?" he asked the cabby.

"Is very good car," the driver told him. "Very efficient petroleum usage. Built in America for top-quality performance."

"We're going up to McCormick Boulevard in Lincolnwood."

"Lincolnwood?" the driver said. "Please to tell me, where is Lincolnwood?"

"Oh, Jesus. You don't even know where Lincolnwood is?"

"Please, not to harangue driver. I am new to this country. My brother bought me this cab. He has very good business in convenience grocery. I will determine to make good."

"Take the Kennedy north," Blake sighed.

When the puff-box cab reached its top speed of forty-eight miles per hour on the expressway, Blake wished he had sent it away and called another. As the wind picked up, blowing mist through the top crack of his window and rocking the little car, he wished it even more.

"The Changing of the Millennia Ball," the driver

said nervously, making conversation. He pointed to a billboard of the elegant dancers, like the one atop Blake's office building. "You will go?"

"No." He looked up at the billboard, and suddenly something about it disturbed him. The concept of the ball had always irritated him, but now it was the poster itself. Something about the look of the couple. What was it?

As they passed by the billboard, another gust of wind rocked the taxi heavily.

"Do these little shit-boxes blow over in the wind?" Blake asked.

"Once in a while, yes, these shit-boxes are known to blow over."

"Great."

When the taxi finally reached Midland Waste Reclamation safely, Blake promised himself never to take another tri-wheeler.

"Don't bother to wait," he told the driver.

"We haven't had any kind of repetition," John Dwight said. He sat behind his desk with a coffee in front of him, looking considerably better than the last time Blake had seen him, just two days before. To the detective, that seemed like a long time ago.

"You look like hell," Dwight told him.

"It's been a rough couple of days," Blake replied. "Rengore's name keeps coming up. However, Frambeen claims he wouldn't bother you because you're his remora."

"What's that?"

"Some bullshit about sharks. The best I got so far is a tip the mercury was an inside job."

"Here?" Dwight asked.

Blake nodded. "Anybody been acting suspicious?"

"Not that I can think of."

"Who's been interested?"

"Well . . ." Dwight shrugged. "Everybody's curious. I don't know."

"Who hasn't asked about it?"

"There's a lot of people who work here, Blake," he said.

The detective sighed. He stood up and gazed out Dwight's window over the plant. "I want another look at the tank," he said.

They went into the uniform room and put on the required gear for entering the plant. At the bottom of the office stairs, Dwight went to mount an electric shop cart. "Let's walk," Blake said, his voice squawking through the wafer on the chest of the protective suit he'd donned. "I want us to think on the way."

"All right," Dwight replied.

As they proceeded down the safety aisle, Blake asked the executive if there were any workers who had reason to be in the mercury-tank vicinity on a regular basis.

"Sure," Dwight told him. "Midge Steiner, one of the plant engineers, is responsible for the maintenance and operation of a lot of the equipment around there."

"Let's talk to her."

They walked the remaining distance to the mercury tank in silence, like two men on the surface of the moon. Blake found it nearly impossible to get past the strangeness of being inside the suit. It made it hard to compose a clear thought. When the tank came into sight, Dwight stopped at a phone and paged Midge Steiner. Blake climbed up on the platform over the tank to look around. Nothing seemed changed. He reexamined the whole area, still finding nothing new.

Dwight approached him, accompanied by a woman in a white coverall and helmet.

"Midge Steiner," the woman said, introducing herself and extending her hand toward Blake. Through the plastic fabric of the coverall gloves, the handshake felt odd to him.

"Ms. Steiner, either before or since the incident involving the mercury here, have you noticed anyone taking more interest in this tank?"

"Well, yeah," she said. "There's been a lot more traffic here since that happened. Everybody wanted a look."

"Anybody come back for second looks? Anybody look nervous?"

"Pete Gallo came around more than once," she said. "Are you some kind of a cop? This is weird, telling you stuff."

"We just want to prevent this from happening again," Blake said.

"Oh, listen. No problem. If somebody is up to something, I want them to get theirs. No fooling. I don't like sneaky people. It's hard enough to run a business, right, Mr. Dwight?"

Dwight gave a short laugh. "That's no lie."

"Anyone else?" Blake asked.

"Pete Gallo. John Connors, I think. And Carl Edelson. I've seen him here more than once. And he's a nervous guy. I think he has trouble with his wife, though. Or money troubles. I forget. But I heard something like that."

"Who's Carl Edelson?"

"He's one of our chemical engineers," Dwight answered. "He is kind of a nervous guy. But I think he was nervous before the sabotage."

"Doesn't matter," Blake said. "There had to be a planning stage. Anyone else?"

"I don't think so," Midge said. "Those are the only repeaters I can think of. I'll let Mr. Dwight know if I think of anybody else."

"Thank you," Blake told her. And thank God for the self-righteous, he said to himself.

"Let's go fishing," he told Dwight.

Back in the office, after the executive had sent for the first of the three men, Blake prepared himself with a half-shot of Dwight's bourbon in a cup of coffee. His ears felt wide open, free again from the hissing of the oxygen in the suit. He read over the men's personnel files and nodded appreciatively when he found things he thought he could use.

"No matter what crap I say," he told the businessman, "you back me up."

"These men work for me. I have to keep their trust."

"I'll just be leading them out, prompting them to tell the truth. Sometimes I might pretend we know things we don't really know. But if they haven't done anything, they won't admit anything. And remember, you haven't broken any trust. Somebody else has."

"Don't we have to respect their rights?" Dwight asked.

"That's for police," the detective said. "And they don't do it either. They just talk about it."

Carl Edelson walked into the office wearing the black coverall protectors which identified him as a chemical engineer. He carried his helmet under his arm. He looked at Blake, then at Dwight. "You wanted to see me?" he asked the boss.

"That's right," Blake answered. Dwight simply looked on. Edelson stood in the center of the room like a schoolboy in the principal's office. He tried to continue to look at Dwight.

"We want you to tell us about mercury," Blake said.

"I don't know anything about that," Edelson replied quickly.

Blake liked Edelson's reaction. The engineer looked like a character, too, his short black beard and upturned mustache trying to make up for a lack of hair on his head. He set down his helmet on a table by the window.

"You're a chemical engineer," Blake told him. "How can you say you don't know anything about mercury?"

"Oh." He looked embarrassed. "You just want general information?"

"Actually, Carl, your instincts were right," Blake admitted. "Mr. Dwight and I have just been looking over the evidence. We know what happened at Chicago Chemical Supply, too."

"I don't know anything about Chicago Chemical Supply."

"We think you do, Carl. We think you know who did the mercury job over there. And we know you can tell us about the mercury job here."

Edelson stood looking uneasily from Blake to Dwight.

"I can tell you want to talk about it, Carl," Blake said sympathetically. "It's a hard thing to keep bottled up inside. How about we start with what happened right here? Or maybe you can tell us about the Rengore connection." Blake felt like he was pushing it when he mentioned Rengore, but Edelson looked startled. That reassured the detective. His hunch was right. He's going to let go, Blake thought.

He took a sip of his bourbon-laced coffee and let Edelson float a minute. He started to think how he enjoyed interrogation. He was good at it. You played on their sympathy, gave them your trust. After a while, they'd open up and let it all out. Edelson might end up in jail, but that was his problem. He'd got himself into this mess.

The detective got up and approached him. "Why don't you sit down?" he suggested. "We know this is tough for you."

The tall man nodded and sat in the plain wooden chair they'd brought for him. Little beads of perspiration rose in a band across the suspect's bald pate. Blake was glad Edelson hadn't removed his coverall. Without the air circulation from the helmet unit, the engineer would start to bake in no time.

"I'm afraid with what we've got right now, if we took you to court, you'd get a conviction," Blake said quietly, evenly, putting himself into his role. "A long one. Is that what you want?"

"No," Edelson pleaded.

"That's what you'll get," Blake said. He could smell Edelson already, smell the hot sweat from the neck of his suit. "Before you came in, I was talking to Mr. Dwight. He wanted to know what would happen to you. I told him a lot depended on the judge, but cases like this, the prisoner usually ended up in Stateville Penitentiary. Then I asked him, should we get the police? He said wait a minute. I want to hear Carl's side first. Carl works for me. I thought: fine. That's the way it should be. Mr. Dwight's a good man."

"Yes," the engineer said. "I've always liked working for Mr. Dwight." He looked uncertainly at his boss.

"Have you ever been to Stateville?" Blake asked.

Edelson shook his head.

"I've been to Stateville," Blake said. "With the evidence against you, you'd probably get five years. Do you have any idea what that would be like?"

Edelson stared. Blake waited.

"You know what that's like?" Blake repeated.

"No. I don't know."

"They keep four men to a cell," Blake told him. "And these aren't nice middle-class guys like you or me, Carl. God knows the kind of cellmates you'd get. Christ." Blake shook his head sadly. "I've seen these guys. Psychotics who castrate children. Torturers. Murderers. Unbelievable. Big sweaty rapists. Puerto Rican mobsters. These guys carry knives made out of Coca-Cola cans in their underwear. And the sad thing is, they will not let a guy like you alone. I hate to say this, but you know it's true: a couple of these guys are likely to take turns fucking you in the ass for as long as you're inside. That's just the way it is," he said. "And if you don't smile the right way, they might kill you."

Edelson's face had gone a puffy pink and sweat lay

on him like a heavy dew. He turned away from Blake. "Who is this man, Mr. Dwight?" he asked.

Dwight looked at him for a long moment. "We know about it, Carl," he said softly. "This is the only man who can help you now."

Edelson looked at Dwight, then buried his face in his hands. "Oh, God," he moaned.

Blake stepped back and sipped from his coffee. He was amazed Dwight had come up with a line like that. He looked at him appreciatively, but the businessman turned away. Blake allowed a moment to pass for Dwight's words to sink in.

"I should have introduced myself, Carl. I'm Gregory Blake. I'm a private investigator who has worked with Mr. Dwight for some time. Now, if we're going to help you, what we need is the whole story."

Edelson sat with his face in his hands.

" 'Interference in the production of a substance important to state security.' One phone call and it's 'Good-bye, Carl.' But you've worked here a long time. Mr. Dwight wants to hear your side."

"You protect me if I talk?" Edelson asked.

"As much as we can," Blake said, knowing any promises he made were not binding. He was just private practice, after all.

"I like working here," Edelson said. "Mr. Dwight has always been fair." He looked at Dwight. "Could I get out of this suit?"

Dwight looked at Blake.

"Take it off anytime you want," Blake said, looking at his watch. He turned to Dwight "I don't have a lot of time left."

"Well, just give me some water," Edelson said hurriedly. "My throat's dry. I feel sick."

Good, Blake thought. Let him roast a little. He filled a cup from the purified-water dispenser. Edelson gulped it down. "I know how sick you must feel, what with everything that's gone on."

"I didn't have anything to do with the mercury at Chicago Chemical," he pleaded. "That was a political group. They thought mercury was being used to make a poisonous batch of QDT. They thought the police were going to use it against them, pretending their deaths to be accidental."

"And mercury *is* used in QDT?" Blake asked

"It is. That made it easy to convince them. They were shown authentic documents to prove mercury was being used. So they did the sabotage."

"Because you convinced them this batch of QDT would be poisonous," Blake said.

"It wasn't me. I never met them."

Blake looked at him silently. "What happened to the mercury?" he asked.

"They used a catalyst and added sulfur." Edelson coughed twice and wiped his bare hand over the sweat on his brow. He put the empty paper cup on the floor. "With the catalyst, it changes fast," he said. "I don't know how they got into Chicago Chemical."

"And you did the same thing here," Blake said, more a statement than a question.

Edelson hesitated. He looked up at Blake, then immediately back down. "Yes," he said quietly.

The detective tossed a plastic bag onto Dwight's desk. "This is the mercury compound from Chicago Chemical Supply," he said. "You can check it against what you've got."

Dwight picked it up. "Looks the same," he said.

"It's the same," Edelson said softly.

"So what's the point?" Blake asked him.

"What do you mean?"

"Why did you do it?"

"I didn't want to," he whined.

Blake squatted in front of him and put his hand on Edelson's knee. "We know you didn't want to, Carl," he said supportively. "You've worked here so long."

The engineer stared down at the floor. "There was

supposed to be money involved," he said. "But that wasn't it. The guy threatened me. He threatened me. And then I never got a dollar."

Blake sat back down in the leather chair. He took a sip of his coffee and managed to catch Edelson's eye. "You're doing okay so far, Carl. But you're being a little vague. What was the point? Who was the guy? What political group? I hate to rush you here, but I don't have all day."

"It was the City Action Coalition. Joseph Murray's group."

"That makes sense. They knew about you too," Blake lied.

"They talked to you?" Edelson asked, surprised.

"That's right. But I got mixed truth with lies." He drank some more coffee. "Somebody's going to jail," Blake said reasonably, "and somebody's staying out. We'd like you to be able to stay out."

"You said if I talked, you'd protect me."

"That's right. But we need the whole story. Who was the guy?"

"I don't know his name."

"Come on, Carl!"

"I don't know," he pleaded.

"What was his angle?" Blake asked.

"I don't know that either."

"How did he threaten you?"

Edelson looked at Blake, then back down again. "I don't know," he said.

"Come on, Carl," Blake shouted. "You know that's not the truth."

"He had something on me," Edelson shouted back. "What?"

Edelson looked at Dwight as if for help. "I can't tell you that."

"Does it have something to do with your boss?" Blake asked.

"No," he said. He turned again to Dwight. "I swear.

The mercury is the only thing I've done here, Mr. Dwight."

"Okay," Blake said wearily. "If it isn't anything against Mr. Dwight, we aren't going to care. We won't take you to court on it. But we still have to know what it was. That's the only way we see if you are telling the truth."

"I can't tell you," he said quietly.

Blake waited. He turned to Dwight. "Let's get the district attorney on the phone," he said. "I'm just flat out of time."

"He had pictures, all right?" Edelson screamed. "He had pictures of me being unfaithful to my wife. He was going to show her." The chemist put his face in his hands and began sobbing.

"Okay, get a hold of yourself," Blake said softly.

"I met this woman," Edelson continued. "At the Pittsburgh Conference. She's a chemical engineer for Rengore. We spent a few nights together. Then we met one time back here in Chicago. That was the whole thing. And now this . . ." He began sobbing once again.

Blake looked over at Dwight, feeling embarrassed. Dwight looked out the window at the plant below. The detective waited for Edelson to regain a little composure.

"All right," he continued. "See? We don't care about that. But now, what did this guy with the pictures look like?"

"I never saw him."

"Come on, Carl. We're going backwards here."

"I can't help it. I never saw him. I only talked to him on the phone. I had to copy invoices and papers for him. Documents to prove mercury was being used in QDT. He wanted to convince City Action Coalition that a poisonous batch was being made."

"Who do you think he was?"

"A chemist," Edelson said. "I imagine he was at the convention. But I never saw him."

Blake looked at Edelson for a long moment. "You still have your extra security men?" he asked Dwight.

"Yes."

"Put one of them guarding Carl somewhere. Twenty-four-hour lockup until we solve this."

"You can't lock me up," he said miserably, wiping tears and sweat from his face. "That's against the law."

"We could have the police lock you up, Carl. Would you prefer that?"

"You said you'd protect me if I talked," he whined.

"I want the guy who set you up to this. Otherwise, you're it. That's reality. If I don't get him, you are it." Blake finished his coffee, then stared at the engineer again. "Anything else you remember? I'd sure like to settle this right now."

"I told you. I never saw him. There's nothing else I can say."

"Let's keep Carl locked up until something breaks," Blake said. "He might remember something."

Dwight nodded.

"What am I going to tell my wife? She's so suspicious already."

"Call his wife tonight," Blake told the executive. "Tell her there's an emergency. Carl'll be on the floor all night. And keep holding him. We can't have anyone alerted."

Blake turned back to Edelson. The prisoner looked as though he might faint from the heat.

"Wish me luck, Carl," the detective said. "Otherwise, you might be in the can for one long time."

20

After the interrogation of Carl Edelson, the conversations with Pete Gallo and John Connors cleared them of involvement.

Blake left Midland and got to Sylvia's about noon. The drizzle of earlier in the day had turned to a steady rain. Blake's curly hair was damp with it. His body felt as stiff as if the rain had soaked in and rusted his joints.

"She came out of it about a half-hour ago," Sylvia told him.

"Thank God," he said. "How does she seem?"

"Groggy. Confused. It'll take time."

"Can I see her?"

"Sure." She smiled at him uneasily.

Mona lay on her back on a cot in a small room near the receptionist's office. The red dot in her forehead bruise had enlarged, making her resemble an Indian woman, only her face was very pale. She appeared to be asleep.

"She'll be going in and out all day," Sylvia said. "Go ahead and wake her."

Blake touched her cheek with the palm of his hand. "Mona?" he said. She didn't stir. He took her by the shoulders and shook her gently.

Mona's eyes slowly opened. She looked at Blake, then turned her head from side to side, looking at him with her eyes squinted. "That you, Blake?" she slurred.

"It's me. How are you?"

"Black spots," she said. "Front my eyes." She closed her eyes and opened them again. "Where happened?"

"You took Scott to an old factory on Goose Island. I found you there."

Her eyes widened and her body jerked once in fear. "Carlyle," she cried. "Said he'd buzz. Our office."

"I killed Carlyle," Blake told her. "Don't you remember?"

"He waited behind chains," she said, speaking haltingly. "They hung the ceiling." She closed her eyes and tears ran out the corners.

Blake took her hand and squeezed it. "It's all right."

"Blake," she whispered. "So happy you all right."

"I'm fine," he said.

"Glad." She turned her head as though trying to focus. "Credit card," she told him, sounding like a sleepy child. "They knew."

Blake helped her sit up. "Who?" he said.

"Traced his card. Found factory." Mona's eyes drooped closed, and she relaxed into Blake's arms.

"Did Brubaker trace a credit card?" he asked her loudly.

"Carlyle," Mona whispered. "Said he'd do . . ."

Blake shook her. "Carlyle traced a credit card to find you? Was it Scott's?" he shouted.

"Gregory," the doctor protested.

Mona's eyes struggled open. "Factory," she whispered. "Rented. Carlyle traced." Her eyes slid down again. Blake laid her back on the cot and gently brushed his hand across her face. He stepped away from the cot.

"Was that bad for her?" Blake asked contritely.

"I suppose not," Sylvia said. "It just looked so terrible." She smiled wanly. "Anyway, she sounded better."

"That was better?"

"Did what she say make any sense?" the doctor asked.

"Maybe. I'm not sure."

Blake turned back to Mona and touched her cheek, then moved to Sylvia and hugged the doctor awkwardly. He broke off and looked away. "Take care of her," he said quietly.

21

Blake went back to his office, which felt ever more lonely, the stacks of paper everywhere. He opened the drawer where he normally kept some crackers and chocolate bars. Gone. The office breakers, whoever they were, must have taken his snacks. He hadn't had the heart for lunch after seeing Mona. Now he felt hungry.

The thought of his mother popped into his head again. "Surround yourself with good people," she had told him. "They recur through the ages. You must think of more than just one lifetime."

When the hell had she said that? And why did he keep remembering these things? He hadn't been living his life in line with her ideas. He hadn't really even thought of her in years. It was almost irritating the way these things broke in on his consciousness.

But he had loved her. She was so warm to him when he was little. When she died, she left a hole in his life that had never been filled. He had learned to live with that empty spot so many years ago, he'd forgotten it was there. Mona was the one who'd reminded him of it, he realized suddenly. Yes. He'd remembered the gap simply because he'd discovered maybe she could fill it. But how did she feel about him? And how would she recover from the buzzing?

Blake rubbed his hands over his face and scratched his thick eyebrows. What a fucking world, he thought, that had led him here.

"Let's all dance for the new millennium," he said aloud. He had a strong urge to climb up on the roof of his building with spray paint and deface the changing of the Millennia Ball billboard. He remembered the odd feeling he'd had about the billboard when he'd seen it on the expressway. Maybe vandalizing it was just what he needed. He knew his landlord and former guardian, Quiller, would appreciate that kind of direct action. Quiller was a funny man. He had taught Blake a lot about self-reliance and taking charge. Too bad they saw each other so seldom anymore.

Blake remembered their last encounter. Quiller had been making a personal crusade to create a Halloween Parade.

"I took this idea right to the mayor," Quiller had told him. "I said: 'Mr. Mayor, once upon a time most of the big politicians in this town were micks. All through the Daley years and Jane Byrne, lots of micks were running this town. And so Saint Pat's Day was the big parade. They dyed the river green and all that. But the micks are nowhere today. Today the white politicians are all mixed ethnically. You got Polacks, and micks, and wops, and spics. . . .' And the mayor stops me here for a moment, Gregory. He says: 'Quiller, the Hispanics are not a white ethnic minority. The Hispanics are not white at all.'

"The black politicians don't want you to forget that. They want to keep the Hispanics in their place. So I said: 'Right, Mr. Mayor, but the point is, the micks are out and St. Pat's Day is no big deal anymore, except for the drunks, who always loved it anyway. But now that the biggest contingent of politicians are spooks, we need a Halloween Parade.' The mayor loved it. He roared. He called all his aides in to hear it. There I was, the only white face in that crowded room on the fifth floor, and he made me tell the whole story again. Not everybody was laughing as hard as the mayor. Some of those people just take themselves too seriously."

It always made Blake feel a little strange to be around Quiller, even though he enjoyed him. Quiller had loved Blake's mother. He made no secret of it. And Blake suspected his mother had loved him too. She had told him stories. How Quiller was always taking off on long trips. One time he had set off for Alaska. She didn't hear from him for over a year and a half. In the meantime she'd met Blake's father and they married. When Quiller returned, he told Blake's mother he'd built a home for them in Alaska. An actual house he owned. For the two of them. He had some savings for the first time in his life. He hadn't stopped thinking of her all the time he was gone.

But he'd never written, she'd said. Blake remembered the tone of her voice. The sadness. "He'd never written. How was I to know?"

When she told him she had married, Quiller was crushed. He disappeared for a while; then she found out he was working as a bicycle messenger in the Loop. He never said another word about the house in Alaska. A few years later, he became a lottery winner, then a major landlord.

Blake got up from his chair and stretched. His mother. What a life she'd led. She'd died too young. But he knew what she'd wanted for him. To be a "seeker of truth."

What would she think if she knew he'd become a detective?

He pulled the shade back from the window and looked down at the wet street. The rain fell steadily from a gray sky. Acid rain, Blake thought, apropos mainly of his mood. He left the shade open and sat down on his desk, looking out, trying to bring his mind back to business.

Dwight's problem was still up in the air, although with Edelson locked up, he was probably safe from further sabotage. Whoever had put Edelson up to the job did not likely have another contact at Midland. And Edelson's story that Murray's boys had done the Chicago Chemical sabotage did not seem of any immediate help.

Billy and Scott were still missing. Blake did have the credit-card lead from Mona to follow. And Mona's buzzing gave him a much stronger reason than Billy or Scott to want to get his hands on Brubaker. Of course, with Scott in Brubaker's hands, he was probably a dead issue. By now his organs were probably on their way to some commodities-exchange pit boss. They'd bring a good price. Toxic pollution kept the demand high.

And he wished he had something to follow up on the First National bombing. If he didn't come up with something to clear Murray damned quickly, it would be too bad for him.

Jesus! he thought. He'd completely forgotten the tape from Ahern. He never had entered that co-op call into the computer. If he could find out who'd set him up, it would certainly be a big step toward finding the bomber.

Blake grabbed the tape from the desk and immediately set it back down. The tape could wait. He wanted Brubaker more than anything else.

The detective called Chicago Financial Investigators and asked for Bobby. Bobby was a plump black woman with heavy red lips and the sexiest telephone voice in the greater metropolitan area. Even now it made him smile a little. He sent her a gift every Valentine's Day. She always ran his business fast.

"I want you to run a check for me." he told her. "Jeremy Scott. Run down his credit card. He rented some warehouse or factory space recently. Somebody else ran a check on him too. I need to know about that."

"Sure thing, sweetpie," Bobby lilted. Through the

line, Blake could hear her punching keys. Suddenly he thought he could smell pizza. Someone in the building must have been having an office pizza party. If only he could get a slice!

"You sound kind of down today," Bobby said as she worked. "Rough case?"

"Mona got beat up," he told her. "I'm working with assholes."

"Shit, Greg, I'm sorry. Here it is: Jeremy Scott. Credit cut six months ago. Nothing on renting space. Evicted from his apartment two months ago. This boy's on the skids."

"No space rented?"

"I'm going back three years. No space, honey. Want me to go back further?"

"No. Who else has checked him?"

"I've got one two weeks ago, authorized by Rengore Industries. Then, ranging from three to five weeks ago, I've got a half-dozen banks. Standard loan-authorization checks. All turned down. Nothing before that for six months."

"Is there an officer's name with the Rengore order?"

"Just a Michigan Avenue address. You want it?"

"I already got it. Thanks, Bobby."

"Tell Mona to take care, now," she said. "And say we're hiring over here if she wants to get out of your dangerous-ass office," she laughed.

"I'll tell her." Blake hung up.

Brubaker lied, he thought. They hadn't found Scott through a credit check. But they had tried—with Rengore's authorization. Odd.

Blake grabbed his jacket and took off out of the office.

22

The previous night, just after Mona had been buzzed, Billy had been forced to help load Scott's equipment into the van they'd rented. After they left Mona behind in the factory and secured all the equipment in the van, Brubaker's hirelings handcuffed and blindfolded Billy, then shoved him into the truck. They drove a long way and stopped, finally, in an underground garage. Brubaker led them, with Scott, to a small windowless room furnished with a cot and a chair. The cell smelled like cement dust and sweat.

"He gets the bed," Brubaker told Billy, indicating Scott with a nod. "You touch him again, you're a dead man." Then he walked out, locking the two of them in.

Scott lay down on the cot, clothes on, and stared at the ceiling. A nasty purple bruise spread on the side of his face where Billy had socked him.

Billy fooled with the door for a moment, then tested the heating vent in the upper wall. "What is this place? They do organ redemption here?" he asked.

"Get serious," Scott said. He rolled over to face the wall and wouldn't speak again.

After spending some more time trying to pry open the vent and door, Billy gave up and sat down in the chair and rested his head against the cinder-block wall behind him.

The night dragged on into forever.

Late in the morning, Brubaker and his men came in, clean-shaven, freshly clothed, and led them to an elevator that surged upward long enough so that Billy felt his joints compress. The doors slid open, revealing the executive offices of Rengore Chemical, Inc.

To Billy's surprise, the five of them walked right in past the receptionist and into the president's office. The man inside seemed pleased to see them. He rubbed the fingertips of one hand over the fingernails of the other and smiled like a lizard in the sun.

"Well done, gentlemen," he congratulated. "Welcome back, Jeremy," he said to Scott, equally ingratiatingly. He noticed Scott's bruise, but made no comment.

"The machine belongs to me," Scott said. "I developed it on my own time. I own it."

Billy stood quietly back against the wall. He had to admire Scott his guts, but for an intelligent guy, he didn't seem to know the score.

"Jeremy," Frambeen said. "Legalities. You have no advantage there."

Scott said nothing.

"You must have guessed by now that I own your HRL," Frambeen told him. The executive pulled a document out of his desk and laid it on the surface before him. "Are you aware this is just about overdue?"

Scott did not speak.

"Do you have the money?" Frambeen waited again. "If you don't have it by Monday, then I own *you*," he smiled.

"You can't run the transformer without me," Scott said.

"Nor do I intend to," Frambeen said, waving the HRL. "I'm willing to barter. The loan contract in exchange for your cooperation on the transformer. That plus a disclaimer of ownership."

"It's *my* machine."

Frambeen sighed. "An employee's work belongs to

the employer." He looked at Scott reasonably. "Besides, I'd think your organs must be worth something to you." He got out of his chair and pushed a button on the wall. A panel slid open, revealing the small wet bar. Frambeen pulled out a manila envelope and removed some photographs.

"We have your HRL," he said. "We also have these." He spread them on the table like a winning hand of cards.

Scott leaned forward to look at the first photo, then the second. He sat in the chair by the desk and did not bother to look at the third. He didn't say anything.

Billy took a few steps forward and looked at the photos. Frambeen pulled them away. "Do your men know about this already?" he asked Brubaker.

"No," Brubaker said.

"Let's keep it quiet, then." He looked at Billy's unshaven face and rumpled clothes. "You must have been entrusted with the overnight shift for our Mr. Scott."

Billy took a step back.

"This guy was just locked up with him," Brubaker said.

"What do you mean?" Frambeen lost his smile. "He doesn't work for you?"

"He's Blake's man," Brubaker said.

"Blake's man?" Frambeen stuffed the photos back in the envelope. "What in hell did you bring him in here for?"

"He's a hostage," Brubaker said uneasily. "That woman told us Blake had Carlyle. We kept this guy for trade."

"And you just thought you'd bring him up here and brief him on everything?" Frambeen's face looked cold and white. Billy would have enjoyed Brubaker's discomfort, but he felt too nervous for himself.

"I assume these two men work for you, at least," Frambeen said icily. Brubaker nodded nervously.

"Lock him up downstairs, and one of you keep guard," Frambeen told them.

They each grabbed one of Billy's arms and led him out of the room.

"Let's take care of things with Mr. Scott first," Billy heard Frambeen say in an exasperated tone as the door closed behind them. They walked out into the hall. The fat man rang for the elevator.

23

Blake took a cab from his office over to Biltey's Tavern. It got quiet again as he came down the stairs out of the rain, but not silent like the first time.

"You got food?" he asked the bartender.

"Potato chips and Beer Nuts."

"Two bags of nuts and a short draft," Blake told him. The detective sat down and faced the room. He fingered his bandaged ear where it had begun to itch. His stomach growled. As he had hoped, Ray was there.

"Hey, man, you getting to be a regular?" Ray asked, joining him.

"I need information," Blake said. "Rengore."

"I don't know nothing about no Rengore."

"I hear you and your friends did the mercury at Chicago Chemical Supply because of Rengore's QDT."

"That's bullshit, man," Ray said.

"Look. I don't give a shit about the mercury," Blake said patiently. "I don't work for Chicago Chemical and I don't work for the police. It's no skin off my ass. I know you did it, and I don't care. But if you don't give me straight information, I won't ever get Murray out of jail."

"Okay. But I don't admit nothing to nothing," Ray said, tapping his finger on the bar for emphasis. "You say what you want know. Maybe I say something. But if this cause trouble to me or my friends, you are one dead *hombre*, man. *Comprende?*"

"Who set you up to do the mercury at Chicago Chemical?"

"I don't know thees name."

"Did you meet him?"

"Sure, I meet him. He show us papers, man. Rengore buy mercury to make a poison QDT. The police want this to kill us and pretend it is the accident."

"Yeah? So he convinced you there was a conspiracy."

"Hey, this is no bullshit, man," the Hispanic said angrily. "This guy know his shit. He work for Rengore. He invent some unbelievable bullshit machine, man. It change the chemicals, *de un a otro,* like *mágico*."

"Oh, shit," Blake said. "What did this guy look like?"

"Tall. Blond. He look like a TV star."

Blake slapped the top of the bar. "God damn it, I had the son of a bitch, and I let him get away."

"He has much fear of Rengore, man. They want his machine."

"He told you a lot," Blake said. "I'm surprised. He had another contact who knew nothing about him."

"We don't do nothing for nobody before we believe, man. We make him show proof what he say."

"This is good," the detective said, leaning back to think. "This is going to help me." He leaned toward the Hispanic. "Do you know anything more about Rengore?"

Ray looked at Blake for a while, took a handful of the detective's nuts, and walked silently away. He leaned over a table where three men sat, and talked to them quietly, then came back with the young, skinny black who had showed signs of wanting to talk the first time Blake visited Biltey's.

"I was inside Rengore," the kid said, running the palm of his hand over his short kinky hair, his head cocked back.

"What happened?" Blake asked him.

"I got in at night. Slid through with my little pick-key. They caught me before I could turn around twice."

"You find anything?"

"Shit."

"What were you looking for?" Blake asked.

The young fellow looked at Ray, who nodded.

"Documentation," the kid said. "They was going to pull some murderous scam on us. I was looking for paper. Another guy was doing their plant on the southwest side, same night. Neither one of us got through."

"What happened to you?" Blake asked.

"They locked me up down the basement. A little room just off the right-hand corridor from the truck docks. I spent three days down there. Then they let me go. Just like that."

"Is the guy who did the southwest plant here?" Blake asked.

"Not now. He drop in sometime thees night," Ray said.

"Tell him I want to see him," Blake said. He stuffed the second bag of nuts in his pocket, finished his beer, and walked out of the bar into the rain.

The Blue Island bus pulled up at the corner, heading downtown, and Blake got on, knowing it would be hard to get a cab down here. He could have rented a car, but so far he'd decided against it. Something told him he was *supposed* to do without a car since his was missing, as though accommodating the lack of a vehicle would be the key to stumbling onto something. As though he were playing out some kind of karma. Perhaps the evil of Mona's buzzing might be balanced by something good.

He shook his head. What had happened to his rationality lately? His logic? He missed the damned car. God knew where Mona had left it.

Blake took a seat by a window and thought about what he'd learned in Biltey's. The kid had guts to try to break into Rengore Chemical's offices. Blake figured the kid's real problem was that he went at night. After all, when Blake had visited Frambeen, he'd entered through the basement and no one had bothered him. He hadn't seen any security people at all—only normal workers going about their business.

He wanted to find the lockup the kid had mentioned. Maybe they hadn't redeemed Scott's organs, after all. Blake'd just act like he knew what he was doing. So long as nobody recognized him, he'd probably be safe.

He wiped the steam from the window next to him and came away with his hand greasy from somebody's hair dressing. He tried to wipe it on the seat next to him.

As the bus rolled out of Pilsen, the streets turned progressively uglier. Trash littered the parkways so that no spring grasses could sprout. Hardy weeds grew up in empty lots between sodden papers, used tires, and expanses of broken glass. The bus lurched and struggled to get around a tiny three-wheeled vehicle pulling a trailer at eight miles per hour, ruining its engine. A block later, they rolled past a man who smashed an empty wine bottle on the sidewalk in front of him.

On the back of the seat in front of Blake, someone had scrawled: "Ain't no 2001. End of the Century Is the End of the World."

That would certainly simplify things, Blake thought.

All the way downtown, the bus lurched and braked and accelerated, trying to get through traffic. Phanoline-driven cars stalled terribly in wet weather. The new synthetic fuel required wide-throated carburetors to pull in lots of air, but in weather like this, the moisture made them stall. Some vehicles had trouble dodging them. Heavy gas-driven cars couldn't stop as quickly on wet pavement as light propane-driven vehicles. The bus passed three accidents before they got to the Loop. Blake even noticed what seemed to be a stalled boat on the river as they turned from Canal onto Madison and passed over the bridge.

As the bus turned onto Michigan Avenue, Blake saw a large number of people gathering in the park, despite the rain. Some carried placards and banners protesting the state of the world. Many used the end of the millennium as a theme. He could even see a few Apocalytes preaching from atop park benches, the telltale brands on their foreheads revealing their identity. Blake hoped they would march south past the Taos Pinnacle so that Quiller might see them from his high-rise office. Quiller loved protests of all types, the more crackpot, the better.

Blake got out at Randolph and Michigan and took a last long look at the beauty of the surface world. Up here on Michigan Avenue, people would swear they stood on solid ground. The wide avenue was bordered by broad sidewalks which reached to the front doors of elegant shops and office buildings. Solid. Unbroken.

Illusion.

Blake climbed down a set of stairs cut through a slit in the sidewalk to Lower Michigan Avenue. Here was the true ground level. As he descended, he was engulfed in the smell of dead fish and sewage floating in from the river, mixed with truck exhaust and stale air trapped in this underground world. Here trash blew down from above and collected against the walls to decay. This was the real ground level, in all its secret ugliness.

He walked back on Lower Michigan to the receiving dock and took a moment to settle his nerves before entering the basement of Rengore, Incorporated. Blake headed past the parked trucks, straight for the corridor on the right that the Coalition kid had mentioned. In the first leg of the corridor he spotted a fat man dozing on a chair between two doors. One of those doors had to lead to the cell.

Blake slipped back to the truck dock. He had noticed one of the trucks had its hood open when he'd passed through. Whoever had been working on it had removed the air cleaner to get at the carburetor. The wet weather had it stalled. There was a can of starting fluid on the bumper. Blake grabbed it and scanned the ingredients. Just the kind he wanted. Three different unpronounceable chemicals beginning with "ether-." He sprayed his handkerchief wet with it and gave it a short whiff. Yes. That was the stuff.

He crept back into the hallway and clapped the soaked cloth over the sleeping fat man's face. The fat man's eyes opened abruptly, startled, and he tried to scream, but Blake had his mouth covered too tight. After a number of panicked deep breaths, he went under, etherized by the starting fluid.

The detective gave the doors a quick look. The first had metal grillwork in the bottom panel for ventilation. The second door was sheet metal, cement-filled. Blake took out his pick-keys and set at it on the second door. When he pushed it open, he saw it was incredibly thick and soundproofed.

"Blake," Billy said in surprise. He helped him pull the fat man inside.

"Where's Scott?" the detective whispered.

"Upstairs somewhere. I don't know."

"Let's get out of here before someone comes by." The detective took a moment to relock the cell. "This way," he said. Blake led the big man out into the underground street. They walked around the corner to another building's loading dock, where they would not be easily seen.

"Scott's the one," Billy said.

"Scott's what one?" Blake asked.

"The man in the president's office upstairs . . ."

"Frambeen?"

"He had Scott's HRL. And photographs from the First National. Scott blew up the bank."

"Scott?"

"I couldn't figure what the photos meant at first," Billy said. "I only got a good look at one of them. But that was it: Scott placing the bomb."

"Son of a bitch," Blake said. "Next I'm going to find out Scott was the one who ransacked my office. Where are the photos?"

"The president's office, I guess. He got them out of some little nook in the wall."

"We're going back in there," Blake told him. "I need that evidence."

"What for?" Billy asked.

"It clears Murray, first of all. Besides, I hate to let guys like Frambeen call all the shots. They're too used to that."

"I don't want to go back in there."

"Billy," Blake said, putting his hand on the big man's shoulder, "if you go back in there with me, that means you've been under my employ all the hours since Mona hired you. You get paid straight through. If not, you only get paid up to your capture."

"That ain't fair, Blake."

"Take me to the Labor Board. Then we'll check to see if you've ever paid taxes on the wages I've given you."

"I should have shot you in the subway," Billy said, hitting the side of his fist against the concrete wall in frustration. "Damn it, let's go."

"I knew you'd see it my way," Blake smiled. "We'll go in like real people."

Blake had left the handkerchief near the fat man's nose, so it should keep him out for some time without killing him. But if somebody had discovered his absence, Blake and Billy had a better chance getting through unnoticed in the well-traveled foyer. They walked back to the public stairway and climbed up to the crowded street level.

They walked inside to the elevator and entered with four other people. Blake punched the button for one floor below Frambeen's office. Billy tensed each time the doors slid open. When they reached their floor, he followed Blake out. The detective stopped at the first janitor's closet he found and used a pick-key to open it. He pulled Billy in after him and locked the door.

"What the hell are we doing in here?" Billy whispered.

"You want to walk into Frambeen's office and ask for the photos right now?" Blake asked.

"I want to have lunch," Billy complained. "I haven't eaten since yesterday."

"Yeah," Blake realized. "We should have done that. We have to wait in here until the offices close."

"God," Billy moaned. "I'm hungry."

The detective pulled out the little bag of Beer Nuts. He poured half in Billy's hand.

The two stood in the closet, stomachs growling, for an hour and a half. Then they heard a key in the lock. Blake reached up and carefully turned off the light. When the door opened and the janitor reached in for the switch, Blake clapped his hand over the man's mouth. He pulled him into the closet, and Billy smacked him over the head with a heavy wooden scrub brush. The janitor collapsed to his knees. Blake closed the door.

"You shouldn't hit people on the head like that," he told Billy. "People die from that. Hemorrhages of the brain."

"What's going on in there?" They heard a voice as the door opened again.

Blake clapped his hand around the second man's mouth and pulled him inside. Billy smacked him on the head with the scrub brush.

"I told you not to do that," Blake whispered.

"I'm sorry," Billy said. "I panicked." He pulled the door closed. "If anyone else is out there, it's going to get damned crowded in here." The two men waited silently, listening for footsteps, but the hall seemed clear for the moment.

"Let's tie them up," Blake said. He began stuffing their mouths with paper towels as Billy unwound the long cord off a floor-buffing machine. Blake found a roll of duct tape on the shelf and taped their mouths secure. They wrapped towels around the men's arms and legs before the electric cord to help keep from cutting off their circulation. Then Billy found a full box of duct tape and wrapped the two men like mummies to pipes going up the wall. Even if they tried to kick or bang their heads, they couldn't make a noise.

When the two men looked secure, Billy and Blake sat back down on opposite edges of the heavy sink and waited.

24

At six P.M. Blake opened the door a crack and waited another five minutes. No one passed. Billy walked quietly to the stairwell next to the elevators while Blake locked the janitor's closet door. They went up one flight. From the small glass pane in the stairwell door, they could see Rengore's executive offices.

"Wait here until I get the doors open. Then come across and help me find that stuff," Blake said.

Billy nodded. The big man's throat felt too dry for easy speaking.

Blake tore open a slim foil packet he'd taken from his wallet and pulled out a pair of ultrathin plastic surgical gloves. He pulled on the gloves so that he'd leave no fingerprints. He put his pick-keys into his left hand and walked across to the main office door.

After trying the door, he slid the first pick-key into the lock. He adjusted it four times, but it wouldn't align. He put it into his right pocket. The second key wouldn't go in at all. That one went into his left. The next slid in easily. On his third adjustment, the tumblers clicked. He smiled and felt his jaw muscles relax from clenching his teeth. As he turned the key and the bolt slid out of its slot, he heard footsteps approaching. He pulled the key out and looked casually through the glass door into the office, hoping the person would pass by uninterested.

A man in a white jumpsuit walked up to Blake.

"Excuse me, sir," he said to the detective. "Do you have business in this building?"

"That's right," Blake said. "Are you security?" He noticed the fellow's broad chest and shoulders. Sweat broke out on Blake's palms. Somehow, he felt the guard could sense that.

"Could I see your pass?" the guard asked.

"I don't have a pass," Blake said. He smiled. The guard looked back impassively. "I was sent up to help Mr. Frambeen," the detective explained. "He'll be here in a minute. I'm supposed to wait."

Blake tried hard to keep his eyes focused on the other man's face as Billy crept up behind. The guard's head jerked forward suddenly as Billy's fist hit the back of his skull, and he fell on top of Blake. The detective lowered him to the floor.

"I'm beginning to appreciate your technique," Blake said.

Billy clutched his hand to his stomach and doubled up over it, wheezing with held-in pain. He straightened up again with tears curling out of the corners of his eyes.

"Don't tell me about his fucking skull!" Billy whispered harshly. "I think I busted my God damned hand!"

Blake pulled open the door. "Drag him around behind the file cabinets while I work on Frambeen's office."

Billy curled his good hand under the senseless guard and pulled him into the room. Blake locked the door behind them and took to probing Frambeen's keyhole. By the time he had the door open, he'd sweat his shirt damp and his neck hurt from straining not to look behind him. Billy pulled the guard into Frambeen's office through the open door. The security man's ankles, wrists, and mouth were bound with nylon-reinforced packing tape. Billy slid him across the floor behind Frambeen's desk.

"How did you get him all wrapped?" Blake asked, closing the door behind them.

"There was a desk with mailing supplies back there," Billy said. "If you took any longer, I was going to address him." He rubbed his fist. "That's the last time I punch anybody in the back of the head. I wish I'd had that scrub brush."

"Let's find those photos and the HRL paper."

"There was some kind of cubbyhole in the wall," Billy told him.

"A small bar?" Blake pushed the button which opened Frambeen's refreshment cabinet. The photos were back in their envelope leaning against the inside wall. Blake looked them over quickly. "These are pretty good," he said.

Billy tried to open the desk. "The HRL stuff was in here," he told Blake. "It's locked."

Blake came around and looked at the keyhole. "I don't have anything for that. All my pick-keys are for door locks." He tried pulling hard on the drawer. It wouldn't budge.

Billy took a metallic ruler with "Rengore Industries International" stamped on it from Frambeen's desk. He tried to flex it. "That's strong," he said. "It's so light, I thought it was plastic." He shoved the ruler through the crack above the drawer and bore down on it with his weight. Wood cracked and scraped loudly as he pushed down and pulled, springing the drawer open.

"That's some ruler," Billy said. "I wonder what it's made of?" He stuffed it in his back pocket.

"Frambeen's not going to be happy about his desk," Blake said.

Billy pulled out an envelope and removed a document: Scott's HRL. "This is it," he told Blake.

The tape-bound guard had come to, and he kicked his legs at them with a movement like a lobster on its back. Blake smiled and stepped out of the way. He pushed the button on the wall, and the panel slid closed over Frambeen's liquor cabinet. He took the documents and stuffed them inside his shirt. "Okay," he said.

The door to the office banged open, and Brubaker jumped in, holding a pistol. "Don't move," he shouted. They all froze for a moment, then Brubaker smiled. "You were right, Mr. Frambeen," he said. "They're right in here."

Frambeen walked into the room. The gun in his hand looked as incongruous as if he were holding a banana. "Mr. Blake," he said. "You look almost as unkempt as the last time I saw you." He smiled sleekly. "I met your equally stylish assistant this morning. We just came from looking in his basement suite. Mr. Brubaker's associate was hoarse from screaming. He apparently hadn't realized the cell was soundproofed."

The guard on the floor kicked his legs against the wall. Brubaker took a few steps forward and chuckled. "They got one of your security boys wrapped up here too," he said. Brubaker gestured Blake and Billy against the wall and cut away the tape with a penknife. Frambeen's smile turned sour as the guard got up and rubbed the back of his head. He put a hand on the desk to steady himself.

"Go down to the security office and wait," Frambeen said coldly. "Don't say anything to anyone." The guard nodded in embarrassment and went out.

Frambeen pushed the button for the panel to slide back on his tiny bar. He saw the envelope was missing. He pushed the button, and the panel slid shut.

"I was sorry your assistant overheard this morning," Frambeen told Blake. "I'm even sorrier now you've come into it."

"Where's Scott?" Blake said.

"Mr. Scott is working for me once again. I intend to protect his interests."

"Why did you have him blow up the First National?"

Frambeen looked at the detective quizzically. "I assume you're trying to provoke me. Mr. Scott's bombing of the First National Bank was his own strange inspiration. A poor attempt to delay payment on his Human Resource Loan. He believed no collectors would be sent for him until after the loan actually came due. His bomb was meant to damage the bank's mainframe only—a computer disaster to give him more time. Only he made his bomb a little too big. Surprising for a man of his abilities."

"Scott told you all this?" Blake asked.

"Yes," Frambeen said. "He and I have had some intensive conversation today. Mr. Brubaker was tailing him at the time of the explosion. It was his job to follow Mr. Scott to his chemical processor. He had orders not to interfere until he found the equipment depot. Unfortunately, Mr. Brubaker took orders slightly too literally. Personally, I would have preferred a little interference." Frambeen looked over at Brubaker. Brubaker refused to look back.

"Mr. Scott succeeded in destroying the First National Bank lobby," Frambeen continued, "but his HRL was already in my possession. Eventually he did lead the ever-patient and subtle Mr. Brubaker to the equipment."

"Why didn't you take him then?" Blake asked Brubaker.

"It wasn't allowed," Brubaker said irritably.

"We had to send one of our technicians to make sure he'd found the right equipment," Frambeen said, placating. "There was no rush. We knew Scott would return."

Frambeen cleared his throat and raised the gun awkwardly. "I assume that lump in your shirt represents the photographs. Take them out slowly and put them on the desk."

Blake began unbuttoning his shirt. "You're harboring a fugitive," he told Frambeen. "What's to keep us from cooperating with the police?"

Frambeen smiled. "Aside from the fact you are in my possession?" He waved the gun as though to dismiss the thought. "No need to be coarse," he said. "But you aren't in the best bargaining position, Mr. Blake. I happen also to have a certain tape."

Blake took out the envelope and began rebuttoning his shirt with Scott's HRL document still hidden inside. "The bug in our office?" he asked.

Frambeen nodded.

"Then you're the one who ransacked our files," Blake said to Brubaker.

"Carlyle planted the bug," Brubaker admitted. "Your office was upside down when he went in. Not that I care what you think."

"Has Frambeen told you what came through on the bug?" Blake asked. He felt Billy tense beside him.

"Never mind that," Frambeen said.

Brubaker looked at the president. "What?" he asked.

"Your partner," Blake butted in.

"What about Carlyle?" Brubaker said.

"We'll discuss this later," Frambeen told him.

"Why keep it from him?" Blake asked. "People in our business have a responsibility to their partners. Partners save each other's lives."

"What the fuck are you talking about?" Brubaker demanded.

"Let's not have any more mistakes," Frambeen told Brubaker acidly.

"Does he always treat you like an ignorant flunky?" Blake asked.

"Shut up," Frambeen hissed.

"I'll tell you what happened to your partner," Blake said overloud. "I'll tell you what your 'master' has been holding from you. I stuffed a gun into Carlyle's mouth and blew his brains out."

"You motherfucker," Brubaker shouted, swinging

his pistol at Blake's head. The detective bobbed at the last second and used Brubaker's momentum to spin him around, kicking him forward straight onto Frambeen. A gun discharged, and the two men collapsed, Brubaker on top. Blake jumped to grab Brubaker's gun as it rattled to the floor. Then he pulled Brubaker off his boss and swatted Frambeen's pistol away.

The president sat up, his shirt splashed with blood. Blood oozed out of Brubaker's chest. Blake grabbed the large photo envelope off the desk and used Brubaker's gun to scoot Frambeen's into the envelope, preserving the president's fingerprints.

"I killed him," Frambeen said in shock, still seated.

"Stick to hiring people for the dirty work," Blake advised. He pulled the HRL out of his shirt and stuffed it into the envelope with the photos and gun for safekeeping.

Billy pulled the phone out of the wall and smashed it with the receiver.

"Let's get out of here," Blake said.

25

Blake ran for the hall. Billy followed him to the door and threw the phone under the receptionist's desk. He pulled the Rengore ruler out of his pocket and held it crossways against Frambeen's doorjamb. He slammed the door over it with a bang almost as loud as the gunshot. The metal door and jamb bent around it. The door would not budge.

"That was a hell of a ruler," Billy said to himself. He ran to catch up with Blake. "Are we taking the elevator?" he asked.

"Two cars started coming up before I pushed the call button," Blake said. "Frambeen must have rung a security signal in there somehow." He broke the glass on the elevator-key box with Brubaker's pistol. "Open the door," he told Billy. "We'll climb up on top."

Billy inserted the key in the hole at the top of the door and slid it open. Long cables swung as they pulled the car full of guards upward. Behind, Frambeen began pounding. "I'm in here," he shouted.

On the left wall of the shaft a small red light shone from a button labeled "Emergency Stop." Blake hit it. The cables stopped rising. "I love safety devices," he told Billy. "Open the other one."

They halted the second elevator and hit the call button for the third. "If we stopped them between floors, we might be all right," Blake said.

Frambeen continued to bang on the door. The third

192

elevator stopped at the thirty-fifth floor. "Shit," Billy said. "Somebody's getting on."

"Open the door," Blake told him. "But don't stop it. Wait for me." Blake ran down the stairway and pushed the elevator call button on the floor below. He ran over to the janitor's closet, opened it, and unfastened the two men's mouths.

"Call out for help and keep calling," he said. They looked at him dumbly. "Call out or I'm going to slit your fucking throats," he shouted.

They began yelling for help, and Blake ran back up the stairwell.

"What's all that racket?" Billy asked him.

The elevator stopped just below them. "Salvation, I hope," Blake said. He waited a moment, hit the button again, but the elevator stayed still. "Shit," he said. "Whoever was in that elevator must have put a key in there to hold it." The detective climbed down into the shaft onto the roof of the car. He edged open the trapdoor in its ceiling and looked in. No one. He dropped through and turned the key on the elevator's control panel. A white-jumpsuited guard came running back from the janitor's closet.

"Hey!" the guard shouted. He pulled his gun uselessly as the elevator doors slid shut. The car rose one floor.

Billy hopped in with Frambeen still screaming in the background. Blake hit the button for the basement and turned the key to "Nonstop."

"Push that trapdoor back open," Blake told Billy. "If he opens the door to our shaft, I want to discourage him from stopping us."

"Discourage?" Billy asked. He pushed back the door in the ceiling, and Blake stationed himself below it, his arms stretched over his head, the gun clutched in both hands.

"That'd discourage the hell out of me," Billy said.

"You think he'll know about the Emergency Stop buttons?"

"If he runs upstairs and looks into the open shafts, he'll see them," Blake said. His eyes began to burn as he stared unblinkingly at the red-lit Emergency buttons stretching up away from him into seeming infinity.

"We're almost down," Billy said.

A square patch of light hit the back wall of the shaft high above. Blake thought he saw something stick into the shaft. He fired. It pulled back, but the car stopped suddenly, and he tumbled to the floor.

The doors slid open and a startled guard outside clutched at the flap over his gun. Billy knocked him down with a flying tackle, slapped him hard across the face twice, and took his gun away.

We made it! Blake thought.

Bullets from high above slapped into the top of the elevator car. Blake scrambled out, pulling the envelope of evidence with him.

"Get this guy to open the end garage door," Billy told him. "That's the rental truck we took to Scott's factory."

Billy ran to the truck in the end bay. The door was unlocked, but he couldn't find the ignition key. He climbed in back and pulled the tire iron out of the spare-wheel well. He took it forward and smacked it into the key lock on the steering column. The third crack broke the lock away. Billy pulled a knife from his pocket, stuck it in the hole, and turned where the lock had entered the switch. The engine started. He looked into the rearview, and the garage door behind him slowly opened. Blake got into the truck, pulling his captured guard in with him.

Billy banged the truck into reverse as another set of elevator doors opened. Two guards rushed out. "This is ridiculous," Blake said. He took a shot at them, and they dove for cover. One guard shot out the left back tire as Billy pulled away on the street.

"Keep going," Blake yelled. "Head for the river."

The flattened tire slapped as the van rocked forward wildly around the corner, avoiding a collision with a delivery truck, and shot down the block toward the river.

"Pull in," Blake yelled. Billy turned the truck up onto the sidewalk near a bilevel bridge. "They can't follow us up those stairs with a car," Blake said. He pulled the guard out of the truck and pushed him forward. Billy ran with them through a concrete arch to the bankside.

"This guy'll slow us down," he said.

"No, he won't," Blake told him. As they came up to the stairs, Blake set down the evidence and flipped the guard over the chain, accidentally dropping Brubaker's gun with him. The guard screamed as he dropped into the filthy river water below, his scream blending into the screech of tires behind them. Blake grabbed the evidence, and they headed up the stairs to the upper level of the bridge.

"I lost the gun," Blake called as they ran. "I dropped it in the river."

"You still have Frambeen's gun in the envelope," Billy yelled.

"That's evidence. If I use it, it's no good."

"If we're dead it's no good either," Billy gasped.

They ran out of the stairway, across Wacker Drive, and south onto Michigan as white-suited guards emerged at the top of the stairs.

"Come on," Blake cried. "I saw a demonstration in the park before. Maybe we can lose them in the crowd." The two men darted across wet Michigan Avenue, dodging through the traffic, and sprinted on past the sparse evening pedestrians strolling the sidewalk. They kept a bare half-block lead on Frambeen's white suits as they passed South Water, Lake, and Randolph streets, running until they felt pain clawing through their chests. Blake imagined blood breaking out like a sweat on the surface of his lungs. At least the rain had stopped.

They burst into the long, narrow section of treeless park north of the Art Institute. Here clumps of demonstrators wandered and talked beneath the pink-hued streetlight. As they continued to run, Blake could hear distant chanting and horns. The main action of the demonstration had apparently moved south to the central section of Grant Park. Here small crowds of people gathered around spray-paint artists decorating the sidewalks that crisscrossed the park. There was nowhere near a large enough throng in which to lose themselves here, and the Rengore guards were gaining.

Just past the center of the park, ahead as they ran, Blake saw a group of "millennial dervishes" twirling and falling on the grass. These ecstatics gathered to dance and spin their way to A.D. 2001 in short skirts or kilts with no underwear, whirling exposed until they collapsed in dizziness. A head-shaven nihilist punk had dragged one of the dizzy girls off to the evening shadows at the side of a statue and was humping her jerkily, his black leather pants pulled down just below his ass. Her screams blended with those of her still-twirling companions.

Billy pulled ahead of Blake, running with resolve toward a skinny young guy on a motor scooter. The rider had pulled his little scooter up on the sidewalk to rev his engine and cheer on the punk as he raped the girl dervish. Billy knocked the skinny voyeur from his scooter and kicked it into gear. "End century, end personal property," Billy gasped.

The kid watched from the sidewalk, amazed as Blake hopped on behind and the two men took off on his scooter.

The little scooter was not built for the weight of two, particularly when one of them was as big as Billy, and it strained to pull them along. Blake looked behind to see the guards still gaining, now less than forty feet behind. Blake began kicking his legs to push as they went. The guards were only thirty feet behind. Billy laid on the horn to scatter the pedestrians, his hand twisted hard to turn the throttle all the way up. The engine strained as it pulled them along the sidewalk, slowly accelerating as the guards drew within twenty feet. "Come on!" Blake screamed at the machine.

In front of the Art Institute, the crowd thickened, and Billy drove off the curb into the gutter, hugging the edge of wide Michigan Avenue, driving opposite the flow of traffic. Horns honked and cars veered around them as the tiny scooter sputtered and picked up a little more speed. Blake watched behind him, still kicking his legs to help boost the scooter along. The guards pulled up at the edge of the crowd, gasping for breath, the lead guard trying to use a walkie-talkie.

"They're giving up," Blake shouted gleefully. "We're going to make it!" He looked up at the crowd on the Art Institute steps and their oddness broke through his joy. Belligerent punks were pouring buckets of red paint onto the heads of the brass lions. Blake felt angry at once. Where were the police? At the top of the stairs, someone had set up a high platform. A half-dozen male flagellants stood around its base, beating their own naked backs with whips. Three white-robed "monks" sat atop the platform unmoving, above the heads of the weird rabble.

They're going to burn them, Blake thought suddenly. He just knew it. An uncomfortable shiver of dread shot through his body. Something very ugly was going to happen here. To the south of the crowd, a television-news crew was setting up its cameras.

From the northeast they heard the odd back-and-forth siren of a private emergency vehicle, sounding like a French police car. "They're coming down Columbus Drive," Blake shouted.

"Ambulance?" Billy asked.

"Rengore," Blake said. "It's got to be. No ambulance sounds like that." The siren's volume dropped as it got closer, the huge bulk of the Art Institute blocking the sound. "They'll swing around Congress Parkway. They want to cut us off from the south."

"Hang on," Billy shouted. He turned away from the curb and drove directly into the oncoming traffic.

"Oh, shit!" Blake screamed. Cars veered around them, horns blaring, as Billy weaved from one lane to the next, driving against the flow of cars, moving toward the center median of the eight-lane avenue.

Blake pulled his legs in tight, huddling behind Billy's bulk. He heard the tiny beep of the scooter's little horn as Billy weaved them dangerously around a roaring bus. On their other side, a car's rearview mirror whacked Blake's upper arm, and Billy had to put a leg down to keep the impact from toppling them under the wheels of a vintage Cadillac. He kept their balance, hopping along on one leg until the big car passed, then turned sharply behind it, letting their momentum carry them across the last lane of traffic and onto the median.

Pain ran up Blake's arm and grabbed his shoulder like the talons of a powerful robotic claw. A quick wave of dizziness swept over him, and his face turned cold and sweaty, but he held on all the harder as Billy veered dangerously across the south-bound lanes of traffic toward the intersection at Jackson. Even though they were now going in the right direction, the scooter was much too slow for traffic.

The siren screamed suddenly louder. Blake had been wrong. The Rengore car hadn't gone all the way to Congress. It was coming straight toward them on Jackson. Billy couldn't see it, Blake realized, and his own throat was paralyzed to speak. The Rengore car pulled up at the northeast corner, where the Rengore guards ran up to meet it, just eight lanes of traffic away, pointing at Billy and Blake on the scooter.

The light went from yellow to red as Billy reached the intersection. As he began to slow, Blake's paralysis broke, and he yelled in Billy's ear, "Keep going! The cabstand!"

Billy plunged on, his thumb on the ridiculous scooter horn as traffic crisscrossed around them, deep horns blaring as they crossed the west-bound lanes. Both men jumped off the scooter as they reached the middle of Jackson, leaving it behind to sprint to the end taxi at the cabstand.

A driver sat smoking a medicinal cigarette in the end cab, blowing smoke out the open window. The two men jumped in the back seat.

"Go!" Blake yelled.

"What's the deal?" the cabby asked.

Kitty-corner across the intersection, a guard knelt on the hood of the Rengore car with a tube atop his shoulder. "Oh, Jesus," Blake cried. "Hold your breath!"

"What?" the cabby said.

The grenade hit the side of the driver's door and exploded, billowing deep yellow fog through the window. The driver collapsed into helpless coughing. Billy pulled Blake out the opposite door, and they ran into the Taos Pinnacle, their lungs bursting for air.

"Quick," Blake panted to the information officer at the desk by the elevators. "A man's had a heart attack. Where's your first aid?"

The clerk took a fast look toward the commotion outside. "Of course, sir," he said. He flipped back the counter door of the information desk and led them to an office along the marble hall. Inside he unlocked a large metal cabinet.

"What's this?" a portly man at a desk asked.

"Someone had a heart attack," the clerk said.

"Shall I call an ambulance?" the portly man said.

"He doesn't need a doctor," Blake said, looking through the shelves of neatly stacked bandages and antiseptics. "He's already got a doctor." Blake grabbed a can of spray anesthetic and two round green metal bottles from the bottom shelf. A face cone stuck out from a valve at the top of each. "We just need oxygen."

He led Billy past the lobby of the bank housed on the Taos ground floor to the far west entrance on Jackson. A second grenade burst outside, clogging the air with more yellow fog as gas-masked guards cut off the exit Blake wanted.

"We can't go out. We better go up," Billy said. They ran back past the empty bank lobby, down the marble hallway lined with little shops, their feet slapping loudly on the stone floor, attracting attention from those who had not yet noticed the melee outside.

At the end of the hall by the elevators, a huge Mexican painting of weird characters with electric eyes, looking like visions from an Aztec peyote fest, took up most of the wall. That was Quiller's work, Blake knew. All of his buildings had hallucinatory Mexican art. Every hallway had an "eye of God" in some corner. The elevator doors, dating back to the building's 1929 construction, were done in bronze bas-relief of elegant mythic scenes. They contrasted radically with Quiller's psychedelic nightmare.

As they reached the elevators, Billy pushed back the closing doors of one of the cars and hit the top button.

"How's your arm?" he asked.

Blake held up the anesthetic spray. "That's what I got this for. I don't think it's broken. But that gas is going to be in the ventilation system before long. Once the fans blow it around, we won't see it coming."

"What's going on?" a woman asked. Above the heads of the riders, innocuous music wafted absurdly.

"QDT's been sprayed on the street," Blake said.

"What do we do?" a man asked.

"Get in your office, or room, lock the door, crawl under the desk, or stay in bed," Billy told him.

The two exited on the twenty-fourth floor with those

who were staying in the hotel. Quiller had done the unusual in converting the top six floors of the venerable old office building into a hotel. Since the view was one of the best in the city, it worked. His top-floor restaurant, the Taos Diner, was one of the trendiest in the city. Blake found his way to Quiller's office door and picked it open. They went in, locking the door behind.

The first twenty-three floors of the Taos Pinnacle were quite wide; sixteen large windows ran across the front. The top six floors rose like a triumphant tower out of the broad lower floors, eight windows across. From Quiller's office, Blake opened the side window, and they climbed out on a deck which formed the roof over the twenty-third floor.

"QDT is heavy," Blake said, setting the envelope of evidence against a sewer gas duct and looking down over the edge of the building to the intersection of Jackson and Michigan. The yellow fog rolled in the air currents below like a strange downtown sea, drifting out over Grant Park toward the lake. "It won't reach us up here, outside. And it should take a long time to be pumped up through the building's ventilation."

"We hope," Billy added.

Across the street on a lower roof, the gigantic Changing of the Millennia couple danced on moonlit Navy Pier. Below the handsome billboard and beneath the yellow waves of fog, madness reigned on the street. A last car rebounded wildly off a truck which blocked two lanes diagonally. The car crashed through a large store window. Billy shook his head. "I can't believe they did this."

"Men with power," Blake told him. "They don't give a fuck what they do." Even from twenty-four stories up, Frambeen's men were not hard to pick out: black gas-mask heads on white bodies. They had been joined by dozens of uniformed police in blue. Together they were the only ones able to move with any logic, and they quickly surrounded the building.

"Nice tree we picked," Blake said. "Too bad there's so many dogs barking down there." He took off his shirt to look at his arm. A large black-and-blue patch spread below the shoulder. He sprayed it with the anesthetic, then tested it to make sure the bone was sound.

"They've got to spread out," Billy said, looking down over the edge of the building. "You have any thalamin?"

"No thalamin," Blake told him. "No thalamin, no rocket packs, no cavalry thundering for the last-minute rescue."

"Yeah," Billy said. "And I haven't eaten since yesterday."

26

Blake leaned out over the Michigan Avenue side of the building. "I don't see them spreading out," he told Billy.

"Oh, Jesus, it's Greggy Blake. Now I know I'm hallucinating," came a voice from behind them.

The two men turned to see Quiller halfway out the window. He kept patting the roof with his hand.

"Is this roof here?" he asked them. "I'm not climbing out into empty space, am I?"

"Come on out," Blake told him. "You're all right."

"You even sound like Greggy Blake," Quiller said. "The child of my great unrequited love, out on the roof, when QDT is pumping through the Taos ventilation system. I wish you weren't such an archetypal character. It makes me distrust my senses." Quiller climbed out and leaned his bulk against the limestone of the wall adjacent to the window. He'd aged since Blake had seen him. Quiller's long locks had turned practically white, though his Fu Manchu mustache and goatee were still dark. The wrinkles had deepened down his face. Quiller had to be in his sixties now, Blake realized. But he was still fat, he still wore his Indian headband, and his deepest wrinkles were still the laugh lines around his eyes.

"Did you catch a whiff of the gas?" Blake asked him.

"That depends," Quiller said. "Is that a grizzly bear standing next to you?"

"The nearest thing," Blake said. "This is Billy Rourke. He helps me out sometimes."

Quiller came out away from the wall to shake hands. They all looked over the edge. Below, the scene had grown worse. From their height it looked like someone had sprayed an insect colony with a selective insecticide. Some bugs twitched fitfully on the ground while other bugs moved unaffected: white Rengore bugs and blue police bugs, each with black gas-mask heads.

All across Grant Park, former protesters writhed on the ground. In the grass beyond the band shell, a man stripped to a loincloth hung from a cross. Despite their QDT'd condition, a few flagellants continued to whip themselves at his feet.

"What was the protest about?" Blake asked. "Why were they doing all this today?"

"Weren't you raised a Christian, Blake?" Quiller asked rhetorically. "What was Margaret when you were born?" he mumbled. "Buddhist? Pagan? Freethinker? Today is Good Friday!" he cried. "The last chance to celebrate Christ's crucifixion this millennium —or at least this millennium according to the mayor. It's sort of a reverse Mardi Gras. And Passover just started, so throw that into the pot, as well."

"Crazy," Billy said.

"They were waiting for a focus," Quiller told him. "This gave it. I'm just surprised the police are taking it so seriously. See the 'monks' on the platform on the Art Institute stairs? I've seen cops stand by while those guys lit themselves up. Usually they don't give a shit."

"The cops didn't do this," Blake told him. "Rengore did. Byron Frambeen is after us."

"You?" Quiller looked at them incredulously. The wind picked up his hair and raised it like an absurd halo around his head. "You two? I thought the police had joined the Anti-Christers in a big way. You mean to say the millennium monsters are innocent bystanders?" Quiller sat his corpulent body down on the black tar roof and laughed. "Oh, now I know I must have inhaled QDT. The man who might have been my son seeks refuge from the evil corporate Byron in my Taos Pinnacle. It's too Jungian. An archetypal nightmare of the collective unconscious."

"We hoped to wait out the mess up here until they dispersed," Billy told him.

"It doesn't look like the waiting game is going to work," Blake said. Another police wagon, its siren blasting, pulled up to the intersection. More blue-suits hopped out.

"Frambeen's getting reinforcements," Billy replied. "That guy's a real wart on the ass."

"Come on inside," Quiller told them. "If you've got something against Byron Frambeen, I want to know about it."

"Wait a second," Blake said. "QDT is going to come up the air vents. Why don't we talk out here?"

"I've got separate ventilation," Quiller said. He winked conspiratorially. "Sometimes I smoke a little dope in my office. I don't want the scent to bother my patrons. So my room is sealed." He opened the window and climbed back in.

The inside of Quiller's office smelled of incense or some aromatic herb. Heavy earth-tone weavings of natural fabrics hung on the walls. And in the corner, a shiny kinetic sculpture of flexible chrome rods waved as gently as grass in the breeze, filling the air with a soft tinkling sound.

A large bowl of nuts rested on a coffee table in front of the sofa opposite Quiller's desk. Billy sat and began cracking and eating nuts hungrily.

Blake quickly briefed the old man on Frambeen's accidental killing of Brubaker, Scott's bombing of the First National, and the threat from Murray's Coalition.

"The evidence we have against Frambeen himself—he

knows we can't make any of that stick," Blake said. "But he could put us in jail for breaking and entering. The key item seems to be Scott's machine. If that wasn't valuable, Frambeen would never go to these lengths."

"Don't be too sure," Quiller said. "Byron has something of the *enojada* in him."

"What's that?" Billy asked.

"Down in New Mexico the Hispanics catch these very tasty lizards called *enojadas*. *Enojada* means 'angry.' When these lizards get pissed off, they'll bite down on the thing bothering them and never let go. When they want to catch one, they'll push a leather thong at its face till it bites and use the thong to flip it on its back. Then they put a knife to its belly and gut it. Only when they dip the *enojada* in boiling water, after it's gutted and dead, will the jaws relax and let go of the thong. Byron gets like that sometimes. There's no way in hell to beat him. But sometimes he'll beat himself. Then it's *enojada*-stew time."

"What does it taste like?" Billy asked, chewing a walnut.

"Chicken. Everything you wonder about tastes like chicken. Except pig brains. That tastes like a cross between beef and a spreadable cheese. But a little mushier. Slimy."

Billy put his handful of nuts slowly back into the bowl.

"You know Frambeen?" Blake asked.

"Oh, yeah." Quiller sat on the edge of his enormous dark wood desk and smiled. "Byron and I are like the yin and yang of Chicago's influential businessmen. I agitated to ban QDT a few years back. We've been fighting ever since. He opposes my rezoning requests. I steer city contracts to his competitors. We get a charge out of it."

Blake stepped to the window and looked down at the melee in the streets below. "You think all this might just be Frambeen in panic? Or anger?" He turned back to Quiller. "He was pretty shaken up after shooting Brubaker."

"It might be." Quiller got up and joined him at the window. "It sure doesn't look like a smart move. QDT is for war zones and slum neighborhoods. Frambeen knows that."

"If he's off balance, we've got to keep him off balance." Blake took his evidence to Quiller's copy machine and duplicated Scott's HRL and the photos. "I want you to lock up these copies and Frambeen's gun in your safe. I need these originals for evidence, but if he catches us, I don't want him to get that gun back."

"Why don't you stay in here? You're safe in here until this blows over."

"Yeah," Billy agreed. "Can we get room service in here?"

"He'll have men out here all night," Blake said. "If we wait until morning, he'll be all set with warrants and evidence, and we'll be the ones going to jail." He climbed back out the window to look over the scene again. The others followed.

"Oh, shit," Blake said. He pointed toward the river. A Rengore "bug" in a rocket pack rose from near the bankside and flew up over Michigan Avenue toward them. "We can't stay out here for long either," he said. "We need some uniforms. The gas masks will help disguise us. It's not a good chance, but it's the only chance I see."

"I see a better chance," Quiller said. "Let's get you that rocket pack." He climbed back in the window of his office and hit some controls at his desk. At the top of the pinnacle, the beacon came on. Quiller struggled back out the window again, a dart gun in his hand.

"Rocket boys can't resist that beacon," he told them, slightly out of breath. "When it's on, they've got to land on it. That beacon is the exact same blue as the light in an electric bug zapper."

"Yeah," Billy said, looking up at it. "It looks like one."

"I used to watch night concerts at the Grant Park bandshell, and the beacon would be glowing," Quiller said. "It's supposed to be a beehive—for enterprise— you know. But it looked just like a huge bug zapper. I imagined helicopters being drawn into it. And now, damned if those rocket boys can resist it."

"How do we get up there?" Blake asked. He looked back toward the river. The rocket man hovered over Michigan Avenue, approaching them slowly, as though he were searching the street on the way. Billy grabbed the evidence envelope from the ledge where Blake had set it.

"I've got the key for the roof-deck door," Quiller said. "We can get him with this tranquilizer gun." He held up his pistol and led them through a window into a hallway. An Indian "eye of God" hung inside. Quiller led them into a back stairwell of pink-veined marble, and they started climbing.

"I keep this gun around for when the restaurant features wild-mushroom dishes," Quiller told them. "Once in a while a gatherer makes a mistake and one of my diners goes off on a wild trip." He paused his speech to catch his breath, while Blake took his arm to hurry him up the stairs. "If the victim gets hysterical, I shoot him with this. Calms him right down."

"Remind me not to eat in your restaurant," Blake said.

"Anyway, if we can hit the rocket boy, you fellows have yourselves a vehicle out of here."

"As long as they don't send a helicopter after us," Billy said.

"Fly low, between the buildings," Quiller suggested, puffing for breath. "Then head out along the river. Stay low over the water. You might make it." They

turned another landing at the top of the next flight.
"I'm getting too old for this shit," Quiller said. "And
I've been too fat for years."

Blake felt a slight sting on the surface of his eyes.
The QDT had come up through the ventilation system
much quicker than he'd expected. "Oxygen," he called
out, raising to his face the mask on the round green
bottle he carried. He cleared the mask and took a
deep breath as Billy did the same. Blake offered the
bottle to Quiller, but the old man had not been able to
hold his breath. Quiller's eyes began to dilate almost
immediately.

"Too late," he said, his voice slurred. "It's Byron
mind-expander time." He sank to his knees on the
stairs and fired the single tranquilizer dart into the
floor. Its liquid dribbled out uselessly. "Shit," Quiller
mumbled into the stair. "Shot my load."

Blake took Quiller's arm to help him up, but Billy
shook his head angrily. "Come on," Blake insisted
through his mask. "Off stairs." Billy rolled his eyes
and grabbed Quiller's other arm. The two dragged his
huge bulk one laborious step at a time up to the next
landing. As they slid him on his belly through the fire
door, Blake thought he looked like an enormous sea
lion with his walrus whiskers hanging to the floor.
They set him up by the elevator doors and Billy wrapped
him with the fire hose to help protect him from himself. Blake quickly searched the old man's pockets and
took his keys.

The two men sprinted up the remaining flights of
stairs with their oxygen masks pressed to their faces.
Blake unlocked the top-deck door, and the two stepped
out onto the roof and closed the door behind them.

Far below, on the steps of the Art Institute, the
three "monks" on the platform were engulfed in blazes.
The Rengore rocket man skittered around the flames
like a moth drawn to fire. The stink of burning flesh

and kerosene drifted right to the top of the Taos Pinnacle.

"Jesus," Blake said. "Somebody did that to them. They couldn't have done it themselves. Not under QDT."

"What about us?" Billy asked. "The rocket boy found a brighter light." He looked up at the beacon. The huge blue-lit beehive rested atop four stone-carved buffalo heads. When he looked back at Blake, the detective was standing transfixed, staring down at the Changing of the Millennia Ball billboard.

"Jesus Christ," he whispered.

"What is it?" Billy asked him.

"Looking down on it now, I can see. That dancer. That was him. Going underwater. That was . . . me."

Billy looked at his face staring transfixed at the billboard, and his heart sank. "Oh, Blake. You breathed it," he moaned. A surge of anger churned up through his middle, and he grabbed the detective by the shoulders and shook him. "I can't get out of this alone!" he shouted.

Blake looked at him in shock. "No one's asking you to," he shouted back.

"Well, what's with you? You look like a gooney. Mumbling. You scared the hell out of me."

"I just recognized that dancer on the billboard," he said, feeling slightly disoriented again. The face from the vision flashed into his memory once more. The face of himself as a sailor, seen from above, being dragged to his death beneath the waves. He shook his head to clear it.

"Blake, what are we going to do? That rocket guy isn't coming up here. And we lost the dart gun anyway."

The detective pulled himself together. "I guess we have to take our chances down there. Let's check the floors for Rengore men or police. We need uniforms and gas masks."

"Okay," Billy said. "Let's do it." He took the packet

with Brubaker's photos and tucked it inside his shirt, beneath the waistband of his pants. Blake unlocked the roof door again. "Use your oxygen," he said.

As they hurried down the stairs, feeling the harsh sting of QDT on their eyes, they noticed the door to the top floor was open. An elderly woman in evening dress sat crying in the hall. Her old breasts hung tiredly from the torn front of her gown. Like a petulant child, she tore her dress further. Up the hall, two men in tuxedos lay on their faces making snuffling noises like hogs. Billy and Blake ran down the hall, looking for signs of Rengore men.

The next floor down brought variations of the same weird scene: rich people in odd states of disarray groping about like abandoned patients in a psychosis ward. One man sat on the floor with his trousers undone, holding his erect penis tightly and shaking. "I'm fucking you," he insisted. Next to him, a woman sobbed in misery, crying, "No, no, no," over and over. Neither of them looked at the other. Blake and Billy pressed the cones of their oxygen bottles tight to their faces and kept on moving.

Frambeen had sunk his teeth into this one. Even without memory of the nightmare, these victims would mean trouble for him. Now, if Blake could only use it to flip him on his back and gut him. . . .

On the third floor down, they heard the squawk of radios beneath the confused shrieks and babblings of the patrons: Rengore men with communicators running a room-to-room search. The detective pulled Billy into an open door across from the stairwell. He signaled the big man to hide in the bathroom. Blake lay facedown on the bed, a pillow wrapped around his small green bottle. He heard a passkey enter the lock and took several deep breaths of oxygen.

The door opened, and a guard rolled Blake over. As the detective jabbed him in the stomach, knocking out his wind, Billy ran in to force up the guard's gas mask from behind. Blake clamped a hand over the man's mouth, cutting off the beginning of a scream. He saw the guard take a few startled breaths through his nose. His eyes began to go almost immediately; the concentration of QDT in the room must have been heavy.

Blake held the guard as Billy grabbed his green bottle. The big man clamped it over his own face and ran the oxygen to clear the face cone of QDT, then took a new breath. The bottle ran out at a quarter of a lung full. Billy forced down the panic and signaled Blake to retrieve his bottle.

While the detective took some oxygen, Billy struggled to remove the mask apparatus from the wriggling guard's uniform. Blake tried to help him, flipping out his stiletto, but another radio squawked in the hallway, and the detective flattened himself against the wall by the door. Billy took the knife to cut away the straps on the guard's filtration box.

The second guard burst in, gun drawn, and saw Billy poised with the knife over his partner. At the moment Blake smashed his green bottle down on the back of the guard's head, the guard's gun fired. Billy's arm flipped up like a stung serpent. He took a shocked gasp of air as his arm collapsed back at his side. His jacket sleeve blotted red.

God damn it! Blake thought. He saw their chances diminish as the blood spread. He gave Billy his oxygen bottle, then stripped the unconscious guard and changed into his uniform. This is what happens when you hit someone on the back of the head, Blake thought wryly. Instant bad karma.

He fit the Rengore mask over his face and took the green bottle from Billy, running oxygen into the intake on the filtration box to clear the mask. He gave the bottle back to Billy.

"I'm going to take care of your arm in a minute," Blake said, finally able to speak. "Just as soon as I set you up for some air." His voice sounded tinny through the mask.

He stripped the struggling QDT'd guard and helped his wounded friend into the uniform. Blake's stolen jumpsuit had fit too loose. Billy's fit too tight, and they fought to get him into it. Then Blake put the gas mask over Billy's face and ran the remaining oxygen through the system. He couldn't tell how much QDT Billy had taken in, but his eyes didn't look good. Part of that, he knew, was simple pain.

"How are you?" Blake said. He took the stiletto and slit open the sleeve above the bullet wound.

"Hurts bad," Billy slurred. "Get it out of me."

"The bullet?"

"Get it out, Blake," he pleaded. "I can't stand it."

Blake found the puncture in the center of a swelling halfway up Billy's forearm. Blood oozed from the hole like lava from a fleshy volcano. He felt around the wound with his fingertips. The bullet seemed to be lodged against the bone.

"Damn it," Blake said. Billy's face shone white and sweaty under the gas mask.

"Take it out," he begged again. He seemed on the verge of delirium, whether from shock or QDT, Blake couldn't tell.

"We have to get away," Blake told him. "I'll wrap the wound up good, and Sylvia will take it out. She'll do a better job."

"Can't move like this, Blake," Billy groaned. "You got to get it out."

"All right," Blake said. "I'll take it out." He hated to spend more time in the room, but he couldn't abandon the big man, and he didn't want to waste time arguing either.

The detective got up and double-locked the door. A half-bottle of gin stood on the dresser next to an open suitcase on a stand. He regretted he couldn't drink through his mask. A good belt wouldn't have hurt Billy either.

Blake pulled a man's tie from the suitcase and used it as a tourniquet below Billy's biceps, noticing, oddly, how much the pattern of the tie looked like the "eyes of God" Quiller had hung all over the building.

Blake poured gin over his stiletto.

"I'm not sure this is good surgical technique," he said, "but hold on, buddy." He poured gin into the wound.

The big man twisted on the floor. To Billy, the alcohol felt much more painful than the original blow from the bullet. His outer vision failed him for the moment, and he saw what looked like bright spiky nerves pulsing through his brain. He gasped for breath; the friction slowing the air through the gas mask made him feel he'd suffocate. He tried to tear it from his face, but Blake held it in place and pushed Billy's hand away.

"Hold still if you want it out," Blake said. He wasn't sure he could do it after seeing Billy twist.

He clamped his left hand down on Billy's forearm, adjusting his position until he could feel the submerged bullet against the hard-stretched flesh between his thumb and forefinger. He dipped the stiletto into the gin bottle and tipped it until the liquor bathed the blade again.

"Hang on, pal," he said, then dipped the knife's tip into the puncture.

The blade cut the wound larger as Billy cried out and tried to wrench away from the pain. Blake put a knee atop the big man's arm to hold it in place and probed deeper. He felt the edge of the bullet, and dodged the tip of the stiletto underneath. He pried the bullet up against the flesh compressed beneath his hand. Billy cried out again, his voice echoing tinnily, giving Blake a chill as he remembered the gang boy who'd been shot in Fishman's alley.

He caught the tip of the knife under the slug again and pulled, holding Billy tight. He pried at it again and again, as the big man twisted in his grasp, until the bullet finally rose to the surface and out.

Blake poured more gin into the wound, causing Billy to scream one last time; then he covered it with a clean handkerchief from the suitcase and removed the tourniquet tie to wrap it in place. With two more ties, he made Billy a sling.

27

Sometime before Blake began doctoring Billy, Mona had been wandering through Sylvia Logan's empty offices. She finally had regained her senses. When Sylvia felt certain she would be okay, the doctor had abandoned her patient to go "detecting," as she put it, smiling a bit through her outrage at buzz fluid in the medical profession.

Mona, yawning but jittery, had paced into the reception area and flipped off the heater under the coffeepot. She'd had enough of that, trying to kill the dullness of her "buzzing." Any more coffee and her roots would start to go dark. That's what her mother had always told her as a teenager. Of course now, despite more than a decade of coffee drinking, Mona's hair was still quite blond.

She turned on the medical-dispatch radio to help keep her mind off the horrible memory of her attack and picked up the receptionist's brush to straighten her hair. An emergency alert came through on a QDT situation at Michigan Avenue by the Loop. Mona sat down to page through a magazine. She gingerly fingered the sore spot beneath the Band-Aid on her forehead.

When she'd finished all the photo captions in *Celebrity* magazine, the emergency alert came through again on the radio: QDT deployed in the east Loop, vicinity of the Taos Pinnacle. Dozens of injured and traumatized victims. At least one drowning in the Buckingham Fountain. Medical teams would find police and the Rengore security squad already at the site.

Rengore, Mona thought. She sat up straight in her chair. "Gregory's in trouble," a voice in her head told her. It spoke with too much authority to dismiss as an idle thought.

She rushed to Sylvia's operating room and pulled on one of the doctor's uniforms from the closet. The waistband had to be pinned and the skirt hung a little short on her long legs, but no one would notice in an emergency.

She took a black vinyl med bag from the shelf. Mentally apologizing to Sylvia, she broke the glass on the medicine cabinet, poured half a bottle of thalamin into a pocket on the bag, and swallowed one herself.

I wish I had a gun, she thought, then noticed a box of syringes on the bottom shelf. She quickly appropriated five of them, individually wrapped in plastic and labeled "Letheium," a strong sedative. She tossed them in with the contents of the black bag and ran out of the office to the hospital emergency entrance down the block and around the corner.

A mini-amb pulled up as Mona approached. She opened the driver's door. "Get him inside," she said, indicating the patient. "Leave your engine running. You're taking me to the Taos for the QDT situation."

"We've got to—" the driver started.

"This is just cleared," she told them. "Pick up some gas masks."

"Yes, Doctor."

Mona watched the driver and the other paramedic rush the stretchered patient inside. Once they were out of sight, she squeezed in behind the wheel and took off for the Loop.

"Pretty good," she congratulated herself. She flipped switches on the dash panel experimentally until she found the siren and lights, then laid on the gas toward the Taos. The mini-amb moved fast, and she laughed delightedly as the evening traffic pulled to the sides to clear her a lane. But she slowed down once she felt the thalamin begin to make her drowsy.

As she drove, her legs became painfully cramped. The ambulance driver had been short, and the seat was set for his height. Mona couldn't find the computer input to change the setting and had to drive with her knees against the bottom of the dash.

When she reached the Michigan Avenue bridge, the emergency danced on the other side, lurid as a medieval plague in neon. The wind saved everything to the north, pushing the QDT out over the lake, but from the south bank of the Chicago River on into the Loop, disaster reigned. Gas-masked police, diverting traffic away from the "control zone," waved her through.

She drove cautiously across the bridge, weaving through crazily abandoned vehicles and writhing human wreckage. Red and blue emergency lights flashed beneath pink streetlights, all bathed in a dirty yellow fog of QDT and smoke from a fire somewhere ahead. She threaded a path still being cleared by police tow trucks, and flipped off her siren and flashers when she realized they attracted stray gooneys. Mona had to peel from her fender one fog-crazed man in a three-piece suit who'd hugged onto the mini-amb as she attempted to pass. She tried not to look at the horror of his eyes.

Blake, she thought. How am I ever going to find you? Her pulse fluttered as the fog battled the thalamin in her system. She turned on the vehicle's air filtration and tried to orient herself.

The chaos stretched down as far as she could see. She maneuvered along Michigan Avenue through all the screaming humans and frustrated police, not knowing where to look. The number and variety of victims amazed her. The well-dressed theatergoers, late-evening business people, and general meanderers she expected.

But there were so many weird-looking people. Skinheads. Leather freaks. Oddballs in biblical dress. What were they doing on Michigan Avenue? It didn't make sense. Of course, women in furs worth thousands rolling in the gutter didn't make much sense either.

Mona noticed that many of the banners hanging from the streetlamp posts were splattered with paint. These were the mayor's banners with silhouettes of the slick dancers from the Changing of the Millennia Ball advertisements.

As she got closer to the Art Institute, it seemed the museum itself was on fire, with smoke and flame streaming out the front door. But as she edged her way up to it, she saw the platform blazing on the top front landing, with three lumps engulfed in flames atop it. The stench of burning flesh overpowered even the abilities of the ambulance's high-efficiency atmosphere filtration and began to nauseate her.

Then she saw the red paint that had been poured over the Institute's lions' heads and splattered on the museum's front. She saw banners protesting the state of the environment, the nuclear threat, and American militarism, and she damned the protesters for making the world worse. Why pick on the Art Institute? She wondered why Rengore would be involved in this protest scene, and why Blake would be here—if, in fact, he was.

For the first time she began to doubt the voice that had told her Blake was in trouble and that he was here. She wanted to turn back, to get out of this mess, but she remembered the night she felt driven to go to Blake's apartment, the night he'd rescued the "brainwashed" kid. She'd never been there before. Or since, for that matter. But she'd gone, and Blake *had* been in trouble. She had to keep going now.

The Taos Pinnacle seemed to be the center of the storm. Mona edged the mini-amb through the melee.

She pulled right up on the sidewalk near the hotel entrance and went inside.

Near the front desk, a man in a business suit and gas mask gave orders to men in white jumpsuits with full face shields. A dozen patrons rolled and crawled on the floor, gabbling and moaning.

Two of the men proceeded up the stairs, and the other two stationed themselves in the lobby, sidestepping the roving insane. The man in the suit approached Mona.

"What can I do for you?" he asked.

Mona felt the QDT surge with her nerves. Little white specks appeared on the surface of her vision. Had Blake told her thalamin didn't completely defeat QDT?

"I'm a doctor," she told the man. "Are you with the Taos Pinnacle?"

"Byron Frambeen," the man said, offering his hand. "Rengore Industries."

Mona felt an uncomfortable shock at his name. She noticed he seemed to be holding her hand unnecessarily long.

"You've heard of me?" he asked. The mask blotted out too much of his face for Mona to read his expression. His QDT-reddened eyes made her uncomfortable.

"Yes," she said. "You're no small fish in Chicago." She cringed at the stupidity of her phrase. He seemed not to notice.

"What can I do for you?" he repeated.

"I'm on an emergency retainer by the Association of Loop Hotels," she lied, wondering if there were such an organization. "They called me in."

"I see."

Did he sway or was it her imagination?

"You don't wear a mask?" he said.

"I had one pulled off by a victim on a QDT site once," she told him. "Suddenly it was four hours later, and I was strapped to a couch."

Frambeen laughed oddly. "I'm using both," he said "The mask and the antidote. I must say, none of it is very entertaining."

"You should know," Mona told him.

A crash and a scream echoed from an office beyond the desk, then ripples of absurd laughter. Mona rushed back, followed by Frambeen. A portly gentleman lay shivering on the floor next to a metal cabinet, a gash in his head streaking his face with blood. A younger man sat giggling on the floor in the corner. His eyes looked frighteningly hysterical.

Mona rolled the heavy fellow onto his back. His arms twitched. He covered his face, then his crotch, then his face again.

I'm a doctor, Mona told herself. I've got to look like a doctor.

"Hold his arms," she said to Frambeen. She dug into the med bag as the executive knelt delicately by the victim. What the hell would she do? Frambeen hesitated. "Just grab him," she said. Atop the other paraphernalia lay the hypos.

"We've got to remove his jacket," she said. She straddled the man, wrapped her hands behind his neck, and pulled him to a sitting position. Frambeen stripped the jacket from the man's shoulders. The worry in Frambeen's eyes gave Mona strength.

"Roll up his sleeve," she told him. She cracked out an alcohol swab and moistened the bare arm. High up near his shoulder she tied a rubber tube tightly. A small green vein stood out inside his elbow. She tore the plastic off one of the hypos and pulled the cap off the needle.

What the hell am I doing? she thought as she pushed the plunger and spurted liquid into the air.

"Hold him," she told Frambeen. She took little pleasure in the sickness of Frambeen's expression as she inserted the needle and pushed half the liquid into the man's blood. She recapped the hypo and searched through the med bag for an antiseptic and a gauze. The man's twitching stopped abruptly.

God! Have I killed him? she wondered.

"What was that?" Frambeen asked.

"A sedative. Keep him from further injury."

"Sounds like a good idea." He laughed oddly again.

Mona pulled out a stethoscope and listened to the man's heart. His pulse sounded skittish, but strong enough. Then again, what did she know about it? She washed and bandaged the gash in his head, deciding what to do next.

"Is there an intercom?" Mona asked. "I should have associates already in the building."

"I haven't seen any medical people," Frambeen told her. "But there is a system at the information desk."

She followed him out, and he showed her the equipment. Frambeen watched her with an odd expression as she reached for the microphone. Had he seen through her cover?

"Is something wrong?" she asked him.

"You're the most attractive doctor I've ever met," he said. "Even with that little bandaged bruise on your forehead."

"With that mask on, you look like a praying mantis," Mona replied. "Let's stick to business." He shrugged and went to talk to the guards in the lobby.

Mona flipped the switches on the intercom to the position for an all-floors announcement. She raised the microphone to her lips and hoped the message she was giving would raise Blake. At the same time, she couldn't give herself or him away. She completed the announcement and set the microphone back on its stand. If he was at the building, she thought, her message ought to bring him in.

Mona practiced pseudomedicine for twenty long minutes, hoping Blake would appear, but her sense of urgency finally allowed her to delay no longer. She decided to try the streets. With vague misgivings, she walked out of the Taos Pinnacle lobby, pulled two gooneys off the hood of the mini-amb, and climbed in. The stink of QDT mixed with burnt kerosene, wood, and human flesh made her gag, and a chill shot through her. She flipped on the air conditioner to filter the stench, and tried to think. Again she began to doubt the voice that had told her Blake was in trouble.

She looked out the window. All across Grant Park, all up and down Michigan Avenue, the strangest assortment of people crawled and fell, drooling and babbling like idiots. Police walked among them, flipping them over and comparing their faces with photographs. Twenty feet ahead of the mini-amb, a young businessman in a three-piece suit sat on the sidewalk crying like a baby.

Even if Blake is here, how would I ever find him in this mess? she wondered.

28

Over twenty minutes earlier, many floors above in the Taos Pinnacle, Blake had panicked, thinking he heard the squawk of another Rengore radio. Then he realized it was the hotel intercom coming on in the hall.

"I was never meant to live like this," he said aloud, though he knew Billy had passed out from his amateur surgery. Blake went into the bathroom for cold water to revive his patient.

"Code 29," a female voice said. "All 29-assigned personnel report to the main floor for evacuation instructions."

Code 29. That was a computer code Mona had made for him. The announcement repeated. That's her voice! he thought. It must be her. Maybe they had a chance after all.

Blake splashed cold water onto Billy's wrists and chest, wishing he could remove the big man's helmet to splash his face. Billy's eyes seemed glassy, and his face looked a wet, pale green, but he was coming around. Blake stuffed the evidence into his own jumpsuit and helped the invalid to his feet, steering him around the guards in their underwear on the floor.

"How are you feeling?" Blake asked him. Billy didn't speak. "We got places to go, buddy," the detective said as he led him into the hallway. One well-dressed gooney sat on the floor, hitting himself in the face with an ashtray. From every direction, Blake could hear people wailing and screaming.

The detective punched the button for the elevator and waited. On the wall next to the elevators hung another huge Mexican painting of wild-eyed peyote gods with their arms and legs at abrupt angles. Quiller had lived only two years in Taos, New Mexico, spending his time chewing peyote buttons, throwing up, and having visions, but those two years had set the tone—decoratively, at least—for the rest of his life. Blake looked back down the hall. Blood ran down the face of the gooney with the ashtray, making a livid mask. Quiller's peyote art fit right in.

After a few minutes Blake realized all the cars were frozen at the bottom. Frambeen wasn't going to let them slip out that way. Blake took Billy to the stairwell, snatching the gooney's bloody ashtray on the way. As they started carefully down the stairs, Billy walked with the docile clumsiness of a trained bear.

Blake wondered how Mona had found out they were in the Taos Pinnacle. Or did she, in fact, really *know*? How long would she wait? Sweat broke out on Blake's palms and his stomach tightened. The look of Billy's eyes told him he was lucky the big man could walk at all.

A door swung open one flight below and two sets of footsteps began climbing up, accompanied by the squawk of a radio. Blake clicked off the safety on the pistol in his jumpsuit holster and delicately unbuttoned the hold-down strap.

"Play it cool," he whispered to Billy.

Two policemen rounded the stairs below them. Blake kept his hand on Billy's elbow and his face averted.

"What's wrong with him?" one of them asked.

"Let's eat corned beef," Billy slurred.

"His mask leaked," Blake told them. "He fell and hurt his arm."

The first officer stopped Billy and looked into his face through the mask. He frowned.

Blake felt the hairs all over his body stand up and push against his clothes. He rested his hand on the butt of his pistol and tried to keep his right leg from shaking. The two officers stood too far apart for his comfort. If he had to shoot one, the other might get him.

"He don't look too bad," the first said. "He can't of got much." The officer stepped aside to let them pass. "He's still on his feet."

It took Blake a moment to realize he could move again.

"I keep telling them," the second said as they continued up. "You got to seal the masks with Vaseline."

"Forget it," the first replied. "Feels like it's slipping off all the time with that stuff."

"You just don't adjust it right." A door opened and their sound faded into another floor.

"I don't know about you," Blake told Billy, "but I was ready to shit in my pants."

As they climbed down, he wondered how Quiller was doing. He'd once told Blake he'd experienced QDT. He rushed over to his hypnotherapist the next day. The hypnotist helped him achieve total recall. Quiller said it was an amazing trip. He wouldn't have missed it for the world.

As Blake helped Billy step around another gooney crawling on the floor, they passed under the last of Quiller's "eyes of God." Blake tried to rush Billy onward, but trying to hurry the drug-shocked Billy was like trying to run in a horrible frozen dream.

Much later, when they finally came out of the stairwell onto the first floor near the elevators, Frambeen stood there facing them, as though he'd been waiting the whole time. The executive wore a small gas mask that covered only his mouth and nose. His eyes looked red and watery from QDT irritation. Thirty feet away in the lobby stood two more police. The end of the road.

"What's wrong with him?" Frambeen asked Blake, pointing to Billy. He sounded slightly drunk.

"His mask leaked, sir," Blake said, unable to hope the ruse would work. "He fell and injured his arm."

Frambeen squinted hard at them, shifting his gaze from one to the other. He wiped a tear from the corner of his eye.

"Take him in there," he said, gesturing toward a conference room. Frambeen dipped his handkerchief in the drinking fountain and washed his eyes as he followed them in, not noticing how Blake tried to hurry the somnambulant Billy. As soon as he'd wiped the sting from his eyes, he saw the ill fit of their jumpsuits, the dark curliness of Blake's hair, their relative sizes. He reached forward and snatched the pistol from Blake's unsnapped holster as they crossed the threshold into the room.

"Move away," he said, pushing the gun into the detective's back. He unsnapped Billy's holster and removed the pistol, tossing it on a sofa behind him. "You've been damned inconvenient," Frambeen said. "Take off his mask."

Blake stood, just looking at the other man.

"Take off his mask," Frambeen repeated. "Remember, I have little use for you alive."

Blake still didn't move, trying to figure his odds. Frambeen seemed slowed, possibly by thalamin—though he'd been quick enough getting Blake's gun.

"You can take off his mask, right now," Frambeen said, "or I can shoot him. Your choice." The executive cocked the pistol.

Blake didn't think much of Frambeen's abilities with a gun, but at point-blank range he didn't need much ability. The detective moved over and unfastened the straps behind Billy's head. He held them in place with his hand. Frambeen stood cautiously back. "Go ahead," he ordered.

Blake pulled away the mask as Billy dumbly held still. The big man took four slow breaths, collapsed to his knees, then crumpled to the floor, moaning softly.

"Now yours," Frambeen said.

29

How am I ever going to find Blake? Mona wondered. Gooneys crawled through the parks. The police struggled to keep the pavement clear. Even cruising the streets would be a heavy chore.

She looked across Michigan Avenue into the melee in Grant Park. Out of the squirming masses of QDT'd demonstrators, one large man stood up, then fell back onto the ground.

Billy, Mona thought. That looks like Billy. How did he escape Brubaker?

She got out of the ambulance, locking the door behind her, and the stink of burnt protesters and QDT hit her again. Mona crossed the street carefully, wiping tears from the corners of her irritated eyes. About twenty yards ahead in the park, the big man was crawling away from her on his belly. Was it him? It was hard to tell in the late-evening darkness. Directly in her path a man stabbed the ground repeatedly with a stick, screaming and grunting in rage. Mona walked around him in a wide circle.

Now that she was in the park, Mona was for the first time surrounded by gooneys in great numbers, crying and shrieking and falling down. It looked like a scene from a horror movie: having climbed from their graves, the dead stumble blindly among the living. Mona felt a chill go through her. She hopped over a woman who seemed to be vibrating and hurried on toward the big man.

When she reached him, the man had stopped moving and lay still, facedown on the wet ground. Mona crouched down for leverage and flipped him over. A long stringer of snot hung from his nose, which Mona, with a wrench of disgust, first thought was a worm crawling from his nostril. She stepped away.

It wasn't Billy.

She shook off the thought of the worm and wondered again if the QDT were beginning to get to her.

She screamed as she felt a hand grab her arm from behind.

"Sorry," the young police officer told her, his voice hollow through the gas mask. "I didn't mean to frighten you."

Mona regained her composure. "That's all right. I wasn't expecting you."

"Are you a doctor?"

"Yes," she said hesitantly.

"We have an emergency center set up in the lobby of the Goodman Theatre, behind the Art Institute. There's a lot of injured people back there. We sure could use your help."

"I can't," she told him. "I'm sorry. I can't."

A woman came tottering toward them, her arms outstretched. The young cop calmly grabbed the woman's arms and laid her on her back on the ground.

"Why not?" he asked.

Mona looked at him blankly. Why not?

"I was brought in here by the hotels," she blurted. "I have to work for the hotels. That's my mini-amb across the street," she said, pointing.

The cop looked at it slowly. He looked back at her. "Then what are you doing over here in the park?" he asked.

Mona felt her face go hot, and she knew she must be blushing. "I'm looking for someone," she said, scrambling for thoughts. "My paramedic. He was wearing a mask instead of taking thalamin. It must have got pulled off."

"You thought this was him?" the cop asked, tapping the big gooney with his toe.

"That's right."

"Wasn't your paramedic in uniform?"

"No. He was called in on emergency. There was no time." It was hard to tell through his gas mask, but Mona thought the young cop looked suspicious. "I'll be glad to radio in for help for your station, officer," she promised. "I've got to radio in about my paramedic now anyway."

"Thanks," he said unappreciatively as he watched her walk away.

Mona got back in the mini-amb and breathed a heavy sigh of relief. It felt good to have the security of the vehicle surrounding her again. But that didn't solve her problem. What to do?

Mona looked over the switches on the instrument panel and under the dash. She got out and checked the assembly on the roof. No megaphone. A megaphone would extend her range—assuming Blake were in earshot and in any condition to understand her call.

She grabbed the med bag and went back into the hotel. At the far end of the lobby near the elevators she saw Frambeen disappear into a room with two men. If anyone could get a megaphone, Frambeen could. Too bad she hadn't used more charm when he confessed his attraction, but she had never cared for sleek men like him.

She reached the door of the conference room and stopped dead. Billy lay on the floor, unmasked and incoherent. Frambeen held a gun on Blake, who was removing his mask. Couldn't Blake see her? If he took off that mask, she'd never get them out.

She reached into the med bag.

"Mr. Frambeen?" she said. The executive scratched

at his eye with his gun hand. He immediately directed it back at the detective.

"Take it off," he told Blake. "Page my men from the intercom, please, Doctor," he said, keeping his eyes on the detective. "I need them here."

"Is this man injured?" she asked, walking toward Billy. Immediately at Frambeen's side she spun and grabbed the pistol. He pulled the trigger, and the hammer slammed down on the web of skin between her thumb and first knuckle. It stung like hell, but the gun didn't fire. She stabbed the hypo into the exposed back of Frambeen's neck overhand, like a dagger, and pressed down the plunger with her thumb.

Frambeen shrieked, but his gas mask muffled the sound. He dove forward, trying to escape, but Mona clung to him like an avenging harpy, landing atop his back on the floor, pushing Letheium into his flesh. Blake pulled the pistol from their hands. Frambeen spun Mona off him, the needle hanging from his neck like a dart. He stumbled sideways, fell, and Blake pulled away his mask.

Mona ran out into the hall and closed the door behind her. The two police officers from the lobby approached to check on the disturbance.

"Go and get my stretcher," she told them. "One of Mr. Frambeen's men has been injured." She led them across the lobby, pointed out the mini-amb, and gave them her keys. "It's in the back," she told them. She hurried back to the conference room. Blake knelt over Billy. Frambeen was nowhere in sight.

"What happened?" Mona asked.

"Billy took a bullet in the arm," Blake said. "I took care of Frambeen. He's under the couch." He tightened the compress where Billy's fall had renewed the bleeding. The police officers hurried into the room.

"Mr. Frambeen asked that one of you follow him to the fifth floor," Mona said. "A QDT victim got his hands on a gun."

"I'll go," the younger one said. He ran off toward the stairs. Blake helped the other snap open the stretcher. The three rolled Billy on and strapped him to it.

"The gooney shot him?" the officer asked.

"Yeah," Blake said, grabbing the back of the stretcher. Mona took back her keys and led the way out of the lobby to the ambulance.

"I've got to go with him," Blake told the officer, climbing into the back of the wagon.

"I guess I'd better get back inside," he replied, speaking loudly to be heard over the insane racket of the street as sirens blared from fire trucks trying to reach a blaze on the other side of the park. Then something about Blake caught him, and he looked carefully through his gas mask. He looked down at Billy, faceup and unmasked on the stretcher. "Wait a minute," he said, backing off and reaching for his communicator.

"Here, don't be a jackass," Blake called, lunging to grab the air hose on his uniform. He wrenched hard, tearing the face shield from his head and pulling him into the ambulance.

"Help!" he screamed. Blake stuffed gauze into his mouth. His cry was echoed uselessly by a man in a business suit, lying in the gutter and flailing his arms as though he were drowning. Forty feet away on the corner, two other police officers didn't even turn to look.

The cop's eyes lost focus, and his struggles grew random as he breathed. Mona started the engine, and Blake rolled him out on the curb. He closed the back hatch, and she pulled out into the street.

"I was glad to see you," Blake said, catching his breath. He tossed the fingerprint-covered hypo he'd taken from Frambeen's neck out the window and pulled the envelope of evidence from within his jumpsuit. "How did you know we were here?"

"I found out Rengore was here, and that caught my attention," Mona told him, pulling a U-turn. "Then I heard a voice, inside my head. It was strange. I felt I *had* to come here. That you were in danger."

"Well," Blake mused, "I don't know what it was, but I'm glad you took the call."

Mona smiled and shrugged. She dodged a woman crawling in the street. "Will Billy be all right?" she asked.

"I hope so. Sylvia ought to be able to take care of him."

She drove the insane blocks up to the bridge over the river where two police officers blocked their path, waving them down. Mona turned on the siren and hit the gas, and they jumped out of the way. The mini-amb drove out of the madness as the 2000 Fest couples on the streetlight banners danced blithely on into the night.

30

"Let me ask you something, Gregory," Sylvia said, ministering to Billy's wounded arm. "Where did you learn your medicine? Old John Wayne movies? Honestly. Pouring gin into a bullet wound."

"Not a good idea?" Blake leaned forward in his chair and felt the bullet press snugly against his thigh from inside his pocket. When the guard who'd fired it came back from gooney-land, he'd remember nothing of the incident. A shame Frambeen had taken thalamin. Memory lapse on his part would be a true blessing.

Blake leaned back and breathed deep. He felt light-headed with hunger and fatigue. The aroma of medical alcohol tingled in his nostrils.

"Well, gin's not the best," Sylvia said. She looked him in the face and gave a short laugh of pity. "Oh, hell. You did fine." She finished off with Billy.

"Let me see your hand," she told Mona. Frambeen's pistol hammer had bruised and torn the flesh, leaving a large black blood blister on the palm side. "Very pretty," she said.

"What did you find out?" Blake asked her.

"I went to med school with a fellow who's up to his hips in buzz business," she said as she dressed the wound. "I told him what happened in Mona's case. He started confessing like a Catholic with the last priest on earth. He's lived for years in unrelieved guilt."

"What did he say?" Blake asked. He rubbed his eyes with the butts of his palms.

"He has nightmares from the redemption process. He's recycled too many organs from people who still needed them. First they pump a detoxification fluid into the buzzed person's veins. That causes the organs to excrete poisons into the blood. And it jars the person awake into horrible, shrieking pain. Not until the end of the long, hideous process is the brain dead, burnt out."

"My God," Mona said. "I thought buzzers destroyed the ability to feel anything."

Sylvia wrapped the last piece of tape onto Mona's hand. "The original buzz fluid did," she said. "It was a corrosive. Fast as a bullet through the brain. But it often damaged other organs as the fluid circulated in the blood. Now collectors are just rough anesthetists. The doctors torture and kill. It makes me sick."

"And secrecy covers the physicians' guilt," Blake said.

Sylvia unlocked a cabinet by the instrument table and pulled out an envelope. "This is dangerous," she told them. "Documents on the process. Damning evidence. By moving to anesthetic buzzings, they doubled the successful transplant value of redeemed organs—and doubled their profits. Not even the collectors know about the change. It's a shame what it does to our humanity."

"It was murder before. It's still murder now," Blake said.

"It's *torture* and murder now," Sylvia told him. "Administered by physicians. There's a difference."

"What are we going to do?" Mona asked. Blake opened the envelope and looked at the documents.

The doctor walked up to the window and stared into the night. "I'll have to speak out," she said. "I can't let this continue."

"They'll slap you down," Blake told her, still looking at the papers. "You'd be a useless sacrifice."

"It's a small number of doctors involved. I'll get my acquaintance to come forward. He'll tell the truth." She looked at Mona. "You should have seen how eager he was to confess."

"Did he tell you not to mention his name?" Blake asked. Sylvia looked at him. "You haven't mentioned his name," he said. "He made you promise, didn't he?"

"He just needs a push," she said.

"That small number has heavy legal clout," Blake told her. "Organ redemption is a prosperous business. They'd stop you. Probably they'd kill you. Let's see if I can find someone who can use this."

31

Blake and Mona left Billy to ride out the QDT in Sylvia Logan's office. They retrieved Blake's car, still parked outside the agency where Mona had rented Scott's van. Then they went to an all-night carry-out chicken joint, Blake explaining that chickens were not such repositories of poison as pigs.

Blake pulled into the drive-in lane and stopped next to a large icon chicken on its nest. An electronic pad on a flex-neck glided from a slot in the nest to their window. Blake pulled it into the car, and they punched in their menu selections. He tried to put his twenty-dollar bill into the chicken's mouth but had to get out of the car to reach. Then the chicken cackled electronically as Blake's change tumbled into a cup on its breast and a box of food slid into the bottom slot on the nest.

As ridiculous as the transaction seemed, somehow it depressed him as he drove on toward refuge at the Heart O' Chicago Motel.

"What do you think Frambeen will do?" Mona asked.

"Maybe he'll send his goons to kill us," Blake said. "I don't know."

"Wouldn't that clash with his sense of personal elegance?"

"It's Frambeen's personal elegance we've wounded the most. But maybe he'll just have us arrested."

"On what charge?"

"Who knows? I wanted to keep the pressure on him, to keep him feeling threatened, so he'd make some fatal mistake. Maybe he's made it. Now all we can do is get our evidence to the right people in the morning and hope."

"You don't want to take it to the police tonight?"

"No. He's too well-connected tonight. The cops are working with him. The bank bombing is Ahern's case. We'll go to him." He pulled up at a stoplight and leaned his head back against the headrest. He closed his eyes, feeling physically and spiritually exhausted. Mona touched his arm reassuringly.

"Let's be human," she said. "Let's go over to my place. I don't want to hide in that faceless motel room tonight."

Blake looked at the surety in her face and felt his courage return. He felt the tight boundaries around himself expand to include her. It made him feel larger, and warm, and he wanted to hold her in his arms.

"Good," he said. "I feel exactly the same way."

She gave him directions, and as he drove he felt the restrictions of his personal rules drop away as though they were falling out the bottom of the car and being left on the pavement. If romance were to come to him and Mona, so be it. He looked at the side of her face, looking straight forward, a small enigmatic smile curling at the edges of her lips. He realized that before it came to love, there was something else he had to settle.

"I think we may need a new secretary," he told her.

"Is that so?" She smiled over at him, curious.

"You're so good at saving my ass, I thought I'd better make you my partner."

"Wise move, partner." She looked forward again, still smiling, then laughed aloud with delight. She squeezed his forearm. "Of course, if you hadn't tracked me down at Scott's place, God knows where I'd be today."

He winked at her. "Well, I'd hate to see you partner with anyone who wasn't the best."

Mona laughed delightedly again. She showed him a place to park, and they carried the food up to her apartment. They entered through the back door, sat down at the kitchen table, and immediately set to eating, the smell of fried poultry and grease thickening the air.

When he was finished, Blake got up from the old wooden table and stretched. "Do you mind if I look around?" he asked.

"It's a mess."

"So is mine."

Walking into the living room, he was surprised to see no couch, no chairs, and no coffee table, just a wide expanse of Oriental rug and thick pillows lying along the walls. Newspapers, magazines, paperbacks, and coffee cups littered the floor. A small television set sat abandoned in one corner. A tangle of blankets and sheets piled up in another. On the walls hung photographic prints of waterfalls, mountains, and dancers. The rug was so thickly padded, he could see the indent his shoes made where he stood. He slipped them off out of respect and put them over near the wall.

"Furniture doesn't interest me much," Mona said, walking in behind him. "I like being down at floor level." She kicked two big pillows out into the center with her bare feet and sat down on the floor. She scratched lightly at the bandage over the bruise on her forehead. Blake knelt in front of her.

"How does that feel?"

"Itchy," she said. "Especially where Sylvia dug away at the bone."

"I'm sorry," he said. "But how do *you* feel? You were still incoherent this morning."

"I was just groggy," she said. "The anesthetic hadn't worn off. The worst is the memory of that buzzer coming at me." She shuddered, then stiffened, the memory taking her. "It's like being shot in the face at point-blank range."

"You don't have to talk about it if you don't want," Blake said, seeing the change in her eyes.

"You recognize you're dead," Mona went on, staring far past him. "Finished. But in that last instant, I felt terrified of being scattered—my organs, my body— like I had something more to lose than my life." She looked him in the eyes. "This is such an odd thing— but I felt it. I felt my soul would be cut in pieces and lost."

Blake took her hands and held them tight. "I know," he said. "I had a dream like that. Just before I woke up, before I left Sylvia's office. I saw Carlyle being cut apart while they redeemed his organs. His spirit was mutilated. And then I saw your face. I was terrified that would happen to you."

She looked at him, feeling a tingle of fear up her back. "It's strange. When I heard what was happening around the Pinnacle, I felt relieved to think you were in trouble," she said. "Just for the distraction. I had no doubt at first."

"You saved our lives."

"I was so low." She pulled his hands to her and pressed his palms against her cheeks. "At Dr. Sylvia's I was so full of death, I had to stop thinking or be crushed. And the QDT. It was like those victims weren't even human anymore. Horrible."

She knelt up and hugged him abruptly around the neck, tight. He sensed the moisture of her tears on his skin. "Oh, Blake," she whispered to him. "I'm so tired of death."

He took her fully in his arms and kissed her on the mouth gently; then she curled her head under to rest it against his chest. He felt the bittersweet desire to hold and protect her like a child mix with his growing hunger to make love to her like a woman. They clung tightly to each other until he raised her face to him, and they kissed again gently, and then again forcefully, with an intensity near desperation. He plunged his fingers into her thick blond hair and brushed his lips over her face, feeling the small dampness of tears beneath her eyes, cool against the warmth of their skin. Inside his chest he felt he could burst with the longing to make her a part of himself—and make himself merge into her.

"I love you," he told her. "Is it crazy to say that?"

"Not if you mean it." Her eyes were red, and she looked on the verge of crying, but she was smiling at the same time. He hugged her tight to him.

"I love you," he said again. "It feels so good to say it."

She opened his shirt to feel the plainness, the honesty of his flesh, and with the touch she began trembling. The trembling infected Blake, and they began undressing each other purposefully, slowly, caressing each other's bodies with a sense of wonder and desire.

Mona's whole body hummed with an invisible vibration of want, a vibration in harmony with Blake's own. They lay down on the carpet. She clutched her arms around his waist and pulled him tight to her, wanting to explode her boundaries and become one being with him.

"Make love to me. Please," she said. "Make love to me and don't stop." Tears dampened her face, filled with a want she'd never felt before. Her legs parted around him, and he found her moist and open as she raised herself to meet him.

32

In the morning Blake awoke to find himself between sheets on the floor, soft blankets atop him. Their long night of lovemaking had been so intense, he remembered nothing of this bed-making. From the kitchen he smelled brewed coffee and bacon frying. It filled him with such a sense of well-being, he forgot what the day might bring.

He found a robe lying next to him on the floor, put it on, and went into the kitchen to wrap his arms around Mona from behind. He kissed her neck as she turned the strips of bacon. "Don't you dare tell me anything about poisons in pork fat," she warned him, then turned to kiss him tenderly. "Want some coffee?" she asked.

"I'd love some."

She poured out two cups, then stretched, fluffing out her thick blond hair with her fingers. "How do you feel, Blake?"

"I feel good," he said. "It's like a whole new day."

She smiled. "A whole new day. That sounds nice."

"I don't even remember you making the bed on the floor last night. I suppose I passed out too heavily to get me to the bedroom."

"The bedroom!" She laughed as she ladled up the eggs. "That *is* the bedroom. You've seen the whole place."

*   *   *

After breakfast Blake called Quiller at his office. Quiller insisted Blake and Mona come to pick him up before they went to the police. When they arrived at his office a half-hour later, Quiller was on the floor in the lotus position. The air was filled with the sweet scent of joss sticks burning behind him. His eyes slowly opened, and he unwrapped his legs and stood to embrace them.

"Thank God we all made it through the night. I was just practicing Hakomi mindfulness," he said excitedly, gesturing toward his prayer mat on the floor. "I've reconstructed practically the entire QDT episode. I've conquered the memory block in Byron's fog."

"You're something else," Blake told him. Mona sat on the couch and rose again to remove a cracked walnut shell from beneath her.

"I'm doing my personal best to advance the evolution of the species," he said.

"What about Frambeen?" Blake asked. "What happened to him?"

"He was in the building last night, but that's all I know," Quiller said. "I just want to come along when you take in the evidence. I had a QDT vision of you vanishing. I want to keep it from coming true."

Outside the window, the 2000 Fest Ball billboard caught Blake's eye. "Quiller, do you remember the story my mother used to tell about the past life vision I had?"

"Christ, yes. Margaret never tired of that one."

"That same story you told me last night?" Mona asked him.

"Yes. Look at the dancer on that billboard. I think it's the exact face of my past-life sailor. The sailor who drowned."

Quiller and Mona moved to the window and looked. The dancers were painted in a style that recalled the art deco of the 1920's. The male dancer looked down at his partner with a superciliousness impossible to imagine in a drowning man.

"All those years, Greggy. I won't even say it's a coincidence. Whatever your memory has done to the face of that vision—it's like a dream now. Your mind has made some connection, but I doubt it's the same face."

"You think that dancer means something?" Mona asked.

"To his subconscious mind, yes." He put a hand on Blake's shoulder and looked back out at the billboard. "Your mother was always finding odd things like this. Things that indicated meaning in the universe—but you couldn't make it out. Psychic coincidences. She said they proved there *was* meaning to the universe. Life was revealing itself to us, but we were too dense to get it." He clapped a hand on Blake's back. "Let me grab Frambeen's gun and we'll be out of here."

Blake nodded and picked up the evidence against Scott as Quiller opened his safe. What good Frambeen's pistol would do without Brubaker's body, he didn't know. Surely the executive had sent the corpse to be dried and chipped. By now the former Brubaker was probably on his way to an Iowa farmer, transformed into a bag of fertilizer. Still, they had played hard for the cards they'd got. Blake wasn't about to suggest they throw any away.

As they drove, Quiller read the materials on buzz fluid which Sylvia had collected. Blake figured if anybody knew who might be able to use it, Quiller would.

The skies had cleared from the previous day's rain, and the pavement was dry when Blake pulled into the parking lot in front of the police detectives' headquarters. Behind them, traffic rumbled across the Western Avenue overpass. Blake watched as a bus crossed Belmont, a 2000 Fest Ball ad with a blowup of the dancers' faces pasted to its side. He felt irritated by it, as though it were a perverse exploitation of some better, more ideal version of himself.

"I'm not entirely happy about going in here," Mona said. The ride had left them all very quiet.

"Don't worry, children. Uncle Quiller is here. I'm much too big a man to disappear."

"In more ways than one," Blake said.

"Never mind," Mona said. "Let's get it over."

Blake stuffed the duplicates they'd made of Brubaker's photos under the seat.

At the front desk of the station, Detective Lieutenant Ahern approached them, smiling. "Blake," he said in greeting. He took the envelope from Mona's hand. "These the photos?"

Blake and Mona looked at each other in surprise as Ahern slipped them from the envelope. "Great. Just what we needed," he said. "Thanks for bringing them in." The lieutenant began walking away.

"Hold on," Blake said. "What's happening here?"

Ahern laughed. "What's the matter? Don't you know?" He stood enjoying it a moment. "Byron Frambeen wants you to phone him before you start telling any lies." Ahern winked at them.

"Frambeen called you?" Blake asked.

"He brought Scott down here himself." Ahern went back to his desk and sat down.

"How about that?" Mona said.

"Looks like he let go of the leather thong," Quiller said.

"Yeah," Blake agreed. He followed over to Ahern's desk. "What about the QDT?" he asked the lieutenant.

"What about it?"

"You know that was Frambeen's party at Grant Park last night?" Blake said.

"What's the matter? You catch a whiff?" Ahern laughed in his face. "They had court approval to deploy QDT. Those Apocalytes were setting themselves afire. They damaged the Art Institute. The whole thing was about to turn into a riot. Besides that, Scott was operating with a group of terrorists. They planned to attack the protesters. He was alone when they got him, but everybody's pleased enough with the way it came out."

"Particularly Lieutenant Ahern," Blake said.

"How did Frambeen get court approval?" Quiller asked.

"The Justice Department always appreciates civilian aid." The lieutenant gave them an oily smile. "Besides, Frambeen and Judge Brentwell are very good friends."

"So Brentwell's on the take?" Quiller patted his belly appreciatively. "We'll roast his ass."

"Who's the fat guy?" Ahern asked Blake. Then he turned to Quiller. "Have I seen you around here?"

"You'll remember this face later on," Quiller said, arranging his mustache and goatee.

"Yeah," Ahern said. "Next time I see a Charlie Chan movie. Don't forget, Blake, Frambeen wants you to call."

"Sure." Blake walked out to the foyer and got the executive on the phone.

"Blake," Frambeen said. "Good to hear from you. You're at the station?"

Blake was amazed how jovial he sounded. He felt tempted to ask how his neck felt. "Yeah," Blake said. "You brought Scott in."

"Of course. Once we realized his guilt."

The detective rolled his eyes. "What about Scott's machine?"

"I've had my people working with Scott ever since we got it. Unfortunately, our best scientific minds have concluded the processor is worthless."

"So out goes Scott with the trash. Our evidence on him means nothing to you anymore."

"That's right."

"Too bad you didn't know that last night. You wouldn't have had to turn the Loop upside down."

"That was unfortunate. I count myself among the victims."

Blake fought down the urge to hang up. "Where's Brubaker?" he asked.

Frambeen paused. "The police have his body. Mr. Brubaker was regrettably killed in the action at Grant Park." Frambeen paused again. "Where's Mr. Carlyle?"

"Is anyone interested?" Blake asked.

"They don't need to be. Business is a mad scramble sometimes. After all the bodies land, everyone makes the best of his position. I'm impressed, Mr. Blake. You scrambled to a better position than I anticipated. But it's over now." The threat was clear beneath his voice. Blake didn't say a word.

"You're an effective worker," Frambeen went on. "Perhaps you'd take an assignment sometime."

"We'll see," Blake told him. "I'm not sure I'd feel safe. I'm not a remora, after all."

Frambeen chuckled. "Well, please remember me to your doctor friend. I'd like to share lunch with her sometime. Tell her I love the battle—I'm not a man bitter over a single lost skirmish." He chuckled again as they hung up.

Kinky son of a bitch, Blake thought, recalling Mona astride Frambeen's back, stabbing the hypo into his neck.

The detective returned to Ahern's desk. Quiller sat off to the side, reading the buzz-fluid file. "They got Scott to confess," Mona told Blake. "Everything's pretty tidy."

Ahern pulled two file folders out of his desk. "Somebody left these in the lost and found," he smiled. "I think they might be yours." He held out the missing Murray and City Action Coalition files.

"Figures," Blake said. "When you want to know who robbed you, look to the police."

"We're happy to help."

"Have you freed Murray?" Blake asked.

"I haven't," the lieutenant sighed. "But I guess there's no avoiding it." He got up from his desk and led them down to the lockup, leaving Quiller to his reading. On the way to Murray, they passed Scott's cell. The blond man jumped up from his cot.

"Frambeen cheated me," he shouted. "Where was my protection?"

"The world needs protection from you," Mona said.

"That bomb was not my fault. It was only supposed to damage the bank's mainframe. The men who sold me the wrong explosives are to blame."

"You just needed to buy time until you processed the mercury, right?" Blake asked.

"What do you mean?" Scott asked suspiciously.

"I know all about Edelson and the Coalition," Blake told him. "I know about the poisonous-QDT story. You are an A-one bullshitter. How'd you get photos of Edelson with his girl?"

"What? Am I going to get prosecuted for that too?"

"Not by me," Blake said. "I'm just curious."

Scott sat on his cot. "I never even had any photos," he said with a little laugh. "Edelson met Karen Kreskey at a chemists' conference. I worked with her at Rengore. She was always talking about him. Her 'beloved baldy.' She said he was terrified his wife would find out, so I pretended to have photos. I needed fast money to cover my HRL. I knew my processor could purify mercury, so I cut off Rengore's source at Midland through him."

"I heard your machine doesn't work."

He rose from the cot. "It would work. If I was able to finish, the processor would work. Those idiots don't even understand the concept."

"Sure," Blake said. "Here's the protection you hired.

It's more than you deserve." He pulled Scott's HRL out of his pocket and stuffed it through the bars. Scott grabbed the document and tore it to pieces.

"I just want to know why you picked me," Blake asked.

"It was your ad in the yellow pages. It said *No HRL's*. I figured that meant you wouldn't turn me in for the bounty."

"If you were relying on my help, why did you give my name to the police when you co-opped Murray?"

Scott looked at him blankly. "Why? Did that cause you trouble?"

Ahern snorted a laugh.

"Let's go," Blake said. "This guy's an idiot."

As they approached his cell, Murray was sitting bolt upright on his cot, his eyes closed. "Fucking Murray," the lieutenant muttered under his breath. He unlocked the door. The prisoner looked up in surprise.

"What's this?" Murray asked.

"Field trip. Outside," Ahern said.

"You're free, Mr. Murray," Mona told him. "The real bomber has been found."

Murray looked at the three, eyeing Blake particularly. "I don't believe it," he said. "You really came through."

They all walked out to the front. "I got something for you, Blake," Ahern said. They went to his desk while Mona and Murray went out the door. Ahern pulled a cassette tape out of his desk and tossed it to Blake. 'Carlyle' was printed on a Rengore label stuck to its side. Frambeen had given Ahern the tape of Carlyle's death.

"Frambeen wants his gun back," Ahern said. "I won't ask what that's about."

"What if I tell you you should?"

"I still won't ask what that's about. The scramble's over, Blake." He winked at him again. "We're all done with you here."

"Glad I could help out."

"Don't think we owe you a favor. Frambeen gave us Scott, not you."

"Sure," Blake said. He walked out to the front steps. Murray stretched his arms and inhaled deeply, pushing his hands through his nappy hair.

"Your information on QDT was planted to manipulate you," Blake told him. "Mercury is a regular part of the QDT process. It doesn't leave a poisonous residue."

"Why are you telling me this?"

"Midland Waste is off-limits."

"I can accept that," Murray said.

As they shook hands on it, a police car came rocketing toward them on the sidewalk, blue lights flashing atop. They jumped out of the way as its horn blared and it screeched to a halt right where they'd been standing. The door swung open and Quiller tried to climb out. He fell to the sidewalk, laughing hysterically, then struggled back to his feet.

"Thanks, Bernie," he said, gasping for breath. "That was perfect."

"Sure thing, Mr. Quiller," the officer at the wheel said.

Quiller waved as the car backed away, then turned to his friends and began laughing hard again. "You should have seen your faces!" he screamed.

"Very funny, Quiller," Blake said. Mona stood to the side with her mouth open.

"That was really good," the old man said, wiping the tears from his eye. "You can't put a price on a good laugh like that," he announced, then paused, considering. "But maybe five grand would do it." He pulled an envelope out of his pocket and handed it to Murray.

"What the hell is this, Quiller?" Murray asked.

"You know each other?" Mona said.

"Count it," Quiller told him. Murray pulled a huge

wad of bills from the envelope. "There's five grand there." He turned to Mona, giving her a big toothy grin. "I know *everybody* in this town," he said.

"What am I supposed to do with this?" Murray asked.

"Get in Blake's car and I'll tell you."

They all got in the car and Quiller turned on the radio. "I'm sure the detectives are all battling for space at the windows with their shotgun microphones," he said. He pulled the file on buzz fluid from his inside jacket pocket, unfolded it, and slapped it with the back of his hand. "This is fantastic stuff, boys and girl. And the best part is, there is only one firm licensed to produce and fill buzzers: Rengore Pharmaceuticals of Oak Brook, Illinois. And I happen to know that the divisional president in charge of Rengore Pharmaceuticals reports directly to Mr. Byron Frambeen." Quiller let out a whoop and clapped his hands together.

"We're going to get him, after all," Mona cheered.

Quiller began clicking his fingers together over his head like castanets and wiggling around on his seat as though he were doing some Mexican jig. "Oh, Byron, I'm going to taste your lizard chicken meat yet!" he shouted, tossing the file to the mystified Murray, who began reading it immediately.

"All you have to do to win that five thousand dollars in your lap," Quiller told him, "is use that information."

"Oh, this is good," the activist said as he read. "HRL's, buzz fluid, redemption. It's a desecration of the human soul. I will definitely use this."

"And if you two want to help him on that," Quiller told Blake and Mona, "you can bill me for your hours."

"I might take you up on that," Blake told him.

Quiller grabbed Murray's arm and began dragging him out of the car. "Come on," he said. "Let's use some of that money to buy lunch. We'll let these professionals get back to work." He pulled two one hundreds out of Murray's wad and stuck them under Blake's windshield wiper.

"Quiller, wait," Mona called. "Do you always carry five thousand dollars with you?"

He leaned back in the window. "Whenever I talk to police or politicians I do," he told her. "This is Chicago, after all."

"Good luck," Blake told them. They shook hands all around again, and Murray walked off down the street with Quiller, the freed man stretching and twisting as though he'd just been released from a cocoon.

Blake turned off the radio and flipped the ignition switch, but the engine wouldn't go. "It must be run down," he said. He got out, grabbed the cash from under the wiper, opened the back, and pulled the cord on the gas-powered generator. They waited for the batteries to charge.

"While you were talking to Frambeen on the phone, Ahern told me he'd matched Scott's voice to the co-op tape," Mona said. "Scott bombed the First National and called the police not long after. He implicated Murray to throw the trail off himself. He was holding our ad to call us next when the police asked him for ID. So he blurted out your name."

"And that's what dragged us in."

"That's what dragged us in." She took his hand. "It's all over, Blake."

"It's all over so suddenly," he said. "I feel like I'm in shock."

She gave his hand a squeeze, trying to reassure. "We did pretty good."

"Frambeen ought to be in jail."

"We might still get him."

"I hope so. I'm glad Scott's processor didn't work." He flipped the switch, and the engine came on.

"The strange thing is," Blake said, looking into her eyes, "I feel I'm supposed to learn something from all this. I've been thinking about my mother's death. And that weird billboard. But I can't put it together." He leaned forward and put his head on the steering wheel.

"If the drowning sailor was you and he has the same face as the dancer, then the dancer is somehow you too. Right?"

He leaned up from the steering wheel. "I guess so," he said.

"So maybe the dancer fulfills what the sailor lost in drowning. *You* are supposed to dance us into the new millennium."

They looked at each other a moment and burst out laughing. Blake put the car into gear and pulled out into traffic. Mona slid over on the seat close to him.

"Gregory Blake, Seeker of Truth. Guide to the New Age," he said. "I don't know about this."

"You could just dance *me* into the new millennium," she suggested. "Why don't we get away? Think about it a little. We could fly south and take a vacation."

"You got to come back from a vacation," he said. "I want a new world."

About the Author

Richard David George Patrick Engling was born on St. Patrick's Day in 1952. Since then the city of Chicago has seen fit to dye the river green every year on his birthday. He was educated at Northern Illinois University and at Indiana University, where he earned his M.A. in Creative Writing. He now lives in Chicago with his wife Gail and dog Gertie and is a founding member of the Chicago Writers Group. His play, *Ghost Watch*, was produced by the Chicago Actors Ensemble in 1987. He is currently at work on a new novel featuring Blake and Mona.